I0659274

YOU STOLE MY THUNDER

Ophelia Finsen

Also by Ophelia Finsen:

Lovers of Old Films
This is Living
Society of Lost Causes
The Women of Jimanac
Skye
The Romanian
At the Upper Villa Tyde
Perception

ISBN: 978-0-9934120-1-1

Arabella had just finished fixing her hairpiece when Shazia entered the changing rooms. The door banged shut. The music flicked back to bell jar level, as if their ears were submerged in water. With a jangle of gold bracelets, swoop of Indian silks and a film of glowing, perfumed sweat upon her flesh, Shazia swung into the empty chair beside Arabella and slapped the leaflet on the dressing table with particular glee.

Arabella gave the piece of paper the slightest of glances. A big breasted woman in a red loin cloth and what could only be described as a bra made up of string and two pogs was holding a fifties siren pose. Arabella sniffed. "Looks a bit a slapper."

Shazia opened her mouth and laughed. "That's rich coming from you."

Shazia looked exotic. She carried her look of tempting humidity and soaring temperatures, monsoons and musical languages, but as soon as she opened her mouth, you knew she was as Yorkshire as a gang of flat capped whippets sharing a bag of chips on Scarborough pier. "What did that guy call you the other week? A cheeky tart?"

"He was intimidated." Arabella stretched the right of her face by pouting to the left. Preparation for mascara. "Besides, I don't dress like that. Although I don't think *dress* ought to be the verb we're actively using looking at her."

"They're all raving about her outside."

Arabella calmly finished her eye makeup, screwing the brush back into the mascara tube.

"She's only been out two weeks and people are talking about her."

"The photo looks too burlesque for this place." Arabella packed her makeup bag into her rucksack.

"That's where she is, over at the Burlesque Bar. But they reckon she's going to come over here. She's a bit of a fusion artist, multitalented."

"Really." Picking up the leaflet, Arabella examined the photo properly. Cherry Malone was the woman's name. It had to be purely a stage name. The attention-seeker was going for red: alongside her scant red clothes she had intensely styled bright red hair, the colour of tomatoes. 50s cheeky fun, the side tag line promised. "Something and nothing."

"Look at the other side. She's like you."

"What?" Her fury gave a little clench in the centre of her chest. On the other side of the paper Cherry had embellished her act with a standard size bra, covered in sequins and beads, a waist chain of hanging coins and a number of bracelets, armlets, anklets, and metallic bands everywhere else that would hold adornment. She stood with her hips pushed to one side.

"She's a belly dancer."

Arabella's eyes narrowed. "What's that she's got in her hand?"

"She plays the ukulele."

"The fuck she does."

"She's just like you." Shazia grinned sheepishly as Arabella turned sharply, artificial pigtails swinging like whips. "Well, not exactly. She's just new to the scene."

There was a bang on the door. "Two minutes, Arabella."

"I'd better get going." She stood up before shaking the advertisement at her friend. "She damn well better not think she's going to be on the same night as me."

Before the dance started the stage was dark, giving Arabella chance to mount and stand bare footed with her back to the audience. She'd been one of the quirkier belly dancers at the bar for the last few years. Her act was a mix of Egyptian, East Coast tribal fusion and crazy manga-esque dress. She was a casual part timer on the stage, but the people who saw her perform never forgot.

It wasn't a seedy place. Strictly no stripping. Both male and female dancers performed most nights, interspersed with live musicians who would play one or two songs. It was a trendy, popular place in Leeds where people of all ages and sexes came to eat, drink and talk. The dancers were an expensive alternative to art on the walls or televisions showing music videos, but that very fact made it a talking point. The vibe followed the eastern ethnic compass point when collating its dances: Bhangra, Bollywood, Thai, Chinese, belly dance; they'd even had a small Hawaiian troop here at one point. The dancing was on and off throughout the night, and you could watch it or not – no one expected the conversation to stop for the dancers. A kind of floor show if you fancy it. The artists didn't get paid a big wage, but performing here had started a couple of big careers (as well as a lot more minor ones); and if nothing else it gave really competent dancers the excuse to get their glad rags on and dance their latest choreographic masterpieces.

Tonight it was fusion, with a modern electronic underground dance mix with Arabic beats. Arabella was dressed like her version of a manga character, with waist-length electric blue pigtails with silver ribbons threaded through. The hair piece was the most expensive part of her ensemble. The more modest pieces were the black leggings, floor length grey loin cloth threaded with silver, coin belt and bead sash all tied at the low waist. Halter neck top, necklace and armlets. Proportionally, hip to waist to bust she had an hourglass figure, a tidy trim waist the fad dieters would envy, thinking it had to be down to surgery or pills. In reality it was due to genetics, the dancing and the clothes she wore, but people never wanted to hear that anything took time and effort.

As the music started, Arabella stepped bare foot into the centre of the small stage and began her performance. She twisted her body at the waist, only her torso moving because of the all important isolation of the belly dance. Her arms moved in snake strobe effect. She let her eyes flitter over the audience. It was the usual mixture. Some completely ignored her, others gave the occasional glance, those that pretended they were watching, and then the real audience members, all the way through from a distraction, to fun, to appreciation, amazement and unadulterated lust.

At the large round dining table there was a group of wannabe lads – men who wanted to be young and cool, but were too close to forty and too well employed to be fooling anyone with the carefree flicks. They were laughing and pushing one another, pointing at her as if this was the kind of place where you put notes into the belts of the dancers. It had a touch of the pathetic. A ball of horror lodged in the back of her throat as she recognised one of the men in the centre of the group. He looked her straight in the eye as he put down his bottle of larger and the cat was out of the proverbial bag.

Ian worked on the same open plan office floor as Arabella. Everyone had a day job. He was tall and the cliché of alpha male. He was married with three children, but still enjoyed a roving eye at work. He liked to think he was every woman's friend, but deep inside beat the heat of a bitter misogynist. An opinionated smart arse who swore too much and who now knew what Arabella did on a weekend.

Damn it. She put her face back to a mask, but inside she could feel the irritation flood her system. Not that her dancing was a secret. It was certainly nothing to be ashamed of. But she didn't feel the need for people like Ian to know details of her personal life. Arabella enjoyed a distinction, a very sharp divide between work (and in this she meant the paid employment that paid the bills) and life (and this meant all the things she enjoyed doing). It simply didn't do to get the two things mixed up. She'd seen a lot of messy ends where people hadn't considered the consequences.

She rolled her body up through a reverse undulation. Ian grinned as if she was doing it for him. She would have given him a smack had she not a set to complete.

Dance finished, she left to applause and whistles. Paranoid the response hadn't been quite as warm as it sometimes was. Were they saving the cheers for Cherry? What nonsense. Coming off the stage and into the slightly less glamorous backstage, Arabella shrieked as something bit her. Stumbling to the side of the corridor, she lifted her right shin onto her knee like she was a horse to be shod. A thick, sturdy piece of glass protruded from the sole of her foot. She'd never been one for feinting at the sight of blood. It was almost a badge of honour that she wouldn't admit to pain, but glass in bare feet was pushing it. Swearing under her breath, she looked around for someone to shout at. There never was anyone available when they were needed. Grimacing, she slid the glass out of her flesh. "Shit," she swore as the cut welled up with blood that splattered thickly on the linoleum floor. She wiped at the wound as if a quick touch would stop the gushing.

"Shit," she repeated, tossing the offending piece of glass into a rubbish sack. She hobbled back towards her dressing room. She could feel the blood slick between her toes, making the tip-toe step of her right foot slippery underfoot.

At the dressing room door, Pritesh, the assistant manager was leaning, grinning like a used car salesman at whichever poor sod, probably Shazia, was inside. He looked back out to the corridor as Arabella approached. "Woah, girl," he shook his head, laughing at her. "With a face like that you're not going to charm the customers. You need a walking stick? Hop-a-long belly dancer? Not sure that's going to sell."

"Fuck off, Pritesh."

"Very charming. You old birds are grumpy. Someone told me you're not in your twenties."

Arabella shoved past him into the dressing room. It was something of a sore point that she would be turning thirty this year. She hobbled across to her chair and flopped, grabbing at a towel to rest her foot on as she set it on her knee. Her foot wept blood.

"Arabella!" Shazia looked horrified. She was back in her civvies: jeans and a big fluffy jumper, hair tied back and make up off. "What have you done?"

"This moron needs to hire cleaners. I just stepped on a piece of broken glass out there."

"You not heard of shoes?" Pritesh chirruped.

She squeezed her skin together, watching the blood flow lessen to virtually nothing. She wrapped the towel tightly around her foot and held it in place.

"You want to be careful," Shazia told him. "She could do you. Accidents in the work place."

"Yeah yeah yeah. It's a restaurant. Glasses get broken. She needs to buy herself a pair of shoes."

"Such a considerate boss."

"I'm not her boss. I never hired her. She was working here long before I started working..."

"Give it a rest," Arabella interrupted, before he got started on the usual line of age-related jokes. Twenty nine ought not to be the tragedy point for jokes. She certainly wasn't considered past-it at the day job. But the fact remained that dancers tended to quit in their twenties. Moved up or grew up. Arabella was considered one of the old crew at this place. It was bizarre to think in relative terms she was 'old' here; most days she felt as though she'd barely gotten started with life.

Pritesh shuffled awkwardly. "Yeah, seriously though, I could do with your opinion. What do you think of this one?"

Arabella looked up. He had hold of another one of those leaflets about Cherry Malone.

"We might book her for a couple of nights."

"And?"

"Well, sounds like a new act. She belly dances and she plays the ukulele."

"So?"

"So it's two different things. A belly dancer who plays."

"I play the banjo."

"Yeah, but not at the same time."

Arabella stared up at him. He was engrossed in staring at the leaflet, or rather the curves of Cherry's scantily clad figure. He was fickle, distracted by the new. Distracted by the pornographic, she thought sourly, feeling a bad mood coming on. Thank god she was only signed up for the one dance set this evening.

"Anyway girls, got to go. Good seeing you."

"Wish we could say the same."

"Bye, Pritesh," Shazia tinkled.

Arabella looked at her friend with a touch of disdain now that they were alone. "Bye, Pritesh? What's up with you?"

She shrugged. "Just being friendly."

"I worry."

"*I worry*," Shazia corrected. "What are you going to do with your foot?"

"It'll be fine," Arabella muttered. "It's probably stopped bleeding now." She released the pressure and unrolled the towel to open a fresh flow of blood.

"You need to go to A and E."

"I'm not wasting hours of my life watching drunken arseholes having punch ups with their own vomit." Arabella pursed her lips.

"That needs stitches."

"Fine."

"Oh no," Shazia whined, watching as Arabella started rummaging in her rucksack. Every dancer had a small sewing kit with them at all times for costume malfunction emergencies. There were no wardrobe mistresses here, and no one wanted to go out there with a loose strap or unreliable clasp. "Stop being a baby. You don't have to be afraid of doctors."

"I'm not afraid."

"Then don't try stitching yourself up."

"How is do-it-yourself surgery being cowardly?"

Shazia wrinkled her upper lip and shuffled in her seat so she wouldn't have to watch. Arabella poured herself a glass of vodka, splashed a bit on her foot, which made her yowl. She wiped off her needle and thread, downed the rest of the vodka and stuck her courage to some foolish board. "Jesus!" She yelled with the first stitch. The needle was a lot duller and heavier than the neat, feather-light slice of glass had been.

"You've really got to get over your fear of doctors," Shazia repeated as Arabella stubbornly worked on her own foot, barely able to see through the tears. "It's silly."

"I just want to get home. I'm tired." Arabella put down the needle. She had her first aid kit open on the dressing table. Pressing a roll of cotton wool, she bound it tightly to her foot with gauze, fixing in place with a safety pin. Florence would have been damn proud. "There. Sorted. Five minute job, rather than a soul destroying five hour wait. Doctors are such arrogant pricks, I simply can't be doing with them." She stood up and put her full weight on her right foot, the sensation making her eyes bulge unpleasantly.

Shazia didn't look convinced. "You should probably get a taxi to the station."

Sunday morning arrived as a thumping bore. Arabella was woken by daylight and a blackbird twittering near her window. Sunday morning already? It must be early in the morning, for she didn't feel ready to get up yet. Lying flat out on her stomach, a stranded starfish, she did a push up to get a view of her clock. Ten in the morning already. Increasingly she'd noticed that late nights were really knocking her out. Is this what happened when you got old, when you were nearing thirty?

Rolling over, she sat up in bed and finished off the last of the water in the pint glass on the bedside table. What she really needed was a large mug of tea, but she couldn't find it within herself to get up. She picked up her mobile phone and toyed with the idea of ringing downstairs for service. She caught sight of the nail varnish stain on the carpet near her dressing table and thought better of it. Probably better to wait until she'd bought that little rug she'd planned on to cover the stain. Not that Adam would have said anything even if he had seen it.

Tossing the phone down on the fluffy rolling valleys of her duvet cover, she turned on her CD player with the remote and got some music into the room. She had some Finnish crispbreads in a bag by the bed that she'd meant to take down to the kitchen but hadn't quite gotten to doing. Nibbling on crispbreads and picking up on her current read where she'd left off – Madame Bovary – Arabella gradually got in synch with Sunday. The music, which was set on random shuffle, started up. John Newman's take on Northern Soul was probably a bit energetic for first thing, or perhaps this was what was needed for a Sunday. She'd been pondering on using one of these tracks in her act; going completely away from any Middle Eastern influence, but wasn't sure whether people would get it or just think she was some confused stripper. If she was a stripper, confused was the active word as she never took her clothes off on stage.

No matter. She started undulating her feet under the covers, as all of the best bed dances started out. A throb pulsated up her calf from her right foot. She'd forgotten about last night and the laceration in the corridor. She didn't quite dare look at her foot. DIY surgery had seemed like a good idea in the adrenaline-fuelled Saturday night dance, but on a sober Sunday morning it was embarrassing. She'd never be able to admit to anyone of the medical profession what she'd done. She wiggled her toes to be sure the appendage wasn't dead and went back to her book. She'd look at it later in the day. When she'd arrived home last night – technically this morning – she'd smothered her foot in antiseptic cream, bandaged it up thoroughly and gone to bed. She didn't want to undo all that good work too early. That foot dressing had been applied to survive the duration.

When John started singing the same songs again, and Emma had grown to be a bit of a bore, it was time to get out of bed. Walking to the door, her foot so thickly bandaged it looked like it was in a pot, she thought to herself how it didn't really hurt that much at all. Wrapping her pastel blue dressing gown – all ruffles and layers, a glamorous but OTT affair she'd found in a vintage shop – around her body, she left what she liked to refer to as her apartment and started downstairs.

With each step she tottered lop-sided, and each descent reverberated through her leg, to the point it was quite painful when she got to the bottom of the stairs. The entrance hall was a clutter of umbrellas, shoes, various flotsam and her own boots. Arabella had a thing for boots and it had been commented upon that from the knee down she ought to have been a cowboy. As she moved off the staircase, her damaged limb caught on one of Adam's legs and she lost her balance, shouting out as she grabbed the end of the banister, sweeping around and kicking out a spray of shoes. Adam's leg went skidding through into his room.

"Arabella, is that you?"

Adam's voice filtered down the hall from the kitchen. Arabella cursed and muttered under her breath, pulling herself up. She ran a quick hand through her distressed hair and straightened her dressing gown. "Who else could it be?" She glared at his one remaining leg in the hallway. Why did he have to leave the things out in the shared space anyway? It wasn't as if Adam could ever have been described as an exhibitionist over his disability.

Adam Kepwick, owner of the semi-detached house, and Arabella's landlord, was at the kitchen sink in full uniform of marigolds and apron. His mother may have been dead these last five years, but her influence still reigned unchallenged. He twisted around to look as Arabella flounced into the kitchen, catching sight of the mood on her face, and nervously focusing intensely back on the washing up. Arabella busied herself with the tea paraphernalia, getting the kettle on to boil and taking out her largest mug from the cupboard. It was a chunky white mug that was probably weapon enough to brain burglars, with the words "PMS Monster" emblazoned in red. It had been a not-so-secret Santa present from an ex colleague about three years ago. A pretty boy waster with too much spare cash. He'd seen no harm in laughing at colleagues who hadn't heard of the designers he liked to buy. Sneering and arrogance were bad enough in themselves, but for someone who wasn't sure which countries bordered onto Wales, he was on very shaky ground to claim any degree of intellectual authority or general superiority. In his early deluded days, he'd fancied his chances with Arabella, but had been put down in no uncertain terms. To save face he'd decided she was a frustrated, frigid old woman (definitely had to be more than his twenty-one years) and probably a lesbian to boot. He'd bought the mug as a joke that ought to have hailed him as the heart of the office, gleeful that he'd gotten her name in the Christmas game selection. The atmosphere had been tense when the gift had been opened, many knowing better than to laugh at the badly-placed joke. Arabella hadn't said a word, but had left the mug prominently displayed on her desk, and every morning had pointedly had her ten o'clock cup of green tea whilst glaring at the boy over the rim, the red words growling in his direction. He hadn't lasted long, and had decided to seek other employment elsewhere a couple of months later. Arabella didn't feel any guilt. After the way he'd spoken to people in the office, she considered him fair game. Of course, the mug hadn't lasted much longer at work, the final straw being when her colleague Ian had jovially assured her that all women were a bit angry and frustrated until they'd had children. The mug had gone home that night to be replaced with an inoffensive article with stars. But misogyny is not to be stopped in its tracks that easily, and a week later Ian had been scolding her on her choice of teabags, feeling it was his duty to tell her she needing to quit the green tea as it was inhibiting her ability to conceive.

Anyone who thought that sexism had been eradicated from the work place in the United Kingdom was living in a fantasy land.

Arabella set herself at the head of the kitchen table, mug of tea in front of her like a chalice. Her foot was throbbing, so she set it up on the little stool. The toaster popped and Adam removed his washing up gloves, and fetched the two slices of slightly burnt toast onto a plate. "Toasted teacake?" he asked, walking over to the table. "Oh, what have you done to your foot, Arabella?"

She glanced at her sickly foot. She had rather overdone it with the bandages. It looked as though she'd broken her ankle. "It's nothing," she waved his worry frown aside. "I just stepped on a bit of broken glass last night."

"It didn't need stitches?"

"I did it myself."

"Shouldn't you have gone to A&E, Arabella?"

"I know what I'm doing," she retorted, ending on a sense of uncertainly as Adam clunked his way over to the fridge for the butter. He was wearing one of his oldest legs. She didn't know why he didn't just throw it out or sell it on EBay as a vintage medical curiosity. It was probably just his answer to the comfort blanket quandary, but he did so sound like the portent of doom as he clonked his way along the downstairs corridor at night with the damn thing on.

Adam was an amputee, having lost his left leg from just below the knee. It had happened in his tenth year of life, so he was quite accustomed to his one-footed nature now at the grand old age of thirty-six. The loss of a limb had been a somewhat minor episode in comparison to what came next. The accident had turned an already over bearing woman into a disturbingly protective single mother, and Adam had grown up into a stuttering, timid recluse who was terrified of loud bangs, crowds and angry women. It made it all the more surprising that after the death of his mother he had decided to take in a tenant for the upstairs, and even more of a shock when he offered the place to Arabella Mangella, four years ago.

Placing the butter dish on the table, Adam sat down opposite her. "Have you planned anything for today?"

"Nothing much."

"Arabella, would I be able to borrow your car?"

She picked up a slice of teacake. He used to drive her crazy with his over use of her name in every question, but she'd grown deaf to it with time. "I suppose." She started to spread butter on the tea cake. "Was this just to butter me up, then?"

Adam laughed lightly. "Of course not. I made that last night."

She took a bite, and looked over at him. "It's very good, but it was Saturday night last night. And you were baking tea cakes?"

He got up from the table, avoiding looking at her. He unhooked the apron up over his head. "I'm not young like you are anymore."

Christ, Arabella thought, is this what I've got to look forward to for my thirties? At least Adam was heading in the right direction. From what she'd heard and seen, he'd been positively middle aged in his twenties whilst his mother was still around. If anything, he was getting younger.

"I need to go to B and Q to pick up tiles." Adam was renovating the downstairs bathroom from the early eighties horror it had been. It was a substantial bathroom, thankfully not one Arabella had to use. The house was divided between the two quite neatly. Adam had the large sitting room as his living and sleeping area, the downstairs bathroom and one of the upstairs bedrooms as his studio. The other two bedrooms had an archway knocked through between the two, creating a mini flat for Arabella, along with sole sovereignty over the upstairs bathroom. They shared the kitchen and back garden.

"No problem," Arabella said. "I wasn't doing anything today."

Andrew was laughing as Arabella pulled into the car park. Monday mornings were grim enough at the best of times, but she could do without seeing his tanned face wrinkled up into chortling roars. Driving to work, listening to ELO and singing along, she had almost convinced herself that she wasn't heading straight into another truly shit week. Andrew's face suggested otherwise.

Arabella turned off the engine and stepped out of her vehicle. Andrew, nearing pension age, scruffy in jeans and T-shirt, stomach hanging over the waistband, worked in stores and no one expected him to be beautiful, respectable or anything other than reasonably productive. He remained in place, pointing at her car as if she hadn't noticed.

"Good weekend, Arabella?"

"Sod off, Andrew."

"That good, eh? There's certainly something to be said for women drivers."

"Oh, come on, Andrew," Arabella snapped as she got her handbag out from the back seat. Normally she didn't mind Andrew. He swore too much, was too opinionated in the wrong direction, had little to no understanding of political correctness or why it sometimes was important. He told it how it was and could be quite funny with his dry, cutting comments. A bit of banter with him could be misleading, creating an assumption that you could be immune from his scorn. "Is that the best you can come up with? That old cracker joke? Besides which, this wasn't made of woman." She stood at the end of her car and waved an arm dramatically at the damage. "This is man-made."

"Too busy winking at the boys to look where you're going?"

"I'm not even going to waste my breath..."

"Sure as hell I'm not getting a lift with you again."

"I'm not offering."

Andrew stuck his hands in his jeans pockets and started to amble off to work. "Just make sure you don't park anywhere near my car in future," he called back over his shoulder.

Arabella curled her lip. "Tosser."

"Morning!" Nicki was approaching from behind. With only the driver's side in view she was unaware of the disaster that had occurred on Sunday. "Another bloody Monday I could be doing without." Nicki was a bottle blonde, somewhere in her early forties and looked like a definition cougar. A single career woman who ate young men for breakfast. And still they kept on coming.

"Nice shoes," she added as Arabella turned around. The feet and the rest of her ensemble simply didn't match. Arabella was small with her five foot three stature, with an annoyingly narrow waist but curvy hips and bust that the current fashion trends simply frowned upon at present. She was dressed in her usual smart-quirky, in pinstriped trousers, blouse with waist-nipping waistcoat, shoulder-length dark hair styled like a fifties starlet. She'd finished off the random mix with a long string of lilac pearls knotted at the bottom and bright red lipstick. Nicki's eyes looked back at her feet, dressed in scuffed trainers.

"I know," Arabella stared at her own feet. She usually wore heels to work, to give herself more gravity. "They're the only damn things I could get on. Couldn't get my foot into any of my boots, and sandals are a bit of a no-no at the moment."

"You injured yourself?"

"Yeah, I sliced my foot open on broken glass at the weekend. It's a bit swollen. But all the bandages don't help either."

"Jesus," Nicki wrinkled her lip. "You been to the doctor about that?"

"No," she said. "I don't believe in doctors."

"They do exist; there isn't any question over it now."

"I don't hold with them. They're a waste of time."

"You don't want your foot to go septic. You could end up like Adam."

"It'll be fine."

They started to head for the building, and Nicki caught sight of Arabella's car, specifically the passenger side. It looked as though a Nordic god had balled up his fist and punched the side of the car. The passenger door wouldn't open now. Painful scrape marks feathered their way up the body work.

"Oh my god, is this why your foot's stuffed?"

"I just told you I stepped on broken glass."

"But your car!"

"Adam happened to my car," Arabella muttered, feeling her fury simmer again. She hadn't spoken a word to him since the incident. There had been a tense moment this morning when they'd bumped into one another in the corridor, but she'd handled it by pretending he wasn't there.

"He was in an accident?"

"He had trouble parking. I think he left the leg with his brain in at home when he borrowed my car."

"You shouldn't mock the afflicted."

Arabella turned on Nicki. "Have you seen what he's done to my fucking car?" She pointed back at the dent the size of a small horse. "He tried to parallel park into a bollard. He's not hiding behind being disabled for such cretinous behaviour."

"You're a harsh woman."

"Yeah, well," Arabella limped to the main doors. "It's a harsh world."

Her smashed up car had provided the neighbours with some entertainment to liven up a dull Sunday afternoon, if nothing else. It hadn't been favourable for Arabella's blood pressure, but that just seemed to make it all the funnier for the idiots across the road, and all the more distressing for Adam. As if it was his car that had been ruined.

Arabella had been in her living room at the time of the accident. Sat on a little padded bench by the window, she'd been removing the blue nail varnish from her fingernails whilst idly watching the world outside. Not an awful lot was happening in Chocolate Town, as Arabella referred to the village suburb in York. When the chocolate factory towards the centre was brewing up all those confectionary delights, there were days when the air smelt intensely of hot chocolate fudge cake. Arabella's pet name for her home owed more to its history. The pleasantly designed housing area, red bricks of quaint houses from the 1800s was a village initially built to house the workers of the old chocolate factory before it had been bought out by a multi-national corporation. This had been built back in the olden days when the occasional flickers of social conscience were beginning to emerge. Actually people were poor because they were paid meagre wages and made to live in slums, rather than because they were lazy, drunk and stupid. Treat a man decently, and you get a decent man. Sadly, as with all trends, they seemed to be going back through the cycle. Now the government and people in power gave the poor the finger and hoped they'd keep their coughing in the gutter.

There had been a dull bang, a kind of crumpled down noise from outside. She hadn't immediately given it much thought; probably just one of the old farts across the road up to something again, for they never could sit still. As if sitting down in the armchair was admitting defeat, that this was the end of days. The most recent episode had been squabbling over the green garden bins. One working family a little further down the road had overfilled theirs, and it looked quite unsightly. Who needed television? This street could provide ample soap opera at times.

Smiling in preparation of the fun to be had, she idly looked out of the window just as the grating of gears and a car trying to reverse out of the problem cut through the Sunday afternoon. For a moment she didn't recognise the vehicle, followed by the sinking realisation that she did. Arabella had lowered the bottle of nail varnish remover to the window sill. "That's my car," she'd whispered in horror. "That's my car." Then the fury had slapped her full force, and she was up on her feet, unhooking the window latch and pushing the window wide open so that she could lean out of building, a seething banshee. "Adam, what the hell are you doing?" she had yelled. Adam had not heard. He was too preoccupied with trying to back the car off the pavement and away from the bollard. One of the retired gentlemen who lived opposite had been standing at the foot of his garden, arms folded in amusement. He had heard Arabella's shrieks, looked up and waved at her. "Practising parallel parking, love!"

"Don't you fucking love me," she had ranted to herself, withdrawing back into the house. Taking a trench coat with her, she had flown down the staircase like a storm, thundered forth from the front door and cut a path, barefoot, to her car. There had been a heavy thud as the car skittered back off the kerb and onto the road, Adam parking up and looking rather contented with his manoeuvres. He might have stayed that way, but such damage was bound to catch up with him sooner or later, and as he had looked out of the window and spotted Arabella tearing towards him, he had realised the painful part was about to commence.

"Arabella, I..." he had started as he opened the driver's door.

The neighbour had been openly laughing.

"What the hell driving school did you go to?" From the road she had been unable to see the damage. It was only when she ran up onto the footpath that she had seen how bad it was. It hadn't looked as though the passenger door would be in a state to be opened anymore.

Arabella had screamed.

"Looks like he could use a bit more practice," the neighbour had laughed.

"Don't you fucking talk to me!"

"Arabella, I..."

20

"You neither! You complete and utter moron. How can anyone park this badly? It shouldn't be possible." She had held her hands out despairingly. She had felt ready to punch someone. Anyone. She had glared at Adam. "I don't even want to fucking hear it."

Arabella closed her eyes for a moment as she and Nicki entered the building. The glass doors automatically opened on the approach of human beings. It had been a particularly shitty end to a bad weekend. First this uncomfortable, unquantified threat of Cherry *tart* Malone, as Arabella liked to think of her; and now a damaged car. Completely stuffed. She was just lucky it was still moving when she turned the engine on. And now she was at work and she'd have to listen to more cutbacks shit.

Nicki glanced across at her. "What did Adam have to say for himself?"

"I didn't let him. I was too mad. I swear to God, I would have killed him yesterday." Arabella paused at the foot of the stairs. This was where they parted. "And now it's Monday morning and we're back at work."

"Doesn't get any better, does it?" Nicki said wryly.

"You're telling me."

Arabella worked in a large open plan office on the first floor. The route from staircase to desk was like running the valley of fear. Snippets of conversations and opinions from work colleagues assaulted her every morning, depressing and devaluing her opinion of the world in general just a little bit more. Her fingers tightened around her handbag straps as she surveyed who was already in. Margaret, the fifty something divorcee cat-woman, soured and full of opinions but not an ounce of sense in her head. Lynn, a heavy smoker and gossip compatriot of Margaret, was unfortunately in as well, which meant the moralising and bitching would already be in full flow. It just had to be done. Arabella put her head down and marched for her desk.

"... I don't know what she's waiting for. Says she's not interested."

"Selfish is what she is."

"She's thirty five at least, I bet. Should have started having children ten years ago."

"That's the problem."

Arabella felt her indignation gag in her throat. She didn't even know who they were discussing, but as soon as women's ages and child count came up, the narrow mindedness of the collective could be horrifying. Sometimes she stood up and argued back, but most of the office, men and woman combined, tended to smile patronisingly and assure her that she was wrong. She was just in denial. Women just weren't like that.

Thumping her handbag onto her desk, Arabella swung her rear end into her chair and flicked on the computer. Someone just kill me now, she thought.

"Arabella, good morning." Christine appeared in front of her desk as if summoned by thoughts of death. She wore her deep purple trouser suit, and was clutching a couple of files to her chest as always. Perhaps she dribbled toothpaste down the front of her clothes every morning, and needed that officious prop to cover the mess. "Concerns over the sales to income figures." Christine, Arabella's line manager, often felt a need to speak as if writing headlines. Either that or weak slogans. "I need you to liaise with Robin. Investigate. Urgent conversation needs to happen to today. Report due tomorrow." She didn't wait for a response; heading off on power heels to bother some other poor soul.

Biting her tongue, already in a bad mood, Arabella forcefully pushed the button in the bottom corner of her computer screen. There was a flash of life on screen as the computer booted up. In normal-person speak, she needed to have a word with Robin and let Christine know tomorrow. Except they already knew what the problem was. She'd been ranting about it for the last three months, but no one seemed to be listening.

The computer pinged to announce it had completed its morning ablutions. Arabella typed in her username and password. Perhaps she'd been here too long. Seven years she'd worked for this company. The things that had annoyed her when she first started here were still annoying her now. But what to do instead? One office job was very much like the other, and once the first couple of month's novelty had worn off, every office had the usual line up of stereotyped characters, management problems and in-house bitching. This job was to pay the rent, but it was hardly a passion and it certainly didn't define her. But the banjo was never going to be able to support her full time, and the belly dancing had never been taken up for anything more than pocket money.

"I hear we have to have a liaison."

Arabella rolled her eyes as Robin's voice interrupted her thoughts. Her credit controller in arms. He was a relatively decent, likeable character, but his real personality was continuously splattered with schoolboy inappropriate comments and awkwardness. Overweight, his stomach continuously forced his shirt to come untucked from his trousers. He was a mischievous 1930s school boy trapped in the body of a thirty-something twenty first century office worker. Thick black rimmed spectacles that used to steam up when he first started work here and had to sit in proximity to Arabella for his initial training. He'd gotten used to her these days, but she could still make him blush for sport when the notion took her.

"What we need to have is a chat," she corrected him as he pulled an as-yet vacant chair up to her desk.

"I think Christine is wanting a proper report. Figures and... things."

She swung around in her chair, raising an eyebrow at him.

He shrugged. "Pie charts."

"Hungry?"

"Not yet. Unless you're offering."

"The problem is sales."

"It's really people not paying their bills."

"Not paying their bills on time," she corrected. "They seem to think it's ok to extend their credit to eight, nine months, and that's simply not ok. I put prepayment terms on companies, and sales let orders go regardless. David sucking up to the Byas Foundation accounts for a lot of my problems."

"Sales are under a lot of pressure to hit targets."

"But targets are meaningless if people don't pay their bills. Orders like those ought to count negative on their targets," Arabella huffed.

"Morning guys." A young woman of Dolly Parton-esque proportions directed her greetings at no one in particular as she sauntered through the office, swinging her shiny black and gold handbag by her side, cup of branded coffee in one hand. She flounced her hair back off her forehead with a flash of a smile, the short blonde waves reminiscent of Marilyn Monroe. Arabella continued talking, but Robin's attention was drawn away, kite strings of focus moving across the room. He watched the new office temp, a week into the job, nineteen year old Charlize, take her seat over the far side of the open plan space.

"Have you met Charlize yet?" he almost whispered the question in awe.

"Can't say I have."

He looked over at her. Arabella looked irritated that he hadn't been paying attention. "She reminds me of you," he started, as an attempt at a peace offering.

"Excuse me?"

"Well, I mean, when I first started here." He could feel the start of a blush flushing up his ample chin. "Obviously not now. She's only 19 and you're..." Arabella's face was thunder. He wasn't quite sure how to retrieve that thought to his benefit. Or even his survival.

"I think we need to put some figures together on our own," Arabella said tersely. "A couple of case studies of our worst customers. We'll put our work together this afternoon."

"Good idea." Robin stood up abruptly. Arabella looked as though she needed some quiet time on her own. "I'll get started on that."

She pursed her lips. She and Robin were level status on job titles and pay, although it was always her that ended up babysitting him through the awkward problems, the testing customers and any demands for reports or presentations. Someone save me from all of this, she thought silently, taking mug and tea bag from her desk drawer. Getting up, she hobbled over to the kitchen area. She needed strong black tea.

As she stepped into the kitchen a small figure darted from the corridor and appeared at Arabella's side, gently taking her arm as if they were about to take a civilised stroll about the building. "Arabella, love, will you put a call in?"

Moira, the Irish cleaner, smiled up at her from her thick glasses.

"A call?"

"The ladies have no soap."

"You want me to order you soap?"

"Oh no," she waved off the thought as silliness. "We've got loads of soap. We're not allowed to put it in till we get a job."

"But you know there's no soap."

"You and I know that would be the sensible thing to do." Moira looked at her from over the top of her spectacles. "But those who know better have a different system. I'm not to know when a job needs doing. I'm to be told. You put a call in, then I can put out some soap."

"Jesus, Moira, do I have to? Have you ever had a conversation with those people? It's the call centre of the damned."

"Never spoken to them. I'm just the cleaner. And don't take the Lord's name in vain." She gave Arabella's arm a squeeze. "Thanks love."

Arabella worked for an office technology solutions business. It was a private company with a national customer base. They rented offices in a building that was part of an office park just outside of town. Originally it had been exclusively civil service housed within these hallowed bricks, but in the last ten years government finances had been tightened. The civil service was shrinking, but their buildings stayed the same and their costs went up. To draw in some extra cash, they rented out space to the private sector, which was how Arabella came to be working on a civil service site. The buildings were all looked after by a private contractor arranged by the civil service who dealt with maintenance, cleaning, postal services and security. The contractor was a national organisation and had a call centre in some god forsaken hole elsewhere in the country. If anything needed doing, a call had to be made to the call centre to request a job. A call made by a client, not an employee. Said job was logged, issued to the wrong site, reissued to the correct site, and in a couple of hours the cleaner would be allowed to put fresh soap in the dispensers at the ladies loos. The system worked and no one had to rely on their initiative.

"I never realised you were gagging for it that much?"

Arabella wrinkled her brow, peering into the darkening brew of tea in her mug. "Soap?"

"Soap?" Ian laughed. "Still a little dazed and confused?"

She turned around, her heart sinking as she realised it was Ian. He who had seen her dancing in Leeds last Saturday night.

"It was you I saw dancing. Crazy pig tails. Erotic dancing."

"Belly dancing." Arabella snapped.

"Of course, 'cause you didn't strip. But that's why you're doing it."

"To strip?" She sounded very unconvinced.

"For sex."

"I am not a prostitute."

"To chat men up. How are you still single?"

You are such a moron, Arabella thought, as she stirred the teabag around in her mug before plucking it out and dropping it into the composting bin. "I don't know. Maybe it's because I tend to eat them after mating."

Ian laughed. "Right, good one."

Arabella walked away, a scowl on her face. She wasn't quite sure what the good one was exactly, but was reasonably confident that he wasn't one of them.

"Are you trying to become a flamingo?" Nicki flicked her cigarette lighter and angled the flame to her afternoon cigarette. After this just one more hour before home time.

"Not exactly." Arabella, standing on one foot, leant up against the fence. She didn't smoke anymore, but she still sometimes felt the need to come out for a break, smell the smoke and pick over life with Nicki. It hadn't been a pleasant journey to the smoking corner today, her foot was really aching. She longed to take off her trainer, but didn't dare to for fear that she might not be able to get it back on.

"Is that why you didn't come for lunch; because your foot hurts?" Nicki looked unimpressed. "You really need to go see a doctor."

"I cut my foot; of course it's going to hurt."

"Arabella, just ring and make an appointment."

"I'll take a look at it when we go back in."

Nicki rolled her eyes. Arabella could be infuriatingly stubborn at times. She started to say something else, but her train of thought was interrupted by a girlish laugh across the way. A Marilyn wannabe was heading over to the post building carrying a couple of late parcels, chatting to one of the younger men who worked in the post room. Nicki flicked her growing column of ash onto the floor.

"Aren't you supposed to flick that into the fag bin?"

Nicki ignored her. "Have you bumped into her yet?"

Arabella looked over to the post building where Charlize and a puppy-eyed lobotomised male (independent thought and identity currently on hold) were walking in through the door. "Not met her. Seen her. Heard about her."

"Sick of hearing about her," Nicki concluded. "The latest twins on the block."

"It's depressing that a woman can be simplified down to two cushions of fat."

"Don't get philosophical on me now. Besides, there was a time when you were the talk of the office."

"Really?" Arabella didn't know whether to be angry or flattered.

"But then you got old."

Angry. "I am not old."

"I know, I know, you're not even thirty. Yet. Try being in your early forties and then tell me about people half your age strutting in and doing a job that's not a lot simpler than your own."

Arabella pursed her lips thoughtfully. She'd been about to comment on the fact that she was ten years older than Charlize. She'd started here when she was twenty three, and one promotion on, she wasn't any further forward. She was stuck in a rut, and the next generation had since rocked up to glow in their own marvellousness. Arabella was becoming old news. Nicki didn't need this explaining to her. She'd already been here, and was on her second run. The next marvellous generation to replace her were now getting old and worn. When the hell had all of this happened?

"It's probably best you missed lunch today," Nicki continued. "You would have freaked."

"Why?"

"Laura had an announcement to make. She's pregnant."

Arabella looked aghast. "But she's only twenty five."

"Lots of people already have kids by the time they're twenty five."

Mousey little Laura, as Arabella saw her. The girl was nice, perfectly inoffensive although a little dull. Standardised with her high street clothes and her straight, shoulder length brown hair. Not so much one in a million as one of a million. Never did too much of anything, and had it been fifty years ago, would have made some man an absolutely darling little house wife. "It's just so deluded. Girls planning their wedding day since the moment they could hold a thought together, like it's the only aim a woman can have. Fairytale romantic bullshit, princesses chasing after princes. And do you notice how the story ends at the wedding? There's nothing more worthwhile to tell after that. Her bloom is over and she's a slave till she dies. This Prince Charming fable and love at first sight is all bullshit. And yet Laura really believes it all, like there's nothing more out there. How can she give up on life already?"

Nicki burst out laughing. Arabella always took things too seriously, like she'd been given the whole weight of feminism and individualism to carry on her back. She could be harsh on the human race, as if everyone was obliged to aspire to a greater calling than love, family and domesticity. "I don't think people see it like that. Having kids, it's kind of creating life, know what I mean?"

"There's got to be more than just creating your own replacement." Arabella muttered.

"Depends on your perspective," Nicki mused, sauntering over to the smokers' bin to dispose of her cigarette end. "Nature's just about continuation of the species, right?

"Not everybody does. You didn't."

Didn't. As if she was already retired from that sphere. Nicki didn't respond. "We should probably be heading back in."

"Jesus Christ!" Arabella swore as she stepped out, putting full weight onto her damaged foot, forgetting for a moment that it was tender. She was immediately back on her good foot, shaking her fists by her side as if pain was something that could be disposed of like water droplets on skin.

"You need to go to the doctor," Nicki told her as she headed indoors.

"I'll take a look at it," she compromised, thinking it probably felt worse than it actually was. But when she got her trainer off in the ladies, hunched over in a cubicle, she decided that it probably wouldn't hurt to go get some prescription antibiotics after all.

There was nothing about this place to recommend it to any sane person looking for reassurance, Arabella decided. Every time she unconsciously shifted her weight, even a millimetre, the movement set the paper sheet crackling under her rear end. It interrupted an otherwise quiet and poignant atmosphere that was ready to hold its hands together, look grave and tell you the bad news. Doctors. Why would anyone want to go there? They were only a step up from dentists, although in fairness, now she reflected on it, they were a step down. Dentists only wanted to look in your mouth. Doctors sometimes wanted to look up your...

"This doesn't look very happy, does it?"

Arabella pursed her lips as if fingernails had just been dragged down a blackboard. There was something distinctly wrong with this man. He had disturbingly cold hands for a man, even with the latex gloves on. Sitting on his revolving computer chair, he'd scooted across to the foot of the examination bed. She was sitting straight up, her left leg bent and pulled back to her body as if wanting to keep out of harm's way. Her right leg was stretched flat out, her foot so far away as if it had nothing to do with her. She was just a thinking head at one end, the rest of her body increasingly a lump of meat to be prodded when those who knew best thought it was appropriate. Was this was what it was like giving birth?

"This needs cleaning up and those stitches sorting out. They're very crudely done." Dr Thaw raised his head and looked across at her. The last time Arabella Mangella had set foot in this surgery was to register her presence. She was one of those people who ignored all standardised testing, took painkillers if there was a problem, and promptly ignored any symptoms. "A&E didn't do this, did they?"

He looked a little horrified at the standard of stitching. Arabella bit her tongue, wanting to say something about the fact for a first effort, it looked pretty neat, especially when you considered she'd done it herself. She doubted this mild mannered, quietly spoken yet smugly over-confident doctor could have done any better. "No," was all she said to him.

"How did you do it?"

"I stepped on a piece of broken glass."

"It's certainly a clean slice."

Arabella winced, drew in air between her teeth as he started to clean up the wound.

"Drop a glass at home; forgot to clean it up?"

"No, I was at work."

His presumption of office girls blanking out another weekend with one too many bottles of wine had fallen wrong. He paused, looking perplexed. He liked to think he could read people. "You work barefoot?"

"Sometimes, on my weekend job. I dance."

"If you're getting bottles thrown on stage, you need to get shoes."

Arabella took offence at that. "I dance well. I don't get booed. Someone hadn't cleaned up in the backstage corridors."

"You need to look where you're going."

He sounded like someone's mother. Not Arabella's mother, who was a completely different case study in the spectrum of motherhood. But certainly someone's mother, the type who would say, I told you so, and then remind you of the need for coasters.

"Accidents happen."

"They certainly do with some people," he said through gritted teeth as he neatened up the stitching on her foot. What an infuriating woman she must be, an absolute nightmare to live with. Contrary and unpredictable, becoming awkward just to prove a point. A point she was probably wrong on more often than not.

Arabella watched him, a mixture of disbelief, pity and fury pulsing through her. She felt as though he was desperate to advise her on changing her attitudes as well as the way she looked after her feet. He would be the kind of man who got a real thrill out of speaking authoritatively at people, thriving on the chance to show off just how much he knew.

"Jesus Christ," she broke out, just as he was completing bandaging her foot up. She had been thinking that really she ought to have gone and seen a nurse rather than bothering him with this triviality. "If everybody followed that thinking, nothing innovative would happen."

"And you dancing barefoot down a corridor is innovative?"

"I'm living. At least I won't wake up when I'm ninety and wonder what the hell I did with my life."

She was making some very grandiose assumptions that she would be waking up at all when she was ninety, he thought, betting she smoked, drank too much, took dubious substances and probably slept around. "Perhaps if we restrain ourselves to the matter in hand." He pulled himself back on his wheeled chair to the desk.

Arabella stuck her tongue out at his back. What an arsehole. She slipped her foot back into her trainer.

"I'm going to give you a prescription of heavy duty antibiotics. It's best if you could start them this evening. Finish the course of pills, even if you think it's looking better." The printer bleeped and started printing the prescription. "Keep off the foot for the next week."

"But I'm supposed to be working this weekend."

"Not dancing you're not." He passed her the prescription. "I'm serious, give that foot a rest. You're lucky you've not damaged any tendons."

Arabella begrudgingly accepted the offered piece of paper. "Right, thanks." She said, moving for the door.

"And if it starts swelling anymore or getting really red, you get yourself straight back here."

What else could she say? She smiled insincerely. "Of course, doctor."

She'd put her electric blue heels on to try and cheer herself up. It wasn't working. Sitting in the window sill, her one good foot tapping against the glass plane. It was the only foot that could fit into her shoes. She hadn't worn these shoes for ages. Wouldn't be wearing them for a while either. Damn that piece of glass.

"Fucking, fucking fuck," she finally broke out, opening the window to let some spring evening air in. Arabella was in her sitting room, which looked out of the back of the property. There was a little garden with well established hedges and trees, a neat lawn and bedding plants, all carefully tended by Adam. She could hear him rustling outside, although from this angle she couldn't actually see him. He was probably messing about with the pots on the patio.

It was Wednesday evening, and she'd still not spoken to him since the accident to the car on Sunday. There'd been some awkward moments in the kitchen in the morning, icy chills hardly broken by the steam rising from the kettle spout. She'd almost forgotten about her car, then some arse at work would make a comment, or she'd happen to catch sight of it, and grow furious all over again. It wasn't as if it was even a proper accident, the kind of understandable thing. This crunch of metalwork was the product of pure idiocy, and God only knew Adam's ridiculousness acknowledged no bounds at times. Sometimes she was sure this dithering nervous state was just the leftovers from his domineering, manipulative mother. She'd just be irritated that he couldn't rediscover his backbone and get on with it. At other, less charitable times, she just thought he was a fool.

She let out a deep sigh and reached for her banjo. Setting her right foot, the bandaged, crippled appendage, the root of a lot of her frustration, on a chair for balance, she positioned the banjo on her lap. Dug her back into the outer corner of the window sill, angling herself to fit the banjo into the space, and wrapped her fingers around the neck of the instrument.

Her foot wasn't any worse, but it certainly wasn't any better and she'd had to admit that she wouldn't be up to dancing this coming weekend. She'd called in, hoping to get the manager but sadly Pritesh, the assistant had picked up. He'd thought it hysterical that she wouldn't be able to work, mentioning some tosh about these older people not springing back from their injuries as quickly. He ought to watch his mouth; it was his fault that this had happened. All that crappy cleaning and poor consideration towards the health and safety laws of this country. He'd just laughed and said he thought he could book Cherry Malone into her slot.

Cherry Malone!

"Over my dead body," Arabella had yelled.

"It'll be over your amputated foot if you come in," Pritesh had responded. "Take it easy this weekend. You've got to know your limits. You can't keep running like you're only twenty-one anymore."

She'd hung up on him.

As if to prove a point, she'd been determined to work the weekend regardless. She called a couple of contacts, and with luck a club in York had been let down by an act at the last minute. They wanted her to sing and play the banjo – nothing too hillbilly yokel, they didn't want a re-run of *Deliverance* on a Friday night – but a few covers and a few upbeat country and western tracks. She could sit on a bar stool and be the acoustic solo female. Her foot could rest, but the rest of her would be working.

There, she thought smugly. I am not too old for it. Whatever *it* was.

She idly strummed the banjo strings, as if her hand had slipped from position, fingers catching on the instrument as they went down. She sighed again. This had been a crummy week thus.

Outside a blackbird sang from the top of the roof. There was a second strum of notes running through the six strings. Six strings of a guitar. It was a tentative, whispering strum as if it did not quite dare admit to making music. A long pause of waiting. Then a repeat, this time more definite, louder. Intentional.

Arabella shrugged to herself. This didn't mean all was forgiven. Her fingers shifted on the neck of the banjo, settling against the strings, adding pressure. A second strum, a little higher.

Six guitar notes, one higher than before climbed up to her floor.

A few banjo notes dropped back down.

A recognisable line on the guitar.

A reply in like on the banjo.

So it continued for a minute or so. Short burst of notes plucked out on the guitar received their reply a moment later on the banjo. A little slowly, cautiously, as if the tune was being learnt for the first time, learning by rote. Chords came into the mix and the pace picked up. There were no more pauses, and suddenly the banjo was lurching at the guitar's heels, not waiting for its turn, but joining in with the lazy snippets. The gates were released and the melody went into full swing, the duelling guitar and banjo tripping and skipping through the *duelling banjos*; fast energetic finger work over the frets, the strings vibrating. This was a musical piece that the banjo was supposed to win, and even if that hadn't been the rule, Arabella would have probably won anyway – both because Adam would have let her, but also as she was a proficient banjo player, a fact that always raised eyebrows when people first started to learn of her hidden talents. She could outplay Adam, not just on the banjo but the guitar and the mandolin. She owned a couple of guitars that she did play, but the banjo was her number one love.

The neighbours in their gardens heard the iconic track played live, and breathed a sigh of relief, knowing it signified the feuding was all over for the time being. Peace had been declared.

Arabella had been playing the banjo since she had first sneaked downstairs late at night aged twelve to watch the film *Deliverance* on television. The strange boy on the veranda with the banjo had captivated her, and despite the film's dark messages and vicious scenes hardly suitable for a young innocent thing just entering puberty, she couldn't get the music out of her mind. She'd been given a second hand banjo for Christmas with the intention of shutting up the constant banjo chatter. A lifetime of love had been cemented.

It was mainly a private and amateur passion, but Arabella's finger work was so fast and strong, that she could hold her own professionally and would sometimes play in local folk clubs, whipping out American bluegrass, British folk and adapted covers. She would turn her hand to anything.

In her twentieth year, she had gone on a month-long road trip through America's Deep South with a boyfriend from university. He was studying social anthropology and wanted to communicate with the country simpletons. He was a classic example of students who didn't really know the first thing about life or the world, strutting out fuelled by their own arrogance and a general sense of immortality. They were young and fresh and always would be. There was no rush to get serious.

Arabella had joined the road trip that summer partly because she wanted to learn some new tunes for her banjo, and partly because she couldn't bear the thought of two long months away from that prime body. As things turned out, it was a body and mind that lost its attraction the following winter. But in that hot sticky American summer, the end of the relationship was a long way off. The boy had not taken her that seriously. She was just the big breasted girl who had a banjo in her room – he'd never heard her play - who was studying Spanish at university. She would probably end up in a dead end job, be someone's wife, pop out a couple of kids and wind down in mediocrity. He'd seen a future, but as it turned out, he'd been seeing the extent of his own potential.

The first evening in the States, staying at a cheap motel that looked ready for another serial slashing, Arabella had sat in the windowsill and started to play. He'd been shocked. She really could play. And as news quickly spread, she'd been their ticket into the local musical culture. Arabella had found herself invited to all kinds of groups who were curious enough to meet the scarlet-haired (the dye colour of the year) English girl who played the banjo. The boyfriend might as well tag along if he had nothing better to do. Her repartee had exploded over that month and she played with a number of local legends. Somewhere there was a specialist, little known CD of a Deep South banjo player, Arabella providing number two banjo on one of the recorded tracks. There was a photograph in the album sleeve notes, the young thing from England who had appeared one day; only to disappear from their world a few weeks later.

Arabella lifted her right hand from the warming banjo strings as she had the last word in the tune. She smiled and shook her head. She was still pissed about the car, but it looked as though this was the end of the silence.

Although not the greatest singer to grace the earth, Arabella could hold a tune and she had the confidence to belt out lyrics without any sense of self consciousness. Her voice was rich, jazzy and a touch exotic. It was occasionally remarked upon that it would probably do better in French. Whatever. She lived primarily for the banjo, but some songs needed the words to bring out the full essence.

She was in her Indian princess gear for the Friday night gig. It comprised of a wig of thick long black hair fixed in a side plait with random beads woven through, and a camel coloured dress with sections scrunched up through a large wooden bangle at the base of her rib cage, revealing some midriff. Loose fitting and comfortable boots kept the bandaging on her foot hidden. The wound was healing really well after a few days of antibiotics, and she probably could have danced after all. But her slot had been booked in by the cursed Cherry, and she'd already promised to do the banjo act. Whether required or not, her foot was getting some rest.

She was coming to the end of a Dolly Parton cover, just before Graham joined her on stage for a quick set. It was a busy night in the bar. In attendance was the usual line up of couples, small groups of friends, stray students looking for something slightly more upmarket than the standard meat market. There was also a group of about fifteen or so men, all in black tie dinner suits. They were rowdy and pound-a-pint happy. They were unconscious of their own volume as a collective and only a few were still able to walk in a straight line. One had a top hat and L plates. She assumed it was one of the many stag and hen parties that chose to descend upon the city these days.

Graham was loitering on the edge, guitar already strapped on, piece of sheet metal in hand. I guess we're doing *Little Bird*, Arabella thought. Propped up, a regular foot tap against the metal gave a good drumming thudding base line to a track, and they always used it on that song. It was a song Graham insisted they do when they played together. Perhaps if she did more gigs in York, the novelty would wear off.

36

"Ladies and gentlemen," she spoke into the microphone, greeted by a roar of cheers from the bachelors, who in fairness would have probably cheered the opening of a door by this point in the evening. "May I introduce to the stage Graham Nicholson, a very fine guitarist, who will be joining me for a few tracks before I say goodnight. We're going to start off with a Swedish song called *Little Bird*."

From *Little Bird*, which sounded like an old Deep South gospel song, they rolled straight into the old familiar run of Irish and Scottish jigs and reels they'd adapted for the banjo and guitar. They were both players who enjoyed a speed challenge. It was the kind of music where Arabella could lose herself to the finger work. The background of an audience only half listening became lost to her just as the music absorbed her.

At the end of the run, Arabella sacrificed the stage to Graham and the rest of his band. She went out back to lock up her banjo for the duration, but didn't feel like going home just yet. The night felt too early. She wanted a drink. Slipping back out into the bar as a regular customer, although still in performance costume, she was caught by a man who seemed to think he knew her. He immediately struck up a lame conversation.

Arabella squinted at him, wondering if she had ever met anyone quite as bland before. Where had she seen him?

"How is your foot?"

"My foot?" How the hell did he know about her foot? Mark Thaw was his name. Her memory kicked into action. "You're my doctor."

"Well, you're not down as one of my patients." He was quick to point out. "You'd just taken a last minute appointment and I was all there was."

That last statement seemed to sum up more than a quick medical appointment to check her foot over. Arabella shivered, feeling her attention already drifting. She didn't want to spend her evening with this man.

He was rolling his shirt sleeves up nervously. "Look, would you like to dance?"

"You told me no dancing this weekend."

"Oh yes, of course I did."

"I'm going to get a drink."

"Yes, of course, let me..."

"No." She put a staying hand to his arm. "I want to sit at the bar alone. I'm not interested."

"But what's wrong with me? I'm a doctor."

And all a woman wanted was suitable husband material. Someone who would erase the money worries. Apparently. As if a man succeeding in the career stakes would be enough reflected glory for a girl. Just as all every woman really wanted was to reproduce. Arrange her replacement. Arabella felt so very weary of the world at times. "You're just not my type."

"I can change. What is your type?" He stepped up close to her. "I've been thinking about you all week."

For crying out loud, Arabella thought. Surely what had already been said was clear enough. He ought to be backing off. She certainly didn't want to hear that he'd been thinking about her all week and was now convinced that she was the one. This needed nipping in the bud. It needed finality. She needed to be rude.

"You're dull. You're not impulsive. Now leave me alone."

She could feel the man's shock boring into her back as she departed, heading for the bar. Harsh, yes, but that was life and she wasn't here to smooth over disappointment for every soul who crossed her path. Life was mean. Deal with it.

"Hey, it's Dolly!" A man in a suit drunkenly cheered her. One of the stag party. "Hey Dolly!"

"You think I'm Barbara Streisand?"

He looked bemused, as if he couldn't focus on her. "Dolly, isn't it; or Barbara? Babs?" He staggered up to her, accidentally sloshing his pint down her dress.

"Great, thanks, brother."

"Oh no, I'm so sorry." He innocently moved forward to wipe the increasing wet patch with his hands, his paws thoughtlessly going for her breasts.

"Keep your fucking hands off me." She slapped his hand.

The man giggled. "You're a feisty one."

Arabella's face darkened as if she was winding up to throw a punch.

"Herman, you need to go back to the collective." A slightly shorter man, also in black tie dinner jacket, appeared and pushed the wavering drunken beanpole in the direction of his fellow penguins.

"I'm really sorry about that."

Arabella flicked droplets of lager to the floor. This one didn't seem to be as drunk as his compatriots. "What are you, the designated driver?"

He smiled lightly. "We came up on the train, so I hope not. I'm supposed to be having a month off the booze, so I'm the sadly sober one."

"Well, I'm stone cold sober too, but I stink of lager, so go figure."

"Let me buy you a drink to make it up."

"You're not really the one who ought to be apologising."

"He's too drunk to realise." He paused, flashing her a little corner of a smile. "Come on, we came up to York to have fun, not to upset the natives. Nice job on the banjo by the way."

Arabella considered the proposal. She had decided that she needed a drink. "All right." She joined him at the bar. The bar man turned in their direction as she appeared. "I'll have a double whisky and coke; he's paying." She looked across at him, feigning innocence. "You don't mind, do you?"

"I offered."

"So you're here on a stag party?"

"Kind of obvious isn't it."

"Where are you up from?"

"London."

"And what's with the penguin theme? Do you all work as waiters or something?"

He was mid passing her the drink, but took it back on her last question. He looked horrified. The shock was feigned, as he was probably just a bit of a flirt. He was amused that the best man's idea hadn't quite worked as intended. "We're supposed to be James Bond."

"What, all of you?"

"Well, there's been a few of them over the years."

"I suppose," she mused, holding her hand out for her drink. "I don't think any of them would have denied a girl her drink though." Receiving her apology drink, she took a fair gulp, sugar and strong alcohol burning a pathway down her throat. She looked back to the sober Mr Bond. "So which one are you supposed to be?"

He straightened up, puffed out his chest and flashed her smile, as if that was how Bond caught the ladies. It was rather endearing. The real James Bond was too arrogant to feel the need for such behaviour.

"Isn't it obvious?"

Arabella considered him. Ash blonde hair, blue-grey eyes, late thirties at a guess, relatively trim. That figure would be the product of the obligatory gym to go along with the long working hours and the over achieving career. She had a couple of friends who'd gone down to London for careers and excitement. Sure, they were doing well, earning lots of money, forever achieving and doing, but Arabella felt exhausted just listening to everything they managed to cram into a week. She tapped her chin thoughtfully. "Mr Lazenby?"

His shoulders sagged at the put-down. He held his hands out at her as if she was beyond hope. "Daniel Craig."

"You think you're Daniel Craig?" She didn't sound convinced, purposefully overdoing the tone of disbelief. She supposed if he had to be one of the Bond actors, he would have to be the blondie, but really he didn't look like any of them. Besides, she felt an unconscious urge to lightly tease.

"You strike me as a hard woman to please."

She shrugged. "I can't say I'm particularly into Bond. I don't get it. I suppose with all the experience he's had, he might be a good lay. But I have a rule that misogynistic psychopaths are generally best avoided."

He burst out laughing. "Just don't tell Alan that, I think he really believes all of this."

"That he's James Bond?"

"He's really an accounts manager."

"Frustrated guy in a suit."

"It's a way to relax."

"Sounds like he's working too hard."

"Something like that."

"And what about yourself?"

"I work in marketing."

"And is that interesting?"

"Not particularly."

She nodded. Finished her drink. They were standing awfully close. She could feel the chemistry, but she had sworn off all this one night stand nonsense. It was just too depressing waking up to another stranger who looked like the ugly secret twin of the Adonis she thought she'd met the night before. Drunken nights were never intense enough, and tended to verge more on the awkward side of embarrassment. He looked like a nice guy. She felt a draw to his body and could already fantasise about the experience. It was best to leave the memory there and not spoil things. Time to bow out and go home. "Well, Mr..."

"Simon," he supplied. "But call me Ben."

"Well, Ben. You have a stag party to attend." She passed him her empty glass. "Thank you for the drink, and apology accepted. I have an act to pack up and a dress to clean, so you'll have to excuse me."

"You can't go so soon."

"I can and I will. I don't usually socialise with the audience afterwards."

"My lucky night."

"Probably not."

"I'll maybe see you around, banjo lady."

Arabella waved back at him as she sauntered away. "Not in London, you won't."

"What are you doing?" Arabella pressed her forehead to the mirror and dared to look herself in the eye. You're beyond a joke, she thought. You'd said you'd quit this. You said you'd grown up. You'd said you wanted something more.

Her hair, a little stiff with hairspray and blue glitter, brushed against the cool surface of the mirror. Her eyeliner had run slightly and crusted around the corner of her eye. Her earrings felt like heavy, leaden weights in her lobes. It had been a long evening. It was a late night. Three am. She just wanted to sleep.

She'd been restless last night, trying to sleep but unable to settle. The following day, Saturday had been something of a write off. There was an itch screaming under her clothes, and by five o'clock she knew that she had to go out. She'd called Nicki from work and they'd arranged to meet in a pub in town at eight.

Arabella had gone onto battle stations alert. The itch demanded it. She was dressed in an electric blue halter neck dress with full skirts and high heeled shoes. Her hair was filled with volume and waved high off her shoulders, crackling like electricity from the amount of hair glitter she'd applied. She looked like the slutty love child of Marilyn Monroe's *Seven Year Itch*, and one of the smurfs. She wasn't feeling much better. Nicki had raised her eyebrows when Arabella made her entrance into the pub. She distracted everyone she walked past from their conversations, some of the drunker patrons wondering if they were hallucinating.

"Jesus," Nicki had muttered as Arabella had sat at the table with a long vodka. "I didn't realise it was going to be that kind of night." She had felt distinctly dressed down, in her skinny jeans, spangly top and a couple of token bangles.

"I need to do this, get it out of my system. I've been on edge all weekend."

"And just which manga did you step out of?"

Arabella had given her a long look.

"I presume we're going clubbing after this."

"I need to dance." Arabella had taken a deep drink. "I need to get laid."

Nicki had rolled her eyes. "Come on. You're going to pick up another looser? Just go to Anne Summers and get it sorted that way."

"Either a DIY job or a permanent boyfriend?"

"This is your life, not a point to be proved."

Arabella had waved off her concerns. "I need to enjoy myself. We're definitely going dancing."

They had gone clubbing later in the evening, although the increasing age gap in appearance had sent Nicki home just before midnight. She felt like she was taking her student daughter out for a night on the town. Arabella's avoidance of something more fundamental was just depressing. Arabella was too loudly coloured to be lost in the crowd that night. She'd danced her way through a few men, probably all from university, before settling on one who had seemed tall and dashing in the vibrating, pulsating smoke-machine-nicotine-free air of the club. Now that she had him back home in her flat with the ceiling lights on, she could see that he still had the remnants of acne on his cheeks and a little boy's uncertainty and bravado hovering in his eyes. He did not know what to do with her. He was not particularly attractive, and his only redeeming feature was his height. She felt her libido spiral down the plughole.

He was waiting in her sitting room. She was in the bathroom taking a good long hard look at herself. The itch was still there but he wasn't what she wanted. What to do? Ring him a taxi and send him on his way? She'd still have her itch.

Gritting her teeth, she left the bathroom and headed for the arena of conflict.

As she entered the room, he jumped up awkwardly, clearly not sure which pose to strike. He'd taken off his jacket. He grinned at her, a slight leer. "You're looking hot," he told her, his confidence cracking when she didn't immediately respond. Had he said the wrong thing?

Arabella was suppressed a yawn. He really was lame, even worse than her landlord. What to do: throw him out or get it over with? It might help her sleep better. She walked up to him. He really was unattractive.

"Look, sweetheart, I'm really tired..."

His smile dropped.

"Will you just take me from behind?" Anything so she didn't have to look at that face again.

He grinned like he'd struck a gold mine. "Sure thing, darling."

"We're going to France this summer. I like to speak a bit of French there. I did it at school."

"I did French as well. I've forgotten a lot of it."

"Oh, languages,"

Arabella glanced up, a barely perceptible upward flick of the eyes, as a third voice joined the conversation. She ought not to be listening, because she wasn't part of the two women discussing holiday plans, but the rather loud interruption from a young temp caught everyone's attention.

"I am just brilliant at languages," the temp continued with no sense of irony. "Soak it up like a sponge."

Arabella rolled her eyes and looked back at the accounts sheets she was supposed to be working through with Jennifer. There had been a couple of payments to the company that they'd not been able to match up to any invoices or outstanding payments. Jennifer had wondered if it was to cover any of the culminative bank charges Arabella had been chasing a number of repeat offenders for. Writing off the occasional bank charge was one thing, but when these charges were adding up to hundreds of pounds of unauthorised discounts, it was getting to be a joke. Not on her watch.

"Oh really," Margaret's tone of voice changed. It was a difference that co workers who had served their time here in years rather than weeks knew did not bode well. "And what languages do you speak, Missy?"

The girl missed the barbs completely, laughing like a donkey as she continued to type at her computer. "None, but I'd be really good if I wanted to."

Margaret sniffed disdainfully and shared a look with her colleague. Arabella doubted their own talents in the language of romance went beyond hello, do you speak English, but their sniffing was perhaps a little justified. The temp was one of the minor irritations in life: braggers who had nothing to back up the boasts.

"Oh, the youth of today," Margaret's friend sighed. "So good at everything."

"I doubt that," Margaret said. "See these envelopes Charlize got ready for me?" She held one up, holding it by the corner as if it was infected. "What a mess. Sloppy job. I'm thinking I should do them all again."

The labels weren't stuck on ruler straight, but it seemed like a waste of time to give it a second thought. Arabella surprised herself by experiencing a stab of pity for Charlize, the busty youthful pinup, lust object of the month at work. At least half Margaret's age, but twice the potential, her very youth insulted Margaret, making her sour and vengeful. Petty office politics. Women sniping at women. When do we get like that, she wondered? Is it when the clock ticked past thirty?

"What about this one?" Jennifer's voice interrupted her musings on the modern workplace. "One hundred and fifty two pounds and fifty two pence."

"Now that's Davidson's, I remember the amount."

"I don't envy you your job."

Arabella was distracted again from her work, as Christine, her line manager strolled through the open plan office in their general direction. She was accompanied by Ian who appeared to be chewing her ear off. Christine seemed to be carrying more paper on her clipboard than usual, and looked a little worried. She was having a bad start to the week, two people had handed in their MATB1 forms, forewarning of coming births and maternity leave. She'd been to see HR already to ask if they could advertise for replacements. The response hadn't been promising. Budget cuts and tightening of belts. Perhaps this was a good thing to start making efficiencies.

"It's a stressful kind of team to manage; mostly women," Ian continued. "It means regular replacements. Training up people, not knowing what you're going to get. Women bring risk and stress. You know," he paused, lowering his voice slightly as if it were a great secret. "Women all want to go off and have babies."

Arabella could feel the hairs on the back of her neck stand up like an angry cat. She wasn't going to bite. Work was making her too angry.

Christine looked distinctly uncomfortable with Ian's observation. "We are an equal opportunities employer."

"I know that," Ian muttered. "But it's true. Women in a team make for stressful management."

"We see the benefits of a diverse workforce."

For whose benefit are you blurting out your slogans, Christine? Arabella wondered. She and Jennifer were finishing up as she felt the presence of management stop behind her chair. She started to gather up her papers, keen to get back to her desk and start ringing some bad debtors.

"You're turning thirty, soon, aren't you, Arabella?" Ian blurted out.

Arabella pursed her lips. Rise above it, she told herself.

"Really?" Jennifer looked surprised. "I didn't realise. I didn't think you were that old. Although I'm not sure how you are, or what I thought you were..."

"I thought you were nineteen," Margaret added.

Nineteen years old? She'd worked here for seven years, Arabella thought incredulously. Did that mean the company was in the habit of taking on child labour? Or was this what happened when you were one of the defunct generations? You didn't want to admit you were moving on in years, so viewed anyone younger as a permanent child.

"And yet sometimes you seem older," the other woman mused. "Quite opinionated."

"Flammable," Ian chuckled. "Arabella's just frustrated."

She stood up abruptly, feeling her fingernails rip into the papers. There had been occasions at work when she'd been so infuriated by someone's condescending remarks that she had seen red and full-on shouted at them. She had to stop letting work wind her up so much. Nicki had told her she would burst a blood vessel one day with all this stress. Now that she was getting old, she supposed she had to consider these things. "Arabella has a lot of work to get through this afternoon," she told them curtly, pushing past and heading for her desk and music player. Oh how she wanted to punch someone.

Ian looked like a deflated balloon. He had been hoping for a better reaction.

It would have been easy to assume that local jobs were the best. One couldn't possibly be late when there was only a ten minute walk to work. Yet this was going to be her worst record yet. She should have been there for quarter of an hour already. As much as she was whispered about in the same breath as the word diva, Arabella liked to think her work ethic was impeccable. She didn't pull sickies, she turned up on time and she got her work done. Whether it was chasing bad debtors, playing the banjo or dancing, she made sure she earned her keep. She didn't expect anyone to carry her.

These heels weren't the best for rushing, but she was going to have to turn up the glamour on this gig, otherwise there was a distressing risk she could start to resemble her band mates. They were a trio of old daddy rockers, in their fifties, thinking about getting motorbikes if they hadn't already. They had uninspired day jobs, just as Arabella. In their free time they liked to play country and western. They took a few barn dance bookings every year. They liked to book Arabella when her schedule matched up to theirs, claiming it was purely for her skill on the banjo, but it was probably also for the fact that her appearance always increased their chances and bargaining powers on future bookings.

She was heading down the tree lined street towards the bridge across the River Foss, banjo case swinging at her side, when she picked up a figure in her periphery. At first this pedestrian casually walked, but on clocking her, picked up the pace. Shit, this person was coming up to her to talk. Really crappy timing.

"Miss Mangella!"

Miss Mangella? This slowed her down, tottering to a moment of surprise. Who was this, an old school teacher? She looked distractedly at the man. He was a standard, average man in every sense. He was vaguely familiar but she couldn't quite recall and she really didn't care. She needed to get to work.

His warm smile faltered a little as he registered the blank look on her face. She hadn't recognised him. "It's Dr Thaw... I mean, Mark," he reminded her.

"Dr Thaw?"

"Mark," he corrected, keen to get away from the patient doctor relationship that they'd never really had. He did not want to cultivate the professional side of their potential relationship. "I saw you play in town a couple of weeks ago."

Of course, she remembered now. The James Bond night. And he'd been there. Had he been trying to chat her up? Things she didn't need.

His head wobbled as if he was trying to attract her attention to something in the background. "Do you have time just now...?"

"I'm going to work." She cut him short and started walking again.

"Oh, you're performing; great. Can I come and watch you?"

"I suppose, if you must," she muttered.

"And we could go for a drink afterwards."

She couldn't remember their last brief conversation word for word, but she was quite sure she'd made it clear she wasn't interested. "No we can't. I told you last time. I'm not interested."

"I know," he hurried after her as she marched for the bridge. "You said I'm not impulsive, but I am. Surely you can see that. I'm asking you out now."

"That hardly counts."

"Miss Mangella," he caught her arm, a little too breathlessly for Arabella's taste, and stepped up close to her. "It's been two weeks since I last saw you and I can't stop thinking about you. I could be good for you if you'd just give me the chance."

Why was he being so melodramatic? Melodramatic and deaf and dumb and so frustratingly irritating. "You are not my type. Leave me alone."

"You said I was dull and not impulsive. You're wrong. I'll show you." He looked around, as if searching for inspiration or checking for witnesses. Dropping his briefcase on the footpath, he scurried off the bridge and onto the path through the grass, scrambling down the bank and splashing into the shallow river.

What the hell, Arabella mouthed to no one. She moved to the centre of the bridge and leant over the brick wall. Down below stood the doctor, river water streaming past his shins and rapidly soaking up his trouser legs. Was he going for the pity vote: the poor man was so damn desperate; she'd have to go for a drink? Or was this a comedy set up? Or was the man deranged or depressed or just unstable? Either way, he really wasn't her problem.

He held out his arms and smiled up at her.

"What is wrong with you? Do you think we're living in Love-Bloody-Actually-Land?"

His smile faltered. Arabella's angry face was in shadow, looming over at him from the side of the bridge.

"Have you been watching too many bloody rom-coms with quaintly eccentric English men who play the fool and get the girl? Do you think that any old twat standing in a river is going to get my pulse going?" The media had a lot to take the blame for, perpetuating this myth of love at first time. She'd never experienced it, and she was pretty sure it didn't exist. It was just pathetic, simpering over one person. Especially when you weren't their match.

His arms dropped to his sides.

"It ain't happening, sweetheart. Just deal with it and get back to being yourself."

"Miss Mangella..." he started as her face disappeared from over the side of the bridge.

Arabella was walking again. "I've got a job to do."

Later that night, or strictly speaking the next morning, Adam Kepwick had tears streaming down his face as Arabella recounted the evening's bizarre experiences to him over tea. He'd still been up when she'd returned from the barn dance gig, engrossed in bathroom tiles. He had finished an entire wall of tiling. He was working out which tiles needed to be trimmed to fill in awkward gaps. They'd put the kettle on and sat around the kitchen table sharing horror stories of the past few days. A dog had made off with Adam's prosthetic leg whilst he'd been waiting at the bus stop. An unbelievably apologetic dog owner had managed to wrestle the limb from the mutt and get it back to him ten minutes later. Adam had been late for his shift, with the particularly lame excuse that he was late because the dog had taken his leg. The said prosthetic limb sported a number of canine dents. Adam couldn't yet decide if he wanted it fixed, or would prefer to keep the leg as it was, complete with war wounds. Speaking of war wounds had encouraged Arabella, a little giddy from the evening of music, to get her foot out on the table, with its line of healing skin down the sole. It was a battle of woe she wasn't going to win, because Adam had a stump. Accepting defeat, she collected her banjo from the hallway and headed upstairs for bed.

The one-night-only show had been sold out for well over a month but Shazia's cousin worked on the box office and they'd been able to get tickets last minute. It was a burlesque extravaganza in Leeds, a variety show of the adult kind with a respectable approval. This wasn't like going to a seedy lap dancing club where greasy men who wanted to talk and bravado lads waving cash liked to go. Arabella wasn't a particular follower of burlesque, but even she had heard of the two headlining names. There was an American who was a trendsetter in the genre, and an Australian who was relatively new but gaining popularity with tremendous speed. Then a list of other acts, their names in smaller print, including the infamous Cherry Malone. That was the real reason they were here, to check out the competition. It had all been Shazia's idea, gleefully informing Arabella down the phone that she'd managed to get these tickets, three of them although she wasn't sure who to invite as the third part. Just to be awkward Arabella had told her that Adam would like to come.

Her eyes flicked up from the leaflet, running over the audience as they queued to get into the auditorium. It was a wide spread of society, and not just men looking forward to catching a glance of a cheeky backside or a curvy breast. There were women, a lot of women. Here for the dancing, for the songs, for the vintage style, for the emancipation of women, a giggle, or maybe just the thrill of watching a stripper. But this wasn't the stripping of backstreet neon signs. It was an art form – so declared the blurb on the leaflet. Whatever, she thought, there were still perverts going in to this performance who saw it as nothing more than naked flesh.

Adam looked terrified as they finally reached the doors. Shazia handed over their tickets. He was still trying to come to terms with the fact that he was going to look at naked ladies, but that it was all right to do in this setting. When Arabella had told – not asked – him that they would be going to a burlesque show that Friday, he'd actually wanted to check that they didn't really take all their clothes off, did they? He had almost whispered the question, even though they were the only two people in the kitchen. The only damn people in the entire house. Adam's mother would be spinning in her grave if she knew what Arabella was exposing her son to. It was a pleasant satisfaction which almost counteracted her feelings when she heard the name Cherry Malone.

There was an excited buzz of anticipation in the semi lit auditorium, people filtering in and taking their seats. It already looked packed and there were still people queuing to get in.

"We're just over here!" Shazia scampered ahead, herding a gathering of already seated ladies in their forties up so they could do the awkward shuffle, hope-my-arse-doesn't-stick-in-your-face slide to get to their seats. Arabella went in last, her attention drawn to the stage where a curtain of vintage artwork, like an elaborate circus poster, hung, gently shuddering. She flopped into her seat, immediately irritated as the woman next to her slopped her flabby elbow onto the shared armrest. On her other side Adam was nervously twitching.

"So, Adam, have you been to anything like this before?" Shazia beamed at her neighbour.

Adam almost swallowed his own tongue. "No, I don't go to the theatre much. Arabella wanted me to come."

"Arabella said you wanted to come. I thought you were into burlesque."

"Arabella?" Adam looked across at his lodger.

"Don't worry, you're here as our chaperone." Arabella winked at him.

Shazia burst out into peals of laughter. "What do you think is going to happen?"

"To be honest, I don't know. Judging from the audience anything could happen. I need to take my jacket off." She wriggled, trying to shrug-shoulder her way out, but the space between Adam and the grim-faced woman was too narrow. Sighing, purposefully loud but the hint unnoticed, she stood up and slipped her jacket off. She suspected it was going to get hot in here, and the halter neck top would be enough.

"Hey, banjo lady!"

The call had come out from somewhere in the rows behind her. The voice was familiar although she couldn't quite place it. A hand went up directly behind, the next but one row further back from where she was seated. Arabella twisted, catching sight of the man as he sat up from his slouch. A smile twisted in the corner of her lips. It was immediate recognition of the best variety. "Ah, Mr Bond I presume."

The man next to the ex wannabe Bond, a bespectacled type with thick dark frames of the latest fashions, looked confused, turning to his friend for explanation. "Why are you Bond?"

"Crap stag do a few weeks ago," he explained. His attention remained on Arabella. "It's Ben Simon, remember?

"Right." She was slightly bemused as he got up and leaned across to shake her hand, oblivious to the irritated expression of the woman sitting between them. How formal. Very gentlemanly. Is this what one did when one unexpectedly met at a burlesque show? "In York. And now you're here in Leeds."

"Enjoyed my trip that much had to get back up to Yorkshire."

"That and I had a free ticket," his friend muttered.

"Oh, you're on freebies too?"

"I'm a journalist. Here for the local rag. Ben's just on the spare."

"And how have you come by freebies? You're not a journalist as well when you're not playing the banjo?"

"Hardly. Friends in the box office."

There was a moment of silence, no words but a definite undercurrent, the journalist thought, as the woman, the banjo lady, folded her jacket and kept Ben's eye as if she was determined not to be the first to look away.

"Do you know, I never caught your name in York."

"Really?" She paused as the volume of the music started to rise. "I think it's about to start. I'd better sit down."

The show kicked off, an extravaganza of solo and joint performances, a live orchestral soundtrack and some smart costumes, at least until they were disassembled. It was actually rather infectious, and Arabella had to wonder if the audience had a few more drinks, whether some of them would be joining the acts in the shedding of clothes in the aisles. By the midpoint break Cherry Malone had already performed, essentially being one of the supporting acts, a small player in comparison to the American. She was irritatingly competent at what she did. There was a little belly dancing involved in her act. It was not enough for Arabella to feel threatened by her skill, she was surprised and relieved to see. Although mediocre ability didn't seem to matter. The crowd went crazy for the local girl, waving her tassels into the air and flashing her Marilyn smile at the fans.

There would be a half hour break for people to discuss what they had just seen, to get refreshments or to relieve themselves, in whatever sense that meant. Arabella leaned over Adam to Shazia. "Do you think they're selling ice cream?"

"At a burlesque show?"

"They're a theatre, they're always selling sweets. Do you want one?"

Shazia paused, her amusement dropping at Arabella's odd moment of naivety. "Yes."

"Adam?"

Adam was still gripping the arm rests. Arabella patted his shoulder. "I'll get you something."

Slipping back past the ladies to the aisle, she weaved her way up the milling audience to get through to the refreshment stall. Third in the queue, not bad for a quick piece of movement. She was feeling a little jittery ever since the lights had warmed up to denote the end of act one. She had to get out of her seat.

"Could I get three tubs of ice cream?" She asked as she got to the front of the queue.

"What flavour?"

"Oh chocolate will be fine," she said distractedly, looking over the array of children's sweets on offer. Crazy days. "So how will this be served, off a stripper's rear end?" She looked up in perfect timing with the end of her jaunty comment to meet the stony and unamused gaze of the usherette. Tough crowd, she thought. Probably why she'd never gotten into comedy. She passed over a ten pound note.

Heading back down the wide steps of the aisle, a stack of three chocolate pots in her hands, she was stopped by a hand to her elbow.

"Enjoying the show so far?"

Her own James Bond, Mr Ben Simon of London. "It's certainly an eye opener."

"I've never been to anything quite like this."

"Really? I would have thought this would have been common place in London long before it hit a backwater like here."

He smiled, if a little wearily. "Don't do the offended northerner thing; I've had enough of that from him." He nodded in the direction of the journalist. "I'm not even from London originally. Anyway, you never got around to telling me your name."

She felt a little irritated by his friendly telling off, disinclined to continue. "Really? I didn't know I'd been planning to."

"Arabella!" Shazia appeared at her side. "Our ice creams are melting whilst you're yakking." She took two of the tubs from her friend before looking at the stranger. "Don't mind me; I'm just her hungry friend."

"Ben."

"Shazia."

"And do you play something as well?"

She looked a little lost by the question. "Tennis," she said, not sure if it was the right answer. "I'd better get back with this," she added, holding up the ice cream tub.

Ben looked equally bemused.

"She's not a musician," Arabella explained, amused he'd thought banjo lady would be friends with violin woman and drumming man.

"And you're Arabella."

"I am indeed, Arabella the banjo lady."

"Also known as?"

"I don't do nicknames; it's just Arabella." People eager for refreshments pushed past her, forcing her to trip into one of the end chairs. She winced as her knee hit the chair awkwardly. One foot healed, on to the next injury. "I don't really think this is a good place for standing around. I should get back."

"What are you guys doing afterwards? We could all go for a post mortem drink, discuss the show, give my pal something intelligent to put in his review."

Arabella held his gaze, her mouth slightly open, her ice cream melting in her hand. Condensation ran down between her fingers, searching for an outlet. Pooling in the curve before trickling over her knuckles. She was very tempted. She'd been tempted last time, but had sworn off one night stands. It hadn't worked as she'd been on the prowl the very next night. But that boy hadn't been anything she'd regret not seeing again. As for this man, it was a lucky coincidence that she had run into him for a second time. It was so lucky that it certainly would not happen again. This was a bit too intense and far too sober for a one night stand. But if it wasn't a one night stand then what was it? He lived in London. The distance would only cause pain. She was skipping too far ahead of herself, she knew, it was just drinks, but she couldn't take any more upset or disappointment.

"We have to drive home after this," she finally responded, feeling her own disappointment in her stomach. This was for the best, she told herself.

He was confused. "But I'm not up this way much."

"That's exactly my point."

"Oh my god!" Shazia shrieked later on in the car as Arabella was giving her a lift home. "He asked you out and you turned him down? What is wrong with you? You've been single for ages and he was kind of cute."

"There's loads of cute people out there."

"I was there whilst you were letting my ice cream melt. He couldn't take his eyes off you."

"So?"

"You couldn't take your eyes off him. It's an offence against all things romantic and..." Shazia shook her hands in the air as if trying to strangle an unseen adversary. "Adam, tell her she's an idiot."

Adam, demoted to the back seat until they'd dropped off Shazia, shook his head. "Arabella's not an idiot."

"You think she did the right thing?" Shazia gasped, lurching around in the passenger seat.

"No, but Arabella knows what she's doing."

Arabella glanced in the screen mirror to the silhouette of Adam. That was the loyalty of the landlord for you. What faith. She really wasn't sure of herself anymore.

"You people are mad."

"Look, where was the point? He lives in London."

"And?"

"I'm not interested in long distance shit." Arabella indicated to turn left, slowing for the junction.

"It was just drinks, Arabella. You can't write your life off like that," Shazia complained. "You've seen enough films to know..."

"...that it's idealised bullshit and not real life." She stopped the car outside of Shazia's house. "Look, stop stressing. I've only met him twice. It's no big deal."

"Please tell me you at least got his number."

"I have no way of getting in touch with him and I will never see him again."

Shazia shook her head at those words and got out of the car. The usual thank yous for the lift, great night, call you soon, were exchanged and she was gone into the night. Arabella waited whilst Adam changed seats, feeling those words grow heavy in her mouth, a bad taste she couldn't spit out. What had she done? She gripped the steering wheel. Nothing to worry about. She was just getting a little giddy with the big three-zero approaching. Plenty more fish in the sea.

Adam shut the passenger door. "Home, James, Arabella."

"Sure thing."

"So, are you looking forward to your thirtieth?"

Arabella, a mouth full of salad and croutons, looked warningly up at Nicki from her lunch.

"It's this Wednesday, you know."

"I'm quite aware of the fact." She put her fork down and took a draught of water. "But the fact is that it's Monday today and Wednesday is in the future."

"It'll come however much you ignore it."

Arabella shrugged. "It's just a number."

Nicki almost choked on her soup. "That's rich coming from you."

"It's like you say, it's going to come whatever. I've got to deal with it."

"It's a tough life, isn't it? Getting old and turning thirty." Sitting a good ten years on, Nicki wished she could complain about the fact she would be thirty in a couple of days' time. Oh to have her thirties to relive again, to try and get things right.

"Listening to the way people talk about women over thirty..."

"You're hardly the type to be concerned with popular opinion."

"I know, but I did have an older person's moment at the weekend," Arabella admitted, stabbing a cherry tomato with her fork.

"You're suffering from dementia?"

"No. I just thought about the long term consequences and walked away from something. Jesus," Arabella grinned at nothing and shook her head. "I don't know what came over me. We'd gone to this burlesque show in Leeds."

"That doesn't sound like old fuddy duddy behaviour."

"No, not that. I bumped into some dude I'd met before. He's actually from London. But anyway, he asked us out for drinks afterwards and I turned him down."

"That doesn't sound like you."

Arabella snorted. "Like I'm some easy slut? No, what went through my head was that London is too far away and I couldn't be doing with it."

"That sounds serious."

"But it's not; I've only met him a couple of times. I was just disturbed that my brain went down that line of thinking. That I considered the consequence of my actions. Do you know what I mean?"

"Kind of. I'd always had you as a bit of a lone wolf."

"Damn right. I'm not one for dangling on a guy's arm. Men have their uses, but I need my space."

Nicki pursed her lips. To a degree she and Arabella were of the same ilk. They were independent women who worked, had their own money, weren't afraid to go out on their own, and if a problem came up or something needed fixing, they didn't need a man to sort it out. They'd get on and do it themselves, or pay someone to do it. But with standard culture revolving around couples, how to catch a man for life, and the urban myths that all women just loved babies and every girl had been planning her wedding for her entire existence, it could get a bit much. The natural reaction of the stubborn was to push back and say no to it all. I don't need that. Need they certainly didn't, but what about want? The pressure sucked out any free space to actually consider how they wanted their lives to be.

"Mind if we join you, ladies?"

A couple of the temps, Charlize the current eye candy of the office, and another girl Arabella couldn't remember the name of sat down at the table. It was busy in the canteen and this was as much out of necessity as a need to be social. The nameless temp had a fashion magazine open at a page with lurid yellow high heels on display. Arabella glanced across. Her tastes were certainly eccentric but even that looked too much.

"Did you read this article about the dancers in America?" the girl asked no one in particular, flicking through to a glossy article: big pictures, small text. "It's about these girls who work in all the R&B music videos. They earn good money. It's supposed to be liberating..."

Arabella snorted. "Getting paid to wave your arse in hot pants for cash?"

Nicki laughed. "I though that's what you did!"

"You dance in music videos?" The temp looked impressed, Charlize mildly curious.

"I do not. I don't shake my arse to make any bling boy in shapeless exercise clothing look good. I perform as a solo artist. It is art. I just don't flash my crotch at the audience."

The temp started to blush. Fashion magazines with articles about issues that would never really affect her were one thing; sitting next to older women who were clearly more relaxed and experienced was a completely different issue. Nicki was just laughing; Charlize was leaning in, as though she wanted to ask questions. She was like the little girl who had burst in on her older sister's party.

"Seriously, have you watched ballet?"

"I think there's a bit more to it than crotch flashing."

"Yeah, yeah, yeah," Arabella muttered, finishing off the last of her salad.

"So what dancing do you do?" Charlize asked.

Arabella glanced up at her. The new youthful beauty of the office. The one that men and women lusted after. Not that being a wet-dream object was necessarily enviable, but it had knocked her off her perch. "I'm on the belly dance circuit."

Charlize pursed her lips. "I thought you looked familiar. It just didn't immediately click, without the costumes."

Arabella felt a little taken aback that she had been recognised.

There was a roar from the other end of the canteen. The four women twisted and strained to catch sight of the drama. One of the workers from the stores department was red faced and shaking. It looked as though he'd knocked some food to the floor. One of the managers was trying to talk to him.

"Jesus, what the fuck is his problem?" Arabella muttered, slipping back into her seat.

"They've made him redundant today," Nicki said quietly. "I think they told them they had to work out the week, but they might be changing their minds on that score..."

"Really?" Arabella's eyes widened. "I know they've been talking about making cut backs and savings for ages. I didn't think they were actually going to go through with anything."

"It's how it goes. A lot of vague talk for months, and then bang." Nicki snapped her fingers. "I think they're going through all the departments this week with the bad news."

"Another thing we can do without." Arabella caught her friend's face. "You're not worried about this?"

Nicki went to brush it off and lie, then faltered. "A bit. Purchasing is a team they've been looking to gut for a while now."

"You'll be fine. They'd be fools to get rid of you."

"That remains to be seen."

"What about you, Arabella?" the temp asked.

She shrugged. "There's really only the two of us. I doubt they could reduce it anymore." She paused, catching Nicki's eye. Nothing was guaranteed.

"Some of the temps were told not to come back at the end of last week," Charlize said. "The rest of us have been told we might be getting some new responsibilities."

"Shit."

"You've known about this for months," Nicki reminded Arabella.

"I know, but I just kind of forgot about it. Thought it would never happen."

"It might not yet. The finance team is probably quite safe. They did a bit of slimming down when Ray retired."

"True," Arabella nodded, not entirely convinced. They were shifting into unsettling times, with a cloud of uncertainty hanging over the building. She was turning thirty this week and she'd stupidly turned down a bit of short term casual fun. She didn't have the capacity to take on any more crap.

CHAPTER THIRTY

The sun was blazing through the window on the day Arabella turned thirty. She'd forgotten to draw the curtains the night before, and was rudely awoken early in the morning. Sunlight crossed her slumbered pose a good hour before she usually started to stir. As if she was a small child over excited by the promise of Christmas, waking up at silly o'clock and too giddy to do anything but wish time would go faster. Arabella didn't want time to go any quicker.

Not that becoming thirty had brought any noticeable difference to her life. In the bathroom mirror the same image peered groggily back at her. She didn't feel different within herself, certainly not from the day before. She didn't feel as though she was old, had suddenly converted to conservative and mature opinions. Her breasts weren't hanging around her knees; her stomach hadn't suddenly pumped out like a balloon. She scowled at her reflection. Whatever.

Showered and dressed, a pristine design for the coming summer, Arabella strolled down the staircase, in neat trousers, polka dot halter neck top and a pair of aviator sunglasses propped up on her styled nest of thick dark hair. It was just a regular day, going to work and doing all the usual crap. She'd be going out on Friday for drinks and celebrations.

In the kitchen Adam was already up and busying himself. He was startled, guilty as she wandered in and straight across to the kettle.

"Arabella, happy birthday."

She smiled, surprising even herself by how calmly she was taking this. Perhaps she'd stressed over this milestone for enough years in her twenties, that when it finally arrived it was bound to be a big anti climax. "Thank you," she said, flicking the kettle on to boil. "It appears as though earlier predictions were wrong and it wasn't the end of the world when I switched decades." Adam had listened to an excessive amount of chatter about turning thirty pretty much ever since she'd moved in. Even now she wasn't convinced he truly understood. Thirty wouldn't seem a big deal for someone swiftly approaching forty. Adam had been thirty once, but didn't strike her as someone who would have ever mourned the loss of youth.

"You should sit down at the table, Arabella."

She turned around, properly observing the kitchen for the first time. Adam was busy at the oven again. The breakfast table was set, with tulips in a vase, a pot of tea already made, and a present and card waiting beside a mug. Her face broke out into wide grin. "Oh, Adam, thank you." As much as she liked to protest she didn't need fuss, she looked after herself; she still got a buzz from presents. She was still a small child after all.

Scampering over to the kitchen table, she sat down, poured herself a mug of tea and turned her attention to the birthday treats. The card depicted a round fluffy bear taking a stroll down a cobbled street through a field – why someone would cobble a path through a field, she really didn't know. The picture was just the kind of thing Adam would give. A shriek erupted as she opened the parcel, gleefully ripping the paper. "I didn't think this was available anymore!" She waved the CD in the air. It was an album by a Deep South American musician, now deceased, with lots of blues and banjos and slide guitars. Something she'd been wishing for a long time.

"I found it second hand," Adam said, setting a plate in front of her. "This is your birthday breakfast, Arabella."

"Thank you so much!" she grabbed him around the neck and kissing him on the cheek, felt him wobble with embarrassment. Never mind that he seemed to think she was three rather than thirty with a birthday omelette, complete with her age spelt out in peas.

Adam shuffled back to his own side of the table, where a regular omelette waited for him.

"Do you think this is going to be the best birthday ever?" she asked him.

Adam grinned. "Definitely."

She was on a high as she pulled into the car park at work, oblivious today to the smirks at her beat up vehicle. The passenger side was still battered and unusable. Waving off Andrew's sarcastic comments, she strolled into the office. Only a few people were in. The background filled with a low hum of computers running and quiet conversations. She was a little earlier than usual, and had preceded the bulk of the office. Flicking on her computer, she sat down at her desk and checked through her phone whilst she waited for the machine to boot up. There was a message from Shazia saying happy birthday, and that she'd be coming over to York for Friday. Another message from her crazy travelling cousin who was working in Thailand at the moment.

Her eyes flicked up to the computer as the log in box appeared. Putting her phone to one side, she typed in her ID and password and pressed enter. An error message flashed up. Incorrect password. She typed it again, and the same message appeared. Grimacing, Arabella slowed down. She entered her password, letter for letter, making sure she didn't skip something or transpose any letters. It was definitely correctly inputted.

Incorrect password.

"Great." A little crack shifted through her bliss. "Now I'm locked out." Three tries and the system locked up. Kicking back her chair, she headed over to the IT section. A section suggested a separately housed crack team, but in reality they were a small team of males, uniformed in baggy jeans and supposedly amusing T-shirts. Their desks were cluttered with sci-fi pictures, cult cartoon character dolls and desk toys of no obvious point. Only one of the IT section was in as of yet. There had been a time when Arabella had only to stroll over and they were all like snails with their eyes on sticks. These days the novelty had worn off, familiarity breeding contempt, and the steady array of ever-younger temps tended to distract them instead.

However at this hour in the morning she didn't have a lot of competition.

The man-child, who was probably in his thirties but still dressed like he was fifteen, looked up as she approached, popping his iPod headphones out of his ears.

She smiled at him. "I've locked myself out of my machine."

"Already?"

She bit down on her irritation. This had never happened to her before. He made it sound like this was a regular occurrence. She wasn't one of those bubbleheads that came and went like the months here. "It's my birthday today. You have to be nice to me."

"Ok, what's your name?"

"Arabella Mangella."

He started typing, and once his eyes had been drawn to the computer screen, she was completely dead to him. There was only the holy alter of the virtual world. What had men done before the invention of computers and internet?

"Oh right, I see..." he stopped, his eyes widening slightly. "Mangella?"

"Yes."

"This is a problem."

"I only mistyped my password three times. I've just locked myself out, it's no biggie."

"This isn't simple," he told her, getting up from his desk. "I'm going to have to see someone about this."

"Oh." Arabella stood at his desk, watching him march away to the offices at the end of the open plan area. Was he a new starter who didn't know what he was doing? Did he have to fetch the boss? She stepped around to peer at his computer screen, but he'd locked it. No clues as to what he had been doing. "Well, I'll leave it with you," she said to no one, and departed in the direction of the kitchen.

Nicki found her in one of the easy chairs, drinking coffee and staring out of the window. "Happy Birthday, old lady!" she cried, brandishing a glittery gift bag with the top of a bottle sticking forth. "You've not dissolved into a pile of aged wrinkles?"

Arabella smiled wryly. "Not yet."

"I'm sure the ticking time bomb will wait off a bit longer."

"No doubt. Thank you," she added, accepting the present.

"What are you doing hanging around here so early? You on strike?"

Arabella finished her coffee. "Just waiting for the computer nerds; my computer's playing up." She rolled her eyes. "It always manages to time it for when I have too much to do."

"You should have taken today off."

"I guess. See you at lunch?"

"Of course."

Arabella strolled out of the kitchen area, bag swinging by her side, her mood upbeat despite the current technology problems of the morning.

"Arabella?" Jeanette, a pristine forty something whose physical perfection put a lot of the twenty year olds in the office to shame, was leaning out of the side office, clutching the door frame as if she might be blown away. "Do you have a moment?"

The computer techies probably wouldn't be finished yet anyway. "Sure," she said, readjusting her route to head into the HR manager's office without a thought. "What's up?"

"Grab a chair." Jeanette closed the door and turned, her straightened, feather-light hair floating around the movement trajectory like a shampoo and styling advert. "Pretty bag," she commented, eyeing the gift bag Arabella had set on her desk, doubting very much it was for her.

"Yeah, it's a birthday present."

"It's your birthday today?"

"Yes." Arabella eyed Jeanette a little suspiciously at the subdued response to the news. Had the rumour got around that she was thirty? It was no longer something to celebrate as the passing years took their toll on her body and mind? And whilst the rest of them aged, Jeanette just seemed to continue to grow younger, an eternally youthful fairy.

Jeanette sat down behind her desk, moving her computer screen with a creak on the pretext of seeing Arabella better, but really she didn't want to have to look at that damned gift bag.

"As you already know we have been making a thorough assessment of the business over the last few months, with a full efficiency audit. These are austere times and we need to know that we are getting the most for our money in all departments. Within your department the new business model has been approved. This does mean a number of staffing reductions. We are dropping to the one credit controller, who will be credit controller supervisor, with an administration assistant..."

Jesus, Arabella thought, poor Robin.

"As a result of this decision, I'm very sorry to have to tell you that we will have to let you go."

"I..." she started to speak, full of condolences about her to-be-ex-colleague, before her brain short-fused. They weren't making Robin redundant. They weren't making Robin redundant? *They weren't making Robin redundant.*

Jeanette was taking paperwork, letters, and official documents out of a file on her desk. "You've been with the company for seven years, so redundancy pay will be the equivalent of seven months pay, tax free as you know. This will be effective as of the end of the month, although from today to the end of the month you will be on gardening leave. That will be taxable as normal...."

"I don't understand this."

Jeanette stopped talking.

"You're making me redundant?"

"That's correct. As I was..."

"On my birthday?"

"I appreciate this isn't ideal timing. I hadn't realised..."

"You're HR. You have my file. Right there on your desk." She was gradually leaning forward, her hands now hooked onto the edge of the desk. "You're keeping Robin on as the credit controller?"

"He will..."

"I've been here longer. I thought it was last one in, first one out."

"Everyone has been assessed according a business need criteria."

"Is this because I'm a woman?"

Jeanette scowled at her. She delicately touched her collar bone midpoint as if she was about to testify. "As a working woman..."

"You've picked Robin over me?" Arabella demanded loudly. "I carry that fucking credit control section."

"I can't discuss Robin's criteria with you, only to say that he was deemed the most efficient."

"Because he's careless and too timid to chase in debts."

"Arabella, the decision is made." Jeanette pushed paperwork across the desk. "I need you to sign this so I can authorise your redundancy package."

"You're making me redundant?" She felt like a stuck record, juddering against the needle and getting nowhere fast. They were kicking her out, after all the fucking sweat she'd put into this job. She abruptly stood up from her chair, snatching the paperwork off Jeanette. "I'll have to read this later. I've got too much to do right now."

"Arabella, we're paying you gardening leave till the end of the month."

"Just as soon as the techies have fixed my password." She stopped talking, feeling an inward groan rise up through her body. Stupid, stupid, Arabella. No wonder that IT boy had looked so awkward when he'd gone searching in the system for her name. They didn't want the discarded logging back into the system, and accessing the client database, the accounts... the havoc that could be brought about. It just wasn't worth the risk. Snip the connection, and then give them the bad news. If they felt like revenge, at least they couldn't get in to destroy anything important.

"Gardening leave means..."

"I know what bloody gardening leave means," she snapped. "We'll pay you, but kindly piss off out of our office and our sight so we don't have to deal with the guilty reminder."

"We'd appreciate it if you could clear your desk and say your goodbyes in the next half hour, to avoid disruption to the working day..."

"Oh, fuck off, you fucking robot corporate fucker." So much for trying to become a calmer person, save her blood pressure and mellow for the impending old age.

Jeanette's face darkened. "I need you to sign those papers or you're not getting your money."

"Fine." Arabella reached out blindly, snatching at a pen and missing, knocking Jeanette's desk tidy over. Scrabbling for a pen, she angrily scrawled her signature and date, not even bothering to read the terms and conditions. She just wanted to be out of this place.

"Try not to think of this as an end, but rather a chance for a new beginning."

Arabella threw the papers at her.

Jeanette let out a long sigh, separating the duplicates out and offering them back. "These are yours. We'll get the P45 in the post."

Stuffing her papers into her birthday bag, Arabella marched out of the office. Back in open plan, a few more people had arrived for the working day. Close to Jeanette's office there was a particular strained, hushed atmosphere. They had heard raised voices, not the words, but would have guessed what had just happened. It wasn't difficult to work out, considering what had been occurring in all departments this week. Smug bastards, sitting there staring diligently at their screens. No one wanted to make them redundant. She was the rejected one. The member of staff who was a bit shit, not as good. Were they all laughing under the surface, catching one another's eyes and nodding? It was only to be expected. It was a good opportunity to get rid of the dross.

Holding her head high, refusing to meet anyone's eye, Arabella strode through the office to her desk. She opened up her handbag, throwing her phone and sunglasses in. Ripped off a couple of personal pictures from the back board; a cup and a couple of silly office presents which all ended up in the birthday bag. Flinging open the bottom draw, she pulled out her personal office survival kit, something that had mushroomed over the years she'd bedded in here: a pair of blueberry blue flats for when her feet ached; body spray; hand cream; hair brush; cheese crackers; green tea bags; paracetemol; umbrella; hot water bottle; half empty box of tampons; mints and a small collection of mismatched random cutlery. She had a couple of tied up spare carrier bags, now suitable to remove her possessions.

Kicking the drawer shut, she straightened to find Robin uncertainly standing by her desk.

"Is everything all right?"

He obviously hadn't been told yet. He was clutching paperwork, probably wanting to go through a problem client. Not her problem anymore. "Congratulations are in order."

"They are?" Robin looked terrified. It didn't seem to be a good thing judging by Arabella's face.

"You're in charge of credit control."

"I am?" He blanched.

Arabella leaned up to him. "All on your own," she hissed.

"But what..."

"I'm surplus to requirements. Although I'm sure the fact that they don't want to have to pay out maternity has nothing to do with anything."

Robin's eyes widened. "You're pregnant?"

"Of course I'm not bloody pregnant. But I'm a thirty year old woman who hasn't had kids yet. What the hell is wrong with me? Of course it's the only thing I want to fucking do. You're a man. Man versus thirty year old woman. It's a no brainer who they're going to keep."

"You think that's the only reason?" Robin looked a little irritated. "You can't blame everything that happens on that."

"Oh fuck off, Robin," Arabella snapped. She was swearing too much this morning, quite aware the F-word was wearing thin. She needed to vent. "Just... the lot of you can fuck off." She started rummaging through her handbag for her lipstick, coming across an arctic red stick. Snapping the cap off, she scrawled 'fuck off' on her blackened screen, as if she were teaching him the essentials, a bizarre dominatrix dungeon of modernity: lipstick and computers rather than chalk and blackboards.

She threw the lipstick back and gathered up her bags. "I'm leaving now."

Robin held up the papers he'd brought over.

"And as for that, I no longer give a damn."

Out in the car park Lynn was leaning against the bonnet of her car, her arm resting on a cardboard box full of potted plants and photos of the family, a cigarette dangling sadly from the side of her mouth. She looked up as Arabella bustled angrily forth from the doors, a rippling mass of plastic carriers and paraphernalia.

"They shaft you as well?"

"Yes." Unlocking her car, she opened the driver's door and unceremoniously flung her bags onto the passenger seat. "Screw them," she added. "I'm done with this shit hole."

Lynn spat the remains of her cigarette to the ground and stubbed it out underfoot. "Indeed. Just wish I knew what I'm going to do for money."

"It's not an end, it's a fresh start, don't you know?"

Lynn smirked. "Yes, I'd heard some nonsense like that."

Fresh start, my arse. Arabella reversed her car out of the space, not caring if she scratched any neighbouring cars. Fresh starts were to be at her convenience and choice. This was just bullshit. Putting her foot to the accelerator, she drove out of the car park for the last time.

"Motherfucking bastards!" Arabella kicked the damaged side of her car, hurting her foot more than the crumpled body work. The metal didn't buckle in the slightest. In fury at the affront, she slammed both hands onto the side of the vehicle as if she might try to roll it over.

A twig snapped, and she looked under her arm, watching the two polite, middle class doggy walkers trot over to their car, obviously embarrassed by the foul language. Bland and boring, they'd be dead before they started living, she thought sourly, for a second wanting to shout something across the woodland car park. Don't be stupid.

Opening the driver's door, she leant in and retrieved her emergency cigarettes and lighter from the glove box. She'd quit of course, but these were not ordinary times. Holding the cigarette between her lips, she lit up, tossing the half empty packet back in the car. She inhaled, then removed the cigarette from her mouth, and stood, arms folded and watched as the four-wheeled-drive glamour jeep pulled out of the car park.

"Motherfuckers," she whispered.

Parked at an angle, Arabella's car was currently under a tree at Strensall Common car park. It was only five minutes drive away from her until-very-recent work place. The car park had been at just the right point for a break as her head neared explosion. She couldn't drive anymore. Her body was shaking with anger. Her mouth needed to roar.

Strensall Common was a sprawling heath land of heather and silver birch, managed by the MOD and popular with the dog walkers of north York. The car park was on the edge of the common, where a stretch of woodland separated heath from fields.

Arabella sat against the car bonnet and stared grimly out into the green, lush woodland. Where the hell had all this come from? She was redundant. *She* was redundant? Someone had decided that Arabella Mangella was surplus to requirements and had thrown her out as idly as if they'd been shaking dust from the curtains in a spring clean. They'd kept on Robin to cover her work. How many times had she held his hand and carried him through that department?

"I am thirty and I have no job," she spoke through gritted teeth. Although it wasn't quite as bad as all that. She still had the banjo and the dancing, but they were hardly permanent contracts. She'd been considering leaving professional dancing as well, in attempt to get more focus and order in her life. To really get serious about her music. She couldn't quit dancing now; she needed every pound she could earn. And she hadn't been fired; she'd been made redundant. There was no shame in that. These days everyone had been made redundant at least once.

"Shit." That was all good and well, but she hated the corporate bullshit that invaded all aspects of office life. You had to live the dream, baby; bleed for your employers and burn for their mission statement. Even if you were just there to answer the phones and file the paperwork. Everyone had to burn as much as the M.D. Otherwise you were not good enough. Not a diligent worker. She'd need another job to cover the bills. That meant applications and interviews and talking the bullshit and gritting her teeth and smiling through all that nonsense. Even when you were bored of your job of several years, at least you could be nested down into it, competent enough to be left alone, to not have to pretend too often. You were in a position where you could say doing my work competently is enough. At least it used to be enough.

Nobody wanted her.

She inhaled deeply and suddenly through her nose, the smell of tobacco rushing to her eyes and making them water. She was surprised to find herself crying, quick to wipe her eyes with the back of her hand. She was a woman. An independent woman, not a snivelling wreck. She'd fix this, move on, because that's what she did. Crying wouldn't get her anywhere.

Frustrated, she dropped the cigarette to the ground, stubbing it out underfoot as she felt another tear roll down her cheek. What an idiot. She hurried back to her car, lest anyone see her in this weak state. Leaning upwards, she checked her eyes in the windscreen mirror, wiping carefully at the running makeup with a tissue. "Just calm down."

When she got back to the house, her mother was sitting at the kitchen table slowly drinking a cappuccino. Adam was out at work, so was Arabella – or at least that had been the presumption this morning. Her mother was something of an enigma. These days she was usually hidden behind dramatic make up and clothing. It was almost impossible to get down to the real living person. Somehow, and either Adam didn't know or was too scared to confess, Arabella's mother had a back door key. Her visits were infrequent and unannounced, sweeping in with swaths of glittering fabric and clouds of Chanel perfume. She'd been vintage before vintage had become en vogue. In the 70s and 80s she had been the go to model for 50s Hollywood style photography, producing the dresses, the hair, the makeup, a twenty four inch waist and a patience for holding a pose that amazed everyone including her artist model friends. The days of waist cinching dresses were over, her modelling no longer required and her makeup and dresses no longer a speciality. Vintage was mainstream. The old styles, copied out for today's market, were everywhere. She retreated into something of a hermitage, swooping melodramatically in kaftans, long shapeless gowns, jackets with fur lined trim, and diamante accessorised turbans. She was an old diva, a Hollywood star that had been left behind in an explored section of the universe that people had grown bored with.

"Arabella, darling," she called, not bothering to get up, as Arabella entered the kitchen. For why shouldn't she be in the house on her own enjoying a coffee? "Happy Birthday."

"Thanks." This was surreal. Perhaps it all had been an awful dream. Arabella set her bag down and turned on the kettle. "What are you doing here?"

"Wishing my daughter a happy birthday; there's nothing wrong with that, is there? Goodness."

"Of course not."

"Just to think, I have a thirty year old daughter." She peered down at her muddy reflection in her coffee. "Just when did I get so old?"

"It's supposed to be me who's distressed about my age today."

"Nonsense. Thirty is a glorious time. This is the decade when you find yourself. Besides, other people are dead. Did you know your great Aunt Agetha is dead?" She watched her daughter make a cup of tea.

"I didn't even know Great Aunt Agetha was alive."

"My point exactly."

Arabella glanced across at her mother. "Did you know she was alive?"

"Of course I did, darling. How else could I know she had died?" Her mother threw logic back at her. "She always was a vile woman; I never had anything to do with her. That's why the two of you never met. She lived in York with those nasty little dogs of hers." Her lip curled at the memory. "She never enjoyed a moment of her life. We must learn our lessons from her, and enjoy ourselves." She finished speaking and corrected her demeanour to something more positive and fitting for birthday celebrations. She waited until Arabella had joined her at the table before pushing a small wrapped box towards her. "Happy birthday, darling."

Arabella smiled wanly. She didn't really feel like her birthday anymore. She'd complained about her age, but a few presents and attention would have helped her through. Now she felt like an utter failure. She would have to make an effort for her mother. She forced her fingers to unwrap the box, flicking up the neat cardboard lid. Inside there was a silver and blue necklace, dripping with small cut stones, flowing across from the main band like water. She held it up. It was actually very beautiful.

"Topaz, darling," her mother explained. "It is just you."

She managed to smile. "It's wonderful."

"I knew you'd like it. And I must say I'm glad to see you're taking your birthday off work today. Really, one must take these days off to appreciate another year."

"I've not taken the day off work."

"Oh?"

She carefully laid the necklace back in its box. "They made me redundant."

"When?"

"Today?"

"Oh really," her mother said, the corner of her lip curling once again. "People simply don't have style anymore these days. One simply doesn't do things like that on birthdays. It's just not done. It certainly wasn't in my day."

"What's done is done."

"Well, I can't say I'm sorry."

Arabella felt her mouth hang open. "Mother, I just lost my job!"

She waved it off as a mere trifle. "You were wasting yourself there. There is so much more to be gotten out of life." She picked up her blue velvet clutch from the kitchen table. "Now that we find we have the entire day free, I think we ought to do something to celebrate. Why not do something decedent? We could have lunch at the Ritz."

"There isn't a Ritz in York."

"Who said anything about York? A trip is in order." She took a mobile phone out of her clutch bag and started flicking through the contacts list. Pausing, she looked up innocently at Arabella. "What? It only takes a couple of hours on the train to London."

"We can't go to London for lunch."

"Yes we can. I'm calling a taxi for half an hour. Go upstairs and get changed. I want glamour, and I want that necklace. Think of a ball." She found the taxi company's number and pressed connect. "I'm calling them now, time is of the essence. Off you pop."

Arabella tentatively picked up the jewellery. Her mind was already flicking through her wardrobe, deciding what to wear. Why not? It wasn't like there was anything else to do.

Perhaps it was the bubbles in the champagne, or maybe the internal joy of a birthday, or even a perverse reaction to the shock of losing one's job and self worth in one swift slap, but Arabella couldn't stop laughing.

They had received some curious stares at York station. Passengers checked with one another, no, the races hadn't started yet. Perhaps they were going to a wedding, but it seemed odd to be dressed up before the journey started. Joining the ranks of teenagers, travellers and business types in drab suits, Arabella and her mother had boarded the train to London. The diamante clasp on the front of her mother's turban sparkled as they strolled down the carriage looking for unreserved seats. Arabella brought up the rear in a strapless, tight bodice, big skirted blue ball gown, the skirts of which bunched up and rustled down the carriage aisle, catching on seat arms as she drifted by.

This was classically her mother. She could go for weeks living frugally, spending nothing, seeing no one, absorbed into her hermitage, trapped in melodrama and memories. Then she would bloom once again, thoughtless with her money. A return ticket to London bought on the day was well over a hundred pounds.

They were in a fashionable part of town, in a trendy restaurant. At least that was what her mother had told her. Arabella didn't particularly care. The food was nice, certainly not worth the price, but it melted in her mouth and danced with the champagne in her stomach. They were in a corner position on the first floor, with tea and cakes, before they'd be heading off to see a show. Outside the world rushed. People were working, commuting, achieving. For today she was completely out of the circuit and it didn't matter anymore. She was just a woman eating cream cakes in London. No one knew that she was surplus to requirements.

"I have to go to the bathroom."

As she was walking through the seating area, footsteps clicking to the rhythm of light piano background music, someone touched her elbow.

A stranger in a suit nodded to her and clicked his heels together. "Good Afternoon."

Arabella paused and pursed her lips. He didn't sound as though English was his first language but she couldn't quite place the accent.

"How do you say, how much would..."

"How much?"

"Perhaps I approach this wrong? Do I speak to the woman?" He gestured towards the corner of the room.

She wasn't following his train of thought. Technically she was still in the same country, but every time she came to London something happened or she met someone who made her feel like she'd just dropped off the moon. "You want to speak to my mother?" Was this guy one of her mother's strange acquaintances? Her mother did have a lot of eccentric friends across the globe.

"Your mother?" He looked surprised. "This is certainly unexpected, but if it makes you feel more comfortable."

"What the hell are you talking about?"

"My business associate and I are in the city tonight. We have completed discussions and are in search of some company. We were wondering how much it would cost?"

There was a moment when she realised what this odd conversation was about. Her mind flicked to the snowstorm channel. There was no immediate snappy response forthcoming. Just the cold gasp as she finally caught up. "You think I'm a bloody prostitute?" She looked over her shoulder back at her mother. "And she's supposed to be my pimp?"

He gave an awkward little laugh, held open his arms as if to say: 'ha, these little cultural misunderstandings: how amusing'. "You girls in London, you dress so eccentric..."

She stepped up to him, pushing his shoulders aggressively. "Have you not been listening to my vowels? I'm not from round here."

"Mr Arias." An Englishman in a smart suit, scuttled across, having assumedly lost control of his charges. He caught the man's arm politely, steering him away from the situation. "We've got a car waiting..."

"Ben, really, I thought the hospitality would have included girls..."

"This isn't the kind of place."

You again, Arabella thought. This was another ridiculous coincidence. She folded her arms as she watched Ben Simon usher the man towards the foyer where a similar looking exotic dandy was waiting along with a painfully British man.

"Mr Simon."

He turned back to her as the client walked out of ear shot. "I am very sorry about that."

"He thought I was a prostitute."

"This is all a misunderstanding."

"Do I look like a prostitute?" She was unsure as to whether she was offended or worried by the suggestion. The champagne bubbles suddenly weren't quite so entertaining. She just felt a bit ill.

"You look beautiful..."

"I..."

"Ben, we need to go," his colleague called from the foyer.

Arabella was on pause, the start of her sentence still stuck in the back of her throat.

He looked at her. "Don't worry, I got the message loud and clear last time." He smiled a little melancholic. "Arabella. What are the chances?" He looked from her to the foyer again, distracted. "I've got to go and look after my clients. It was good bumping into you. I didn't think I would again."

With that he was gone, into a black London cab with the others. Arabella was suddenly sober. Having forgotten why she'd left the table in the first place, she turned and went back to her mother.

The last of the tea was poured into a cup. "So who was that, darling?"

Arabella dropped rather ungraciously into her chair, her skirts bouncing up on impact. "Oh," she said, "just somebody that I used to know."

Shazia slumped into her chair having passed the tissues across the table of drinks. Despite the number of alcoholic units consumed that evening, she looked frighteningly sober and wan. "Is this what happens?" she asked, looking from Arabella to Nicki. The inference in her question was clear.

"For Christ's sake, I'm just having a bad week," Arabella muttered, finishing her drink before starting to dab around her eyes with a corner of the tissue.

"But you're never like this," Shazia leaned forward, eager for reassurance. "You're always so confident. You never regret anything."

Nicki looked bemused. "Everyone has some regrets."

"But I never thought Arabella..." Shazia paused. "Is this just a turning thirty thing?"

"My life's in a fucking shitty place right now. This has nothing to do with my age," Arabella said. It was Friday and she'd only been technically unemployed for three days. She had a couple of dance shifts coming up at the weekend, so it wasn't even as though she was completely unemployed. Only the main source of income had dried up. The one that paid all the bills. She was only out tonight because she'd promised the other girls. It was her birthday, so she supposed she ought to mark the occasion. The others were off dancing, leaving the three at the table. More drinks and the atmosphere had darkened and Arabella had found herself having a panic attack. It was not a very dignified way to start the first week in her thirties.

"Have you looked for another job yet?" Nicki asked.

"It's still early days. I have got several months' money coming my way." Arabella crunched up the tissue and felt her neck sag down between her shoulders. "I can't stand the thought of writing all those bull shit applications and lying through my teeth at interviews for another shitty office job. I mean, who the hell has a burning passion for administration?"

"Only the very dull, but we've all got to eat." Shazia worked as a secretary during office hours.

"I know. It never seems enough to just want to do the work and fuck off at the end of the day. I'm thinking I might get in touch with my agent."

Nicki started to smile until she caught the look on Arabella's face. "You've not really spoken to him for a couple of years."

"I know, but I need to get serious about something. Maybe I could get some more..." she waved her fingers, searching for inspiration. "Gigs or something. I just need to feel like something in my life is working out." She watched a man walk past the table. "I've got no career, no relationship..."

"I didn't think you did relationships."

"Not for a lot of years," Nicki added on Arabella's behalf.

Shazia peered through the semi-darkness. "There was a time?"

Arabella rolled her eyes. "There was an engagement once."

"Christ on a bike, I've not heard this story before. You were engaged?"

"He was an arsehole, it ended the best way. After that I never really felt like getting stuck..."

"Until that guy you're regretting."

"I am not regretting it," she said, sounding a little unconvinced. "I am not a natural relationship person, and I'm definitely not a long-distance shit kind of person, pining away at the other end of the planet. Where is the point in that?" She looked from Nicki to Shazia. "I'm just having a bad week; I might be a little bit drunk, and I am building up things into things they weren't because my brain is that way inclined just now."

"I suppose so," Shazia sighed. "Well, you did blow him off the other week in Leeds when you weren't unemployed so you must know what you want."

Arabella felt her hackles rise. It wasn't her fault he lived in London. Just as it wasn't her fault the engagement had failed. In truth that had been a narrow escape, and she felt ill to think what her life would look like now, if she hadn't made the move to leave him. It had been a big step, not only to shed the security of what could have been a life-long relationship, but also to effectively make herself homeless, for they had been living together at that point. They'd even been house hunting and considering which mortgage to take out. He had been the boy to come along after her university boy who had taken her to the U.S.A. A nice dependable boy who worshipped her, did sensible things like save money, find a good flat lease they could share, look for deals on electricity bills, and do his fair share of the housework. He put up with her flighty moods and when he had proposed to her, she had been so taken aback that anyone would want her for that length of time she hadn't been able to say anything but yes. So they'd fallen into a little love nest of habit. She hadn't danced more than once a month at a time and she played less and less. They liked to snuggle at home. Of course she'd get back into her playing, she told herself. But the realities of what she was getting involved in started to hit and the terror found her.

What the storybooks fail to mention about getting engaged to your prince, is that you're not just signing up to commitment to him. The prince doesn't come alone, but with a whole trailer of baggage in the form of his family. Families are like people and they do vary, but they all have their expectations, and some are more vocal about it than others. Her fiancé was mama's little treasure. She didn't resent Arabella, in fact she was thrilled by this pretty girl with the curvy hips he'd managed to catch. She saw potential. The second the ring was on the finger, the hints started.

One afternoon she'd come over to visit on the pretext of bringing some of her son's belongings with her. She wanted to clear out his clutter now that he was setting up his own home. She'd placed the bags down on the kitchen table and plucked a teddy bear from the top of the collection. This was her son's favourite bear when he had been a boy, she'd told Arabella with a soft, dew dimpled smile. She'd thought they could put it on a shelf to remind him of happy times, or, she'd thrown in, full of breathless and excitable anticipation, Arabella could have a child, and then they could give the bear to the child. She'd passed the bear to Arabella, who had been so shocked she hadn't thought of a sharp retort. And in taking that bear, acceptance was deemed approving. The hints had increased in direct ratio to the decrease of subtlety. The mother-in-law-to-be grew so excited in anticipation of grandchildren that she started to tell her friends that her son and girlfriend were already trying for a baby, and the future wedding would just be fitted around the pregnancy. In her mid twenties, and still on the pill, Arabella boiled over in rage when this got back to her, hearing the gossip from her boyfriend's aunt one Saturday morning on Coney Street in central York.

The fiancé had calmly agreed it had been wrong of his mother to tell people they were trying for a baby when they had told her no such thing. Beyond that fact of a well-meant lie, he was not worried. He had gently smiled and turned to Arabella and asked the deciding question: Would it be so bad if you were to fall pregnant? For Arabella, the cut had been made and she had to leave. They had never discussed the children question, and for her it was still a vague maybe off in the mists of the future that didn't really concern her at this stage of life. That she was being viewed as precious more than breeding stock brought into the family infuriated her. And if that was all they needed, she could not stay. Besides, there'd be plenty of girls willing to take on that role for a bit of security. She handed back the ring and started looking for somewhere to rent.

Back in the club, Arabella had drifted into silent brooding, going over every person and every event that had screwed her over. Forcing a stubborn minded girl to demonstratively head in the opposite direction.

"Look, brooding isn't going to solve anything," Nicki announced. It was time to bring this to a close. "You're getting your redundancy, so you're not immediately in the red, and if you have to take a little temping or something until you get things figured out, then you'll get something."

"A-ah," Arabella shook her head. "I'm going to set up a meeting with my agent. He was an arse, but it's been a couple of years. He'll have improved with age."

Nicki suppressed a laugh. "He'll have seen the light? Welcome you back with open arms?"

"He'll be pleased I'm back."

"Arabella, I'm pleased you're back."

Why was she not convinced by this statement? He spoke in the tone of 'but'. The statement sounded like the start of a long speech that she wasn't going to enjoy. Her defence flicked up, checking for any chink in the opposition's cover.

Jordan Oates, a man anywhere between his late forties and early sixties, pressed his fingers together as if he had delusions of being the godfather. There wasn't anything threatening about the man, in fact it had been his distinct lethargy that had driven Arabella to neglect contact for the past couple of years. Oates had said that it was because she wasn't interested in building a music career. Arabella had said it was because he was more interested in chasing Scandinavian girls than being a music agent.

"Although I have to ask what brings you back?"

"I need to get serious about my music."

"The nine to five getting a bit dull?"

There was a flickering of narrowed eyes in response. "I've been made redundant."

"Recently?"

"Last week."

He nodded sagely. "I'm very sorry to hear it. Redundancy is never an easy time. I always say one should look at it as a new beginning..."

"That's why I'm here."

"Music isn't a get rich quick scam unless you're a teenager allergic to clothes," Oates said sharply. "Realistically you are going to have to get another regular job, although perhaps the urgency isn't immediate as you'll have some redundancy pay, I assume. Perhaps with time the day job might become part time."

"I have my dancing as well."

"You still doing the belly dancing?" Oates looked a bit surprised. He lent back in the well-worn computer chair, the springs creaking and his feet knocking against the side of the desk. "I hate to tell you this, but if you were ever going to be a belly dancing superstar, you'd be it by now."

"There is nothing wrong with my dancing."

"I never said that. What's going on, Arabella? Life crisis?"

"I'm not that old; I've only just turned thirty," she said defensively. "I told you, I was made redundant, and I've been thinking about my life. I can't go back to the day to day trudge of menial office work. I need to do something meaningful."

Oates didn't immediately respond. He'd heard this a lot of times, but when the money didn't roll in and the work piled up, many a musician's will power wilted. Arabella had been on the circuit for eight years. She knew the score, at least. "All right," he finally spoke. "We never did get you set up with a website and downloads, did we? And you'll be wanting to take a bit of a break from work now."

"You still have all those master tapes?"

"Yes. In fairness we could burn the songs back off the CDs though. You still have your back catalogue? I have most of it around here somewhere."

The recordings had been made just before the end of Arabella's ill-fated engagement. It had been a mixture of traditional Deep South songs, covers, and banjo rearrangements of traditional British and Irish tracks. The songs had been recorded over a few intense days. The session musicians had been paid and the studio fees cleared. The in-laws-to-be had smiled at each other as if it were all a phase. She'd get over it and calm down when she had a child. As if the two things – children and a woman's mind – had to be mutually exclusive. Then the engagement had been broken off and Arabella had decided to make a clean start with a lot of things. It was almost as if she couldn't stand to socialise with anyone or anything that had known her during the engagement. The music project had been shelved and ignored ever since.

"Well, if you've just been made redundant, you'll have nothing planned. How about I book you for a music festival starting three weeks from now? I've an opening come up. We can get this into some order so you have something to sell..."

"You can't get more CDs printed in a week."

"No, but everyone downloads things these days. We can get the songs online, small download fee. It'll work just as well. I always meant to get you a website set up. We need you on peoples' iPods."

"I suppose."

"Two week festival. See it as a working holiday."

There was an edge to this suggestion. Just who was doing whom the favour? "So where's the festival?"

"Reykjavik."

"What, Iceland?" Arabella looked aghast. "Do they even have enough people there to make a festival?"

He smiled knowingly. "Believe me they do. It's the in place to be. My girlfriend's looking for a final roommate on the flat she's rented in town for the month. You can stay there."

"I can?"

"Yes. The festival starts in three weeks' time, but you could always go a few days early. Take some time to get to know the place before the work begins."

Arabella sank back in her chair. "This is very sudden."

Oates grinned. "You want be in music? You've got to be ready at the drop of a hat."

It was impulsive, just to up and go, join the music circuit after all these years of working part time on the periphery of the live music scene. The way her life was going, a knee jerk reaction could hardly make anything worse, Arabella reasoned. She bought her flights to Keflavik, Iceland's international hub airport. She would depart in two weeks' time, leaving her room to settle and take a look around before she started working. It also gave her time to scout out the land, get the news out that a banjo player (and guitar if needed) would be in town and up for any extra gigs, backing positions and support. If she was going to do this, she was going to work hard, and she was going to make the trip pay for itself.

In the meantime, she had two weeks empty of standard employment. The slapping insult of redundancy still stung, but only

Arabella lingered over the tragedy. The rest of the world was back at work, running their homes and their cars, tending partners and families. Arabella remained at the window of her rented rooms with a scowl on her face and her laptop on her knee, increasingly feeling like a fuck up.

Two days after her discussion with Oates, she was in Leeds, having badgered her way into an appointment with the owner of the club where she danced. She had gone directly over Pritesh's head with a noticeable touch of glee. At least that had been her emotional standpoint as she'd made the appointment over the phone. She geared herself up for a serious discussion about her career. Daydreaming of negotiations over the boardroom. In reality, they weren't even to discuss business in the back office. Seth instead chose to sit out on the floor, half an eye on ongoing rehearsals whilst Arabella earnestly explained why she wanted more time at the club, and how she was really going to make Leeds the centre point of the progression of modern interpretative belly dance.

Seth, his fingers dressed like knuckle dusters in a chunky array of gold rings, finished his coffee. He took strictly no alcohol before twelve. "I heard you had a birthday recently. Many congratulations."

"Oh, yes..." Arabella stumbled over the closing paragraph of her case as he spoke for the first time in the last ten minutes. He did realise she was there and who she was, which she supposed she could take as a small victory. Had he been listening to a damn word she'd been saying? She was trying to do them both a favour.

"I heard you went over to the thirties' club."

"That may be, but I'm still in great shape for dancing. I'm sure you know better than I do that thirty is most definitely not the end of life."

Seth gave out a loud bark of laughter, making one of the women who was blocking out a new act on stage stumble out of concentration. Seth turned away from the rehearsals to give Arabella his full attention. "You're telling me, darling."

"Right." She felt as though there was a but coming, but he said nothing. "Just as long as there's to be no age discrimination silliness."

"I also heard you'd been made redundant last week."

She found her fingers curling up into fists. "That has nothing to do with this. I am taking this opportunity to develop my act..."

"Thing is," Seth quickly interrupted before she started on another monologue about the importance of ethnic dance, developing the arts in the north, broadening people's perspective and other art babble she was using to avoid the obvious. "When Pritesh mentioned you'd turned thirty, it made me realise just how long you've been working here. We've had some good nights with you. You're a damned proficient dancer, but your act hasn't really changed in all these years."

"Of course it bloody has. I'm working on some new choreography even now."

Seth waved it all aside. "Most of the subtleties of your choreography are lost on the average punter, I'm afraid."

"Well, that's exactly my point; I want to develop this..."

"That's exactly *my* point," he corrected her. "Don't you think if you were going to make a name in this game, you would have done it by now?"

She was shot down. Arabella lent back in her chair, her mind reversing. This wasn't going how she'd hoped. "Is this about me turning thirty?"

"Not in the way you're thinking. My point is you've been doing this part time for years, for fun, for a bit of pin money. Not to revolutionise the world. If you were going to be a star, if you'd wanted to be a star, you would have done that a long time ago. You would have put everything into it long before you got made redundant. Really you should have gone down to London. It's the only way to get anything fucking done in this country. Breaks my heart to say it, come on the north and all that, but it's the way things are. You've hit a milestone, a time to reassess your life, and you've just been shafted by your job. End of the day you'll get another one. You've got to pay for your meat and potatoes, don't you?"

"That's not it..."

"You said you're heading to Iceland in two weeks' time with your banjo. What am I supposed to do then? Where's the dedication."

"I am dedicated. I just need to go to this festival..."

"You're spreading yourself too thin. You need to take this opportunity to decide what's important to you. What you want to do with your life." He leaned in across the table. "I like you, kid, don't get me wrong. I'll take you on now and then for a set like we always do. But you've got to realise this isn't a dress rehearsal. You have to make a decision, pick something and stick to it. Stop with all this uncertainty and not taking a risk. Before you know it, you'll be my age. If you don't do something now, you'll have nothing. Sure some things don't always work out, but winners give things a try, do you know what I mean?"

Arabella was deflated. This really wasn't what she'd come for. "So you've got no work for me?"

"We're really booked up for the next few months. We've taken on a few new acts. I'll tell you about one we've taken on. Cherry Malone."

Her heart was like a lump of malformed lead that sank to her stomach. She didn't need to hear about Cherry.

"Maybe I could get you a supporting slot on one of Cherry's acts. You're both belly dancers."

"I am not performing with Cherry fucking Malone."

He grinned. "Feeling threatened?"

"I don't need to feel threatened by Miss TitsGalore. I am the far more proficient dancer."

"That may be. As to entertainer..."

"Have you finished kicking me down?"

He sighed. "This is actually meant to be a pep talk. Take Cherry, as much as you don't want to. She's just starting out, but already people are talking about her. She's got an act, a vibe; she can go places if she plays this right. She's only nineteen so she's got the time and energy to work hard and make a name for herself, so that when, if she does become big, she'll still have youth on her side to continue performing. I'm not an ageist and I like a big mature woman, but the older you get the harder it is to stay in that kind of shape. Cherry's aware of this. She's quit her temp job so she can put everything into this career."

"So you're telling me to forget it?"

"I'm telling you people who play around end up with nothing. You pick one job, one man, one woman, one life, and you live that. See what I'm saying?"

"Hang up my dancing shoes."

"You never wear shoes; you're a health and fucking safety nightmare. But no, come back and do us a slot now and then like you do. But if you're going to focus on anything, I'd make it the banjo. That's where your real talent is."

Arabella stood up, feeling resigned. "Thanks for your time, Seth."

He gave her a wink. "No problem, I always liked you. Sure you don't want me to see if I can get you in with Cherry?"

"Very sure."

Arabella bumped into a breathless woman hurrying through the front doors as she was leaving. "Oh my god, Arabella!" the woman shrieked. "I was hoping I'd see you here."

The parts of her face didn't make sense for a moment. I know you, Arabella thought. Somewhere in the past of my life I have seen you before.

"It's Charlize," the woman explained. "You remember, from work. I was so sorry to hear..."

"Oh yeah, how is the place?" Arabella cut her off, not wanting to hear more condolences about being kicked out of her job, especially from a temp who was barely out of school.

"I don't know, I quit my job."

"Why would you do that?"

"I need to focus on other things," Charlize couldn't keep the grin off her face. "You know, it's so cool to meet you here away from the office. I've seen you perform so many times. I remember sneaking in underage to a club where you were dancing and I was just blown away. I was only sixteen. You are the reason I got into this."

"Into what?"

"Dancing," Charlize laughed. "Have you seen my act?"

"I don't think so. I work so much I don't get out to watch a lot."

"I got a spot in the big burlesque extravaganza they did recently. My stage name is Cherry..."

"Cherry!" Someone shouted from within the depths of the club. "Are you starting work today or tomorrow?"

"I should go..." Charlize looked like she didn't want to stop grasping Arabella's hands.

"You're Cherry Malone?"

She nodded eagerly. "You've heard of the act?"

"Of course."

"I've got to get in there. But this is so exciting. If we're working at the same club, maybe we'll get the chance to perform together."

"Maybe." Arabella needed to get out of this building before her legs went. She couldn't take anymore kicks today. "I've got a busy schedule. I'm in a rush."

"Of course, I've got to work anyway. I'll see you, Arabella."

When she got home, Arabella went straight upstairs and flopped on her bed. She turned on her music, letting the CD player take whichever CD was currently in. Unfortunately it was a disc of fast fiddle music, which really didn't suit the mood of despondency and self-pity she was getting gummed into. She lay spread-eagled, surrounded by her dancing paraphernalia: shimmering silks and organza, sashes decorated with beads and coins, embroidered cloth. She was a fucking has-been. People were already citing her as a hero that had encouraged them to take up the trade and make it better, make it *something*. And here was the original: thirty, unemployed, jack of all things and master of nothing. Still living in rented rooms. She didn't even have her own place. Suddenly the weight of a decade was upon her and she hadn't achieved a damn thing. And now she was being passed over for the younger models.

She closed her eyes. Despite being completely alone, she was embarrassed by the fact she was now crying. Her strength and independence had always been traits she'd been particularly proud of. Arabella was self assured; she didn't let anyone else's shit bother her. Even those base rocks of her stability were disappearing. She'd never felt so utterly alone.

The C note reverberated out across the garden. The light was just starting to fade. Dusk was drawing in. The air was cooling down and moisture was building in the atmosphere. Arabella felt like a proper hillbilly, slouched into the corner of the wooden bench. Out on the porch with her banjo. All she needed was a pair of dungarees and pig tails and the setting would be complete.

She sighed, letting her shoulders drop, and ran through eight bars of rich, finger-twisting blues. She needed to get her set for Iceland worked out. She had a couple of solo gigs already booked, along with a few backing jobs, and she'd be touting for more work as soon as she got there. There were just too many good tunes in her brain clambering for air time.

"Are you sure Iceland is going to be a good idea, just now, Arabella?"

She raised a solitary eyebrow and looked down the length of the bench to where Adam was sitting, his guitar inert in his lap. "Whadda ya mean?" she drawled with the slightest of hints of aggression.

"There's a lot happening at the moment. You just lost your job..."

"I think I already know that."

"But running away to Iceland."

"Adam, I am not running away." Arabella sat up to attention, her fingers slipping from position on the neck of the banjo. "I will be gone three weeks, a month tops. It's just like an extended holiday. Everyone goes on holiday."

"But you'll be vulnerable, Arabella."

She laughed out loud. "The last bloody thing I am is vulnerable. I can take care of myself. What are you really worried about, Adam? That I won't come back? That I'll stop paying the rent? Don't you worry; I've got plenty of funds to cover the next few months, whatever happens."

"It's not just that." Adam eyed the generous glass of whisky and lime set on the patio at the corner of the bench. It was the middle of the week and all she did was drink and play the banjo. She'd even said that she was going to quit dancing. All of a sudden after all of these years. "You're unsettled, not just about your job."

Arabella strummed her fingers sharply down the banjo strings and looked coyly across at Adam. "What's up with you all of a sudden? You've got nothing to worry about. I'm the one with troubles."

"I'm worried about you."

"I can look after myself."

"No man is an island, Arabella."

She laughed. "I have news; I'm a woman."

Adam stared down at his feet, one real, one artificial. A stammering humming up from somewhere deep in his chest came to the forefront of his mouth. He wasn't able to put into words what he was thinking. When he was alone he could be particularly articulate, but Arabella's domineering presence tended to send his thoughts into a scramble. "I'll miss you, Arabella."

"No you won't," she dismissed it easily. Leaning forward, she picked up her drink from the ground. "You'll enjoy the peace and quiet. Besides, I'll be back before you know it." She drank deeply from the glass, feeling the alcohol rush through her system. Sighing in satisfaction, she leant back against the bench. "Four years, can you believe it?"

"What is?"

"You and me." She looked directly across at him. "Landlord and lodger."

"It doesn't always have to be that."

"Oh I know. Someday all this will end." Slipping her feet back into her flip flops, she stood up, wobbling slightly as she felt the blood rush out of her head. She had perhaps been a little too generous when pouring the whisky. "I'll grow up one day and get my own place."

"You don't have to. We could..."

"I need to pack." Oh no, dear sweet Adam, don't go there. That is not what you need. I would eat you alive. Your timidity would get stuck in my throat. I would use your stutters as toothpicks.

"Good night." She swung her banjo nonchalantly over one shoulder, glass in her free hand, and sauntered into the kitchen.

A jolt, a wobble in the film then the picture and sound disappeared, to be replaced by inoffensively bland elevator music. Arabella looked up from her screen to the interior of the aeroplane, and then out of the tiny porthole window. They'd landed and she hadn't even realised they were descending into Scotland.

90

She pulled out her earphones in time to hear the cabin crew announce that those not disembarking in Glasgow could wait on board. A number of people were already on their feet, scrabbling through overhead lockers for their luggage. Arabella slumped further down into her seat, experiencing a mix of excitement and terror. What the hell was she doing, running away from all her problems to go to Iceland? Branding it as an important career development move, but really, who was she trying to fool?

She was on the Manchester to Keflavik flight, via Glasgow. She was part way through an in flight film about an obsessive ballerina. It helped to pass the time. She'd been on longer flights and survived the inactivity, although not for a number of years. The whole travel and holiday thing had been absent from her life in the last couple of years. All she seemed to do when she was off the day job was work. It wasn't as though she was that desperate for money. Perhaps this would be a good thing, although even on her first journey for years, she was steadily booking up her itinerary with working gigs.

A group of Amazonians boarded the aircraft, chattering loudly as if they were embarking on a night out in town. Arabella couldn't understand a word. It didn't sound like English and it certainly didn't have any connection to the romance of Spanish that she knew. It was probably Icelandic, strange sounding and linguistically unknown to her. She watched the women, a cluster of confidence, Viking maidens, each with long blonde hair, dark clothes and lashings of makeup. Tall women, intimidating tall... Arabella flipped her aviator sunglasses down from the top of her head, suddenly feeling short and dark, and skulked further back into her corner. If this trip didn't work out, she didn't know what the hell she was going to do.

They landed at Keflavik, the airport serving Reykjavik from a barren lunar landscape of black lava fields hundreds of years old. Arabella was behind the Amazonians as she disembarked the flight. She felt like the grumpy, shrunken female shadow of what went before her. Her sunglasses were firmly set on the bridge of her nose, either to hide her bad mood or add a little gravitas to the persona she cut as she stomped through arrivals, tugging her over-packed suitcase after her.

Outside in the real world the descendants of Vikings and Irish slaves waited for their loved ones to return. A shock of blonde and red hair. A number wore knitted sweaters of various colours, all with the same snowflake design around the collar. It was something Arabella was to learn was a national piece of attire for the country. Towards the edge of these Nordic clusters stood a woman with copper hair, a green and white snowflake jumper and a waist length black leather jacket. She held a piece of paper with Arabella's name. She was gazing out of the window. This must be Jordan Oates' girlfriend, the infamous one of potentially the oldest long distance relationship known to mankind. Arabella had been expecting someone older, shorter, rounder...

"Hafdis?"

The woman gave a slight jump. "Arabella. Have a nice flight? You got your bags?" She looked from the bulging suitcase to the rucksack pulling on Arabella's shoulders. She wasn't sure what she had been expecting, but when Jordan had told her a banjo playing English woman who also did belly dancing in her spare time was coming, she had not been expecting the olive skinned diva who had strolled out of the arrivals doors. "Shall we go? I always find airports depressing places if I'm not going anywhere."

"Sure."

She was hit by the full force of the wind as they left the terminal building. Arabella paused, taking off her sunglasses and pocketing them. Surveying the land around the car park, she viewed the black crusty earth, organic and squeezed out of hell. This bleakness was absolutely everywhere, in every direction. There was nothing else to see. The wind went in for an extra blow, pushing her suitcase out of its intended direction.

"Jesus!" Arabella tugged it back. "Is it always this bloody windy?"

Hafdis laughed, oblivious to her long tresses being blown about her head. "Often, yes."

There was no respite from the wind until they were in the car. There was that comforting thud as the door closed in place. The air was still again. Hafdis' hair settling in a stylish tousled set. Arabella caught sight of herself in the windscreen mirror. She looked like she'd just fallen out of a plane.

"People think it's always snowing in Iceland," Hafdis said as she started the engine. "But when the sun is shining, it can be quite warm. We don't get so much snow, not as you'd think. Not in Reykjavik, as it's by the sea." Jordan's long term influence on her English was obvious, the Yorkshire pronunciation having pushed out the school book American English. But as soon as she mentioned a place in Iceland, the vowels changed, making the names sound intensely foreign and unpronounceable. A subtle reminder that indeed English was not her first language.

Arabella peered out at the dismal landscape, the ghost of her own reflection caught in the glass. "Is it like this everywhere?"

"Like what?"

"Dead."

Hafdis laughed again. "No, there's lots of Iceland where we have living things. But you know, this is a very young country. It's still being born. We have volcanoes and craters and eruptions. We're not the finished article yet. After the lava fields have formed the crust, it takes hundreds of years for anything to grow there again. There are older fields where moss grows."

"Moss?"

Hafdis flashed her a grin. "Yes, but this isn't moss like you get growing on your English walls. These are the most amazing cushions of moss."

They drove up the motorway into the capital, past petrol stations and out of town shopping centres, low-lying grey box-shaped buildings. The sky, speckled with grey clouds, seemed endless overhead. In the residential suburbs of Reykjavik the streets were hung with unpronounceable signs. The buildings looked like well-built shacks, started with concrete, then the walls seemingly finished off with what looked like brightly coloured corrugated iron, in reds, yellows and blues. Some of the fully bricked gable ends of houses had murals painted on them. Arabella found her nose almost pressed up to the window as they drove past one house, the end painted blue with a white snow capped peak that literally rippled with a disco ball effect.

Hafdis parked in a small car park at the foot of a collection of block of flats. All were five or six stories high, modern and tidy and giving off a hue of pastel pink. Hafdis pointed to the building closest to them. "That's us, third floor up."

Arabella followed her up to the main entrance, pushing off offers to help with the luggage.

"There's two keys, one for the main door, one for the flat," Hafdis explained as she led the way up the stairwell. "No lift, I'm afraid. Jordan told you that I'm renting this for the festival; that there's other people staying?"

"Yeah, I've been in touch with Marika. We're going to do a couple of day time gigs together."

"Ah, yes, Marika." Hafdis paused outside a door marked 312. She put her palm to it as if checking for heat. Out in the stairwell they could hear the faded out sound of rock music. "There's also myself and another Swedish girl, Elin, staying here for the duration. Jordan will be over later. And there's a friend from Norway, but he will only be here a week or so." She made the decision to unlock the door, twisting the key and pushing the door open. The volume of the rock music rocketed, now accompanied by a candy-high female voice singing along.

Arabella dumped her bags in the front entrance, kicking off her boots. Jordan had forewarned her that Scandinavians could be funny about outdoor footwear getting beyond the front entrance in a home. She followed Hafdis into the living room.

A girl with a gingerbread tan, long blonde hair and a large black tattoo on her right calf that looked like the logo for a racing car, was dancing on the spot, alone in the flat. She had on a pair of shorts and a black tank top, her knees going like pistons as if she was gearing up for a belly dance shimmy. She was singing to *Sweet Home Alabama*. Her head was back, her eyes closed, and she was utterly oblivious to the intruders.

Hafdis pointedly opened a door to the side and let it slam shut.

"*Fan!*" the girl shrieked, staggering back, her hair dropping with the lightness of feathers. "Hafdis!"

Hafdis shrugged half heartedly and wandered across the open plan kitchen-diner-living room. "This is Marika, Arabella. Do you want some tea?"

"Sure."

94

Marika's face broke into a smile as she turned down the music. "Arabella, it's so nice to meet you. What do you think about Iceland?"

"I've only seen the lava fields. Looks kind of dead."

Marika laughed. "Yes. It's a bit shocking. It's the first thing you see." She had a distinct Swedish lilt as she spoke. "But you must see some of the Iceland whilst you are here. It is fantastic. It's like another world."

"I'll see what I can do, although I want to be working whilst I'm here." She slumped down onto one of the sofas. "I've still got quite a few gaps in my schedule."

"That's nothing to worry about," Hafdis said as she prepared the teapot. "All the big gigs are booked, but a lot of the cafes and bars haven't bothered to book up everything. It's fluid here, you know. They like to see what's doing well, and book at the last minute. So keep your phone on."

"The festival doesn't start until this weekend." Marika bounced into the other seat on the sofa with Arabella. "You have some time to explore."

"Get acclimatised," Hafdis added, carrying a tea tray full of teapot, mugs, milk jug and other paraphernalia. This was taking things a little more seriously than Arabella's usual brew in a mug.

"I need to get a hat." Arabella ran a hand through her messy hair. "It's always this windy?"

Marika, her hands now wrapped around an earthenware mug of tea, laughed brightly. "Yes, it's very bad. This place is a rock in the arctic. You must prepare your hair before you go out."

"I don't worry about it," Hafdis flipped her hair back off her shoulder and settled into the armchair. "I guess I'm used to it, being Icelandic. I don't worry about a few tangles."

"I worry," Marika's blue eyes sparkled over the top of her mug. "I always tie my hair back."

Arabella didn't really have the Rapunzel locks Marika had to be able to tie it all back. She poured milk into her tea. "I'll buy a hat."

The search for the hat started that very afternoon. Hafdis had things to do, but Marika wasn't busy. She'd run off to her room to get ready for the great outdoors. Arabella had quickly taken a rece of her room. She dropped off all unnecessary items that had been stored in her pockets. She got a turquoise military style ladies coat out of the suitcase for the stroll into town. Marika had reappeared with her hair plaited, a pink jogging sweater with the words 'cute girlee' emblazoned across the front, and a black jacket over the top. She was still in the rather short shorts.

"Aren't you going to be cold?" Why was she starting to feel like Marika's mother?

"No, it's not cold, just windy," Marika bounded out of the flat.

"Jesus, what the hell was in your tea? You're like a five year old on e numbers."

Marika laughed, her merriment echoing up the stairwell. "Don't be crazy, Arabella. I'm not a child. I'm twenty two."

Arabella grimaced in solitude and shut the flat door. She suddenly felt very old.

Reykjavik felt like a small provincial town rather than a capital city. There were no high rise buildings, no sprawling city blocks across to the horizon, no underground railway system and no imposing financial districts. Instead there were windblown streets. Buildings were all just a few storeys in height. Nothing dared to grow too tall for fear of being blown over.

Marika and Arabella wandered through the streets into the main shopping areas, stopping in a few clothing shops. Arabella had done quick mental arithmetic, converting the prices into pounds and being surprised by how expensive it all was. Hadn't this country gone through an economic crash?

They'd eventually settled for a tourist shop off the main street, catering for tour bookings and Icelandic woollens and winter wear for the foreigners who'd come over thinking that because it was technically summer, the wind wouldn't blow and the temperature would be thirty degrees. Marika was already bored with the shopping, a little irritated that Arabella still hadn't picked a hat. What did it matter if her hair got a bit flat? These things didn't bother Marika, and she still looked great when she took off her hat. Arabella was over-styled like a fifties actress, as if she was overcompensating for something.

Arabella pursed her lips and peered at her reflection in the little mirror. She had a black, double layer knitted hat on. There was a little logo about polar warmth stitched to the outer rim. This wasn't going to do her hair a lot of favours. Thank God she'd brought a couple of wigs with her. She glanced across at Marika, who was in a bored stance, picking at her nail varnish. She increasingly resembled her teenage daughter.

"That hat is made for the Icelandic wind." The shop assistant, a well-built man with closely shaven hair, glasses and stubble, wandered across to Arabella, appearing in the mirror reflection just to her left.

Arabella raised her eyebrows.

"She really needs a hat." Marika appeared, chirpy again as she wandered over, her hips jutting in his direction. "She's never been to Scandinavia before."

"Are you Icelandic?"

Marika beamed. "No, Swedish."

Arabella stared herself in the eye. He wouldn't have asked you in English if he really thought you were, dumb-ass.

"You two touring Europe?"

"No, we're here for the festival. I play the hardanger fiddle," Marika continued, answering for them both. "I sing as well. I've got a few gigs booked. You should come and see me."

"I thought you said you were Swedish?"

"I am."

"But you play a Norwegian fiddle?"

Marika laughed. It was a sound like a gushing brook; the tinkling of ice particles melting in spring sunshine. "It's a long story..."

"I think I'll take this hat," Arabella interrupted loudly, turning neatly on her heel as if about to start a new dance routine. "It should stop me getting ear ache."

The conversation between the Icelander and the Swede ceased, teetering on the edge of uncertainty. Unsure of what she was referring to. Arabella smiled sweetly. "I'm not used to the gales you have here."

Purchases made, Marika dragged Arabella to a little bar a few doors down. On the way a couple of cars in convoy drove past, peppermint green and bright red, long like rockets. American fifties classics, complete with the rockabilly music and the gelled-like-concrete quiffs of the men behind the wheels. Arabella paused to watch them go past. Just where the hell had she landed? Marika rolled her eyes.

"*Raggare.*"

"Sorry?"

"Oh, it's what we call them in Sweden. These people who are wanting to live in America. In the past. They drive old cars and hang out. I guess they've got them here as well." She didn't sound impressed. "Come on. This is where we're going to do our first gig together."

The music festival had a few big concert venues, but more of the events were held in cafes, restaurants and smaller rooms all over the city. Not the kind of thing any non-Icelandic artist would travel over for on an individual basis; however, with enough of these gigs, and the publicity, it made the trip worthwhile. It was also considered a chance to work on spontaneous collaborations, get to know musicians from other countries, and meet the kooky Icelandic producers and songwriters. With European popularity and good flight connections with the US, the tourist trade was a big part of the economy and a big enough draw to make the music festival a viable option for international artists. The festival was never going to get the superstar headline acts that could fill an arena in fifteen minutes, but the up and coming and the world music, the folk music and the purely eccentric could find a melting pot here.

Marika and Arabella spent a couple of hours at the trendy Icelandic bar, paying out an extortionate amount on cocktails and giggling hysterically by the end of the drinking session. The two women, plus the second Swede Arabella was yet to meet were due to play at the bar in four days' time. It was Arabella's first scheduled gig, but in the tradition of all great meetings, there was a switch around due, and she found herself kicking off the festival two days earlier than originally planned.

There was a Canadian trio of acoustic rockers that had been put in touch with her last minute via Hafdis. The drummer and lead guitarist/singer were fine, but their bass player had fallen over and sprained his wrist. It had been a painful swollen red balloon when Arabella met up with them. His damaged joint needed a few days rest and a freezer's worth of peas before it was going to be up to much. Arabella's instrument of choice was the banjo, but she could easily find her way around the guitar, and helped out friends now and then by finishing off the guitar complement when required.

The group of surfer-grunge men were adapted with a woman for their first gig. Thankfully the set list was a selection of covers so the songs were already familiar to her. After a morning practising together Arabella felt confident enough to appear on stage with them that evening. She'd been on the stage enough to thrive on improvisation. The less time she had to think about it, the better she knew she'd perform. Even though she wasn't as used to working with groups, she was glad on this occasion that she wasn't stage centre. It was quite a rowdy rock night with an organic, writhing mosh pit heading up the audience. Tegan, a cute name for an unshaven T-shirt-trim North American who probably wouldn't think twice about head butting friends and enemies alike, was the lead singer and guitarist. The drummer increasingly reminded her of an unwashed muppet as the evening wore on. She was sure he must have halved his body weight purely through the volume of sweat his body expunged. Arabella added a cool dynamic: the moody, silent girl in the group with heavy dark eye makeup and versatility over bass, electric and acoustic guitar. It was taken for granted by the audience but would garner respect from the other musicians. She enjoyed the night; in fact it was fun to do something not too serious. It was just a jamming session of a few classics with the boys. She got a name check and the extra advertisement for her own upcoming gigs was nothing but a bonus. The more people that turned up for her, the better the chance other bars and cafes might book her, and that other artists might want to try a collaboration for a one-off night.

At the end of the gig, the three of them stood to the front of the stage to take the applause. People took photos on their phones. Social media and the festival's own webpage would be covered tomorrow.

Tegan slung his arms around the sweaty drummer and Arabella, speaking loudly in Arabella's ear that he was glad Nick had crippled himself a couple of days ago. She couldn't have asked for a better start to the festival.

Hallgrimskirkja, the cathedral of Hallgrim, was a memorial in concrete, formed like basalt columns plummeting up from the ground and reaching for the sky. It was as new land freshly erupted from the bowels of Iceland. Set up on a slight rise, it felt like the pinnacle of the city. Grey, reaching up to a steel grey sky. It had been sunny this morning, but the clouds had pulled in. Elin had said that it might snow in the night. Arabella hoped she was joking.

Elin, the other Swede who was sharing the flat, set her accordion case on the paving, and pushed her wavy ash-brown hair back over her ear. "You should have your photo taken with him," she told Arabella, gesturing at the statue. "If it's your first time in Iceland."

Arabella, now in a plum coloured felt hat in the style of 1920s flappers, lent back and squinted to get a better look at the green man. Atop his pinnacle, like the figurehead of a ship in search of new lands, he stared off into the distance. High and unreachable, he was immediately identifiable as an axe-carrying Viking.

"If you insist." She passed her the camera.

"It's Leif Eriksson," Elin told her as she backed away to get both Arabella and the iron man in shot. Arabella clutched her banjo case at her knees like an oversized handbag, struck a pose and pouted at the camera.

Elin pushed up her dark plastic glasses back up her nose as she laughed. "You've only had that hat five minutes and it's like you were born in it."

"Not as practical as my woollen hat, but much better."

She'd seen it on a little shop on Skólavörðustígur as they'd walked up from their lunchtime gig towards the cathedral. Elin was adamant they ought to do some sightseeing whilst she was here. Arabella had been half listening to what the Swede had been telling her during the stroll, until her attention had been completely distracted by the pretty hat in the window.

Picking up her accordion, Elin returned her camera to Arabella. The two women walked to the cathedral.

"It was destiny," Arabella added, feeling a little silly that a hat had turned this day into possibly the best in her life thus far. "That shop was next door to the cafe where I'm doing an afternoon jam session with Johnnie O. He's this old blues guitarist; I just can't wait. I didn't think he did things like this; the guy must be kicking on seventy."

"And you know him?"

"Not that well, but I met him years ago when I was travelling in the States."

"You have done really well. This is only your first time here."

They stood in front of the cathedral doors and stared up at the architecture. Arabella glanced across at the Swede. She had picked up on a hint of jealousy. From what Elin had mentioned, it sounded as though she had been coming to this festival a few years. Elin was a very proficient musician. Arabella had first got in touch with her via Marika when they had been planning a collaboration via email. Things had seemed fine then, but when they'd finally met at the flat, Elin had been distinctly quiet and stand offish. It was a trait that continued on the circuit, and wouldn't help her with her music. As a small independent performer, she really needed to market herself better. If only she could be friendlier with people. At first Arabella had wondered if she was ill or something was wrong, but Marika had just rolled her eyes and muttered something about *typisk svensk*.

In fact, outside of the musical circle, there had been a touch of iciness between the Swedes. Marika definitely came across as the more outgoing and confident of the two. The dominant woman. Arabella had just assumed Elin was younger, but had been surprised to find out that she was actually in her mid thirties.

They'd practiced for several hours in the flat, and put together a set list of Americana, Norwegian and Scottish folk, mostly instrumental but with three vocals; two of which Marika insisted on singing. Arabella hung on to the one vocal she'd brought to the set. Unsurprisingly, Elin didn't sing. They'd taken the collection to a lunch time gig in a restaurant. The two elder women were perched on bar stools. Marika preferred to stand, unavoidably taking centre stage. She was impressive on the hardanger fiddle, which to Arabella's ear had a bleaker, harsher tone than the fiddles she was used to playing with. It felt more rustic, of a wilder, back-to-basics time. And Marika carried it well, rolling competently through the set before having to dash off to a solo booking. It was a little odd that she had been so keen on the trio, for she shone in her queen bee throne too brightly to be part of a group.

In the flow of leaving, she'd shoved a bundle of her own CDs onto the girls, telling them to sell them before hurrying out of the door. More than one or two male eyes longingly watched Marika leave, regretful that they wouldn't get an autograph this time. Elin had looked a little put out, but set the music on the little Parisian table where they would meet and greet for quarter of an hour. Arabella had felt her inner angry child step up, and she had bundled Marika's CD's into her own rucksack. "Fuck that," she'd snapped, bringing a smile to the corner of Elin's face. The frost had thawed. With Elin's two CDs and leaflets advertising Arabella's downloads, they'd greeted the public. Regretfully Marika's CDs had already sold out.

"Do you want to go in?"

They continued to stare at the cathedral entrance. Arabella shrugged. "Is it worth a look?"

Elin sighed. "I always feel repressed in there. It's so barren."

"Let's give it a miss. Shall we head back to the flat? I could do with getting a couple of hours' sleep. We're supposed to be going clubbing tonight. There's a Swedish DJ on that's apparently really good. Are you coming?"

"Probably not. It's not really my thing," Elin admitted. "But you should go. If only to annoy Marika."

"I get on with Marika."

Elin laughed. "You're competition. If there's a man in the room, you're her rival. Haven't you seen?"

"I can't say I've noticed. I'll be damned if I'm going to worry myself with her bloody insecurities. Come on, let's head back. I don't want to have a culture overload. This is enough sightseeing for today."

When Arabella woke up from her nap, Marika was back in the flat. By the glowing sheen of perspiration on her forehead, it looked as though she'd run back from her solo gig, giddy by how well it had gone. Elin was at the kitchen table, politely listening with half an ear, although it looked as though her main focus was a long, long way from Iceland. Arabella padded into the living room, dressed in jeans and a woollen sweater a couple of sizes too big for her.

"Oh, hey, Arabella," Marika took a pause in her over excitable monologue. "Did you guys have any of my CDs left?"

"Yeah, they're just here." Arabella unzipped her rucksack that was lying on the sofa, and pulled out Marika's CDs, untouched and unsold for the time being.

"Oh, that's a lot left." She didn't try to hide her disappointment. "How many did you sell?"

"None, I'm afraid," Arabella shrugged and wandered into the kitchen, clocking the big pot of Swedish coffee that Elin had made. "Can I take a cup?"

"Help yourself."

"Really? So, did you guys have any sold?"

"I don't have any CDs to sell."

"I sold three," Elin said quietly.

"Three?" Marika sounded irritated. She paused, breathing in through her nose and tightening her lips. "You're lucky you don't need to worry about this," she told Arabella. "You just sell to the download generation, so you have no stock to carry. I have MP3 files for download as well. But the music geeks love to buy CDs still." She looked at Arabella's attire. "Are you still coming out tonight?"

"Sure. I was just catching up on some sleep."

"It gets hectic during the festival," Marika grinned. "You've got to know when to pace yourself, or else you get burned out. You're not coming out, are you, Elin? My cousin is on sick leave for burn out at the moment. She's so stupid. She won't accept that she's old now. It's like, she's complaining all of the time because she can't get pregnant.

Like it's a big surprise. She's over thirty; of course it's complicated now."

Arabella raised her eyebrows, sat down at the kitchen table and said nothing.

"But that's what you get when you don't plan. It's sad, because she still thinks she's a young woman. But she's not." Marika had one of the cupboard doors open and was peering thoughtfully at a stack of bowls. "I'm so hungry. I think I've got some instant noodles left in my room. Does anyone want any?"

"No thanks."

Arabella watched her skip away to her room, looking forward to her instant noodles as though they were a culinary masterpiece.

"I am trying to be pregnant."

The statement made Arabella jump. Elin was so quiet, and particularly withdrawn this afternoon since their stroll around town. She was now staring intensely at the table top, gripping her coffee cup. "We have been trying for two years."

She was completely out of her depth. Arabella had never considered herself a baby person, and certainly couldn't understand the near dangerous obsession some women developed over the pregnancy question. She'd heard some colleagues talk about pressures from the wider family; parents expecting grandchildren as if it was payback for all the child rearing they'd already done themselves. She'd had her own dalliance with the issue during her short-lived engagement. It was a sensitive subject whatever your standpoint was. All that knowledge still didn't make her the most empathetic person on the baby question. "I'm sorry to hear it's not working out so easily..."

"She knows I'm thirty five."

"Maybe she doesn't realise..."

Elin looked sharply at her. "She knows. I've talked to her about it before now."

"Look," Arabella sighed. "I don't think she means anything by it. Marika's just a bit of a foolish kid."

"I shouldn't have to listen to this bullshit." Elin stood up abruptly from the table. "I need to practice for tomorrow."

Is that my bullshit or Marika's bullshit that offends you so, Arabella wondered. Alone again. The sound of a key in the front door lock distracted her. Hafdis must be home already. Although when the door opened, it wasn't the stylish Icelander who wandered in, rather a tall, blond man with three day stubble and a thick cable knit grey sweater. What the hell? The man nodded to her and walked into the flat, letting the door bang shut behind him. *"Vi har ikke..."*

Arabella raised her eyebrows.

"Ah," the man paused. "You're not Marika?"

"Neither am I Elin. I don't understand Swedish."

"I've met Elin before, and that was Norwegian. You must be the English girl, Arabella, right?"

"Right. And you're the Norwegian friend."

"Arvid."

"Who's that asking for me?" Marika's voice floated down the corridor, an automatic reaction to her name being uttered. Did she listen in on everything, ear pressed to the door?

Arabella watched as Arvid twisted ever so slightly to look for Marika's appearance. She watched his body shift under that knitted jumper, and smiled to herself. Not bad at all. She'd never had a Norwegian before either. Not that she was collecting, and neither was she continuing on her hedonistic one night tour now that she was a mature and sensible person in her thirties. But a person could still look and imagine.

"Hej," Marika appeared in the doorway, her hair freshly brushed and her clothes changed into figure hugging alternatives for this evening. She literally glowed. Arvid's attention was distracted from the barely-finished-school eager pertness to something out of the corner of his eye. Even as he started to speak to Marika, his vision was moving away from her and back to the woman at the kitchen table.

"Who are you?" Marika flashed him a candy-gloss smile, slinking cat-like around him to lean against the back of the settee.

"I'm Arvid," he told Arabella.

Arabella smiled at him over the top of her coffee cup.

"Arvid? *Är du svensk?*"

"Norwegian. We should speak English. I don't believe Arabella speaks Swedish."

"Arabella?"

From Arabella's viewpoint, against the foreground of the Norwegian sailor's stance, Marika's face popped out from his elbow. She was still clinging to the settee, posing to her best advantage.

"I didn't realise she was there."

Arabella swallowed her mouthful of coffee.

"We were just getting acquainted."

"Oh." Marika stepped up uncertainly from the settee and approached the Norwegian. He still had his back to her, despite the fact that they were the only two people speaking. Arabella just sat there like a mute, drinking her coffee and being rude. "Well, we're going out to a club soon. Do you want to come with us?"

"No. I'm meeting some people this evening."

Norwegians were all rude and ignorant, Marika thought as she gazed up at Arvid with increasing irritation. She was standing right next to him, inviting him out and he didn't even have the decency to look at her.

Arabella finished her coffee, setting the cup on the table with a clink. Her fingers lingered on the rim of the cup as she slowly drew her hand away. She rose from her seat. "I'd better get ready. We'll be going out soon, won't we, Marika?"

Marika could have screamed. No one would look at her. "Fine," she huffed. "I need to go do my make up."

Arabella smiled at Arvid. "Maybe we'll see you later."

"*Käften, fy fan!*"

Arabella slapped a sweaty palm against the wall. The irritated, muffled shout from the next room was an unwelcome distraction. "What the hell?"

"Shut up, for fuck's sake."

She pushed herself back away from the wall, rolling her eyes. "Excuse me," she breathed.

"That's what she said," Arvid groaned. "It's Swedish. You can talk."

Arabella felt his hands grip her hips and push down as if to drag her into the belly of the earth.

"I don't mind screamers."

Arabella lurched forward, feeling his hands catch her breasts as they swung towards his face. "Neither do I." She closed her eyes and forced her muscles to contract again. Her toes flexed in an upward curl.

There was the sound of movement from the next room. A sense of preparation as if she was gearing up for the next verbal assault. Arabella pulled herself back up, still straddling Arvid, and slapped the wall angrily. "¡Cierra la boca!" she shrieked, making no attempt at subtlety. "Mojigata sueca."

Arvid roared with laughter, the force of which vibrated its way up through Arabella's body, pushing her head back with a groan. "Oh God."

"Mojigata sueca."

Arabella looked down at him and grinned. They were moving faster for the final climax. "Mojigata sueca," she whispered, her breathing growing heavy. Her inner core tightened and trembled, on the brink of explosion. "¡Mojigata sueca!"

Later, flopped out on the bed, tender and limp, thoroughly exhausted, Arabella closed her eyes. Her head rested on the crumpled mass of her clubbing outfit for Iceland: a pair of blue hot pants and a glittery gold halter neck. She started to idly dream of the evening out to the festival clubbing scene. She and Marika had been the dancing queens, happy friends and musical slaves to the festival, taking a night off to enjoy proceedings from the other side of the fence. It was all long before they were trading insults through the separating wall of their bedrooms. She could still trace the memory of the steady vibration of music pulsating through her flesh.

They had returned to the flat, where Arvid had been in the kitchen with a bottle of brennivín, the Icelandic schnapps flavoured with caraway. The local tipple to pickle the liver. The girls had taken a glass each and joined him. Marika had tried to play footsie with the Norwegian sailor under the table, but hadn't caught a bite. She'd given up and gone to bed. Arabella had downed what remained of her drink before standing up. "You're not shy, are you?"

Now she roamed through her memories and dreams. She was back on top of the Scandinavian, her head flung back in pleasure. When her gaze returned to the pillows, she was disconcerted to discover there was the three of them in bed. Arvid's eyes were shut, focused on reaching orgasm. He was oblivious to the intruder. Stretched out comfortably by Arvid's side lay Ben Simon, his arms crossed behind his head. He smiled up at her as if to say 'good show'.

"What the fuck are you doing here?" Arabella hissed.

"I thought you were missing me."

"Does it look like I'm missing you?"

"You've gone back to one nighters," he said pointedly.

"This is a relationship."

"This is a figment of your imagination."

"Get the hell out of my bed." She hunched forward, pushing him out of the bed, watching him roll away with satisfaction. "And don't come back."

Arvid grabbed her by the shoulders and pulled her back into the bed. "Come here," he said gruffly. "I've not finished with you yet."

The cafe was a compilation of hippies, tea shop paraphernalia, school days, tourists, music nerds, peppermint tea, homemade cakes, languages, second hand furniture and homemade cushions all contained within a tardis-like state. Everything was neatly crammed into a space that felt like an oversized cupboard. Arabella was carefully slotted into a corner, her elbow just tapping against the wall. As she played, she wiped the chalkboard clean. The walls had been painted up like bricks. Every rectangle was filled with chalkboard paint. The corresponding pot of coloured chalks waited on each table, the alternative replacement for the plastic rose in a glass.

Arabella sat on a stool with her folded coat as a cushion (there was nowhere else to put it) and her purple flapper hat still on her head. It had saved having to do much with her hair this morning. Besides it added to the mismatched, eccentric ambience that was going on here. Mismatched and wrong, yet oh so right.

Across the way there was a group of four Dutch students crammed lazily like crumpled blankets into the worn, tatty leather settee. Behind the sofa stood three music fans, having slipped in the narrow space between settee and wall. They were that keen to be in the presence of this performance. All seats were taken. It was standing room only. No one could get out for fresh drinks, toilet breaks or fire escapes.

His head lolled forward, swaying slightly to the music as if he couldn't quite believe it was this good. The sunglasses concealed his eyes, and for all anyone knew, the old man could have been dozing, his fingers left on automatic pilot to dance across the guitar strings. Then he would break into a smile. "Oh, yeah." Deep and rumbling, good old king toad.

Arabella on the banjo was playing second fiddle to his guitar, but she was thrilled enough to be playing again with the man. She hadn't seen him since she'd last been in the States. Johnnie O was an old solider of the southern country blues, hefty, dumpy, leathery and an immense presence. His forehead was filled with deep ravines, each cast in the heavy appreciation of decades of music.

"Well," he started as the song came to a natural end, his fingers idly strumming. "What you wanting to play now?"

This was always the way when she'd played with Johnnie O. Whether they were just jamming on his front porch, meeting up with a group of friends to practice, or giving a pre arranged performance; everything took on the intimate, unplanned feel of an unexpected meet up. The musical answer to getting a coffee together. Despite the fact that they were booked for a lunch time gig, he would provide no set list and just play what he felt like. He'd sit and talk to Arabella, strumming and chatting, and then suddenly he'd break into full song and they'd do a number. It wasn't exactly the easiest way to work, because one never knew what was coming next, or if one was even familiar with the song.

"Goddamn girl," he burst out laughing. "It's been a long time." He lowered his chin even further and looked at her over the top of his sunglasses, his eyes like marbles. "You ain't married that fool of a boy you were travelling with last?"

Arabella smiled wryly and shook her head. It really had been a long time. "We parted company a long time ago."

"That is good to hear. It'd be a tragedy to the world if you'd gotten hooked up with that one. Hear it, y'all, don't get hooked up with no dull man."

There was some tittering around in the room. Arabella smiled, half an ear trying to pick out the beat he was meandering towards. Another song was on the way.

"But you looking loved up, girl. You married?"

She laughed at the thought.

"You loved up."

She was still in a flush from last night. But that had just been a one night stand. These episodes were over in a few hours. There was usually no particular desire to meet again. In normal circumstances. Although she still felt a glow inside, like she couldn't stop smiling. She was actually looking forward to getting back to the flat and loitering in the hope she'd bump into Arvid again. So what was that supposed to mean?

The pace on the guitar picked up, flowing through a few coherent bars. "Is that a rag I hear?"

"He, he he," he laughed as he committed to the next song. "You got it, it's a rag, baby." And so they were off, this time into a Blind Boy Fuller track. Johnnie O was singing, his deep tenor trembling like a frog's low song.

The cafe had offered them a free late lunch after the two hour gig. A small table was moved across to the musicians, and Johnnie O sat like an old king on his throne, his subjects flocking to hear tales of the south. He had an inner charisma that people were unconsciously drawn to, clustering to the deep rumble of his voice. They were in place the entire afternoon and an hour after the cafe usually closed. The manager of the cafe was forced in the end to bring the afternoon's entertainment to a close, the call of child care no longer possible to postpone for just fifteen minutes more.

Instruments packed up, they were out on the street. The audience scattered, a little dazed and confused as if coming off a drug high.

Johnnie O wasn't walking too fast these days, and Arabella ambled down the road with him; the pair of them cutting an odd couple against the citizens of Reykjavik.

"I'm back in that god damned tin can tomorrow," Johnnie O was saying.

"You've barely been here!"

"And I'm missing my home. This cold ain't no good for my old bones. Tell me, girl, when you next coming over to see us?"

Arabella exhaled slowly. God only knew when she'd next be able to afford the time and the money to fly out to the States. The redundancy money was keeping her going for now, but the music wasn't going to sustain her full time. Certainly not if she was wanting to take intercontinental flights. "I don't know."

"You make it soon. There's a couple of new players I want to get acquainted with you. I ain't long for this world."

A knot of panic clutched her stomach and she had to look across at him to make certain he was still there. "Don't be daft, you're immortal."

"The music is, but the flesh hangs on the bones for a mere moment."

"Jesus, don't get maudlin on me."

"Don't you be blaspheming now," Johnnie O scolded good-naturedly. He remembered how Arabella's casual swearing had set some of the ladies a tittering back at the community centre when she'd first turned up. No one had really expected her to get a tune out of that banjo, let alone that she would play so well. Minnie swore blind she was possessed. "You look like you carrying troubles."

Something caught in her throat and she quickly swallowed it back down. Arabella didn't admit to weakness, not even to herself. Johnnie O had always had that uncanny ability of seeing straight through people. Everyone's reliable old granddaddy, he inspired confidences from all walks of life. "Everyone's got problems," she brushed it aside. "You can't have been playing the blues this long and not know that."

He laughed loudly. "Ain't that the truth."

They stopped at the cross roads. This would be the point they would split for their homesteads, and she realised it may well be the last time she ever saw her old mentor.

"I know I said you all loved up, but you look damned lonely to me. A woman without a man..."

"Give over."

"Give over what? Money or my life?"

"It's Yorkshire. You know what I'm saying." There was a smile at the corner of her mouth. There had been some real misunderstandings between the local idioms from two sides of the Atlantic when she'd first arrived in the States. Apparently the same language, but sometimes it felt like they were from different planets.

"I remember your crazy ways. And I know you need a man."

"No woman needs a man. I am an individual, perfectly capable of looking after myself."

"I'm not talking about the repression of women. I'm talking about human affection. Now you listen to old Johnnie O. No man is an island. And no woman ought to walk alone. You make sure you get that man you're thinking of."

Arvid? She'd only known him for twenty four hours. And he already showed up on her face? "I barely know him."

"Mr Graham's been my neighbour ever since I moved in. Fifty long years, let me tell you. Lived there with his good lady wife. No children. Last month, it came out he had another wife over in Tennessee. Three children and everything. All grown up. All this time. We all thought we knew him. Fifty long years. Let me tell you, time means nothing."

Maybe so, Arabella pondered. Perhaps she ought to try and do something more with Arvid. She had missed a chance with Ben, but she didn't have to make that mistake again out of fear of long distances. It wasn't like either of them actually lived in Iceland, so it wasn't like she was setting up a long distance thing with this arctic land. And they had clicked straight off.

"It's been good catching up, girl," Johnnie O brought her back out of her thoughts. "You get yourself over to see us soon, you hear?"

"I will."

She really ought to have been playing a gig or going to a gig or just generally touting her music. Instead, Arabella was with a group of strangers in a cult-like circle around a pool of steaming water. She'd glanced across at her fellow tourists and for a moment thought she saw a familiar face from her life back in the UK. But it wasn't him.

There was a giddy sense of expectation in the air. Arabella had been here for five minutes and nothing had happened. Worse, having brought her up to this desolate mountain landscape, the edges of icy glaciers peaking over the skyline beyond, Arvid had wandered off. The idea had been that they would spend the day together, and yet she felt like she'd been abandoned for the tourist she was.

Damned Norwegian. The wind picked up and she pulled her collar closer to her chin, enjoying a secret smile. What was this exactly? Hanging out? A date? She couldn't quite decide. It was certainly more than a one night stand. At least it had been until he'd wandered off.

The muttering in the ring started to grow focused and a couple of the women took cameras out of their pockets, aiming them at the pool of water. The atmosphere felt pregnant. Arvid had told her that she needed to do this Golden Circle. She'd thought it was a euphemism, but he'd brought her out on the tourist trail instead and left her in the geyser park. They'd walked up past steam vents, rivulets of boiling water and bubbling mud pots that made her think of bad curries. At the top there was a round steaming pool of water with a crater hole in the middle, water draining back down into the belly of the earth.

A translucent, aquamarine dome bulged up out of the central crater like a bubble. There was a moment when it seemed to waver, and the world held its breath. Then a tower of hot water and steam powered forth to the sky, a sudden immense burst of energy. Arabella felt herself involuntarily gasp, for a moment goggling at the wonder before someone grabbed her from behind and she started screaming.

Arvid's laughter swirled warmly into her ear, and she struggled without conviction in his arms. He swung her around and set her down on the ground. "Did that make you jump, little English lady?"

"You fucker," she whacked him playfully.

"I'm showing you the sights of Iceland. Aren't you enjoying the Golden Circle so far?"

"You mean there's more. I don't see how you're going to top a giant waterfall and a geyser."

"Just wait and see."

The first point on the tour had been to a massive waterfall. Gullfoss, as it was called, sliced its way through the lunar landscape of the Icelandic interior. The sheer sense of power from that body of water churning over the rock edge was beyond intense. There had been a tale about a plague of a man who had wanted to set up a hydro electric plant there. A local Icelandic woman had been so against the exploitation of the island's natural beauty that she had flung herself into the waterfall in protest. That was some conviction, to throw yourself into a body of water like that, knowing that it would be the end. Arabella had stood at the viewing platform and peered into the mist splurging up from the plunge pool. She wondered if she'd ever have such intensity within her to take any such risk.

The final part of the puzzle was the National Park, Þingvellir. It was a tract of land rolled straight out from a medieval fantasy film set. There was a mountain surround, filled in with a near endless spread of moorland, moss covered lava fields, rivers and pools, rugged cliffs, sparse trees and a lonely white farmstead set by a lake. Rolled straight out, or lurched straight up from the bowels of the earth, for this park was every so gradually expanding as the European and North American tectonic plates, one on each edge of the park, gently continued to go their separate ways.

They followed a track up the side of the North American plate that led out of the park. This was the vicinity of the old Viking parliament, apparently, Arabella mused, hugging herself and gazing out over the bleak landscape. And this was the good time of the year. Jesus, what would it have looked like in winter? Who of the old Vikings landed here and thought this would be a good place to set up camp? Scandinavians, she thought, turning back to the little pool

Arvid had brought her to. They were a strange collection of people. It probably said it all. Here was the pool at the parliament, where, according to Arvid, women they wanted to get rid of were 'dealt with'.

"You sure you're not a tourist guide?"

"I told you, I work on shipping."

"Yes, your exciting cargo shipping."

"Cargo ships aren't that exciting. It's where they go that is the interesting part. I've been all over the world." He slung an arm around her shoulders. "How much travelling do you do with your job?"

"I made it to Iceland."

Arvid laughed, not unkindly, but in that way that suggested he didn't really care if that was supposed to be the mark of a great achievement. "This isn't a full time job for you. You have a real job. Things that happen here, they're just..." he waved his free hand in the air as if trying to grasp the word before it escaped him for good. "This is a special island. It's unreal."

"Well, I suppose I'm between jobs then."

"That a euphemism?"

She was unemployed. That didn't sound great, as if she wasn't quite fit for anything normal. She'd been dancing around the subject the last few weeks, throwing herself into her music and trying not to think of the ways she'd fucked up. Or perhaps she'd been dancing around the issue of normality for years, avoiding the fact that her peers were getting married, buying houses, building careers. And was that part of the contract in growing older, or was it simply optional? The jury was out, certainly the one in Arabella's mind.

"I got made redundant," she finally admitted. "Seemed like perfect timing to come and do a festival."

"But then you'll be back to the sunny UK and you'll get yourself a new job."

"Most probably. And all of this will have been forgotten."

He flashed her a grin before striding ahead. "Not everything."

She pursed her lips and followed him up the hill back to the car park. She wasn't quite sure if that conversation had meant to be a warning, or if she was over-thinking things. Yet again. The redundancy had knocked her off kilter more than she might have liked to admit. Work and work colleagues weren't meant to have any claim on your emotions or nerves but often they did. They could hurt.

At the breach of the hill, Arvid turned and waved at her. "Hurry up."

"Yeah, yeah, yeah," she muttered, picking up the pace. "You and your fucking mile-long legs can just wait a bit."

Back at the flat there was a new addition to their community. He was half-heartedly helping Hafdis with the cooking, but easily distracted by the arrival of Arvid and Arabella. Jordan Oates, Arabella's agent, offered them both a bottle of beer, before returning to his usual route of talking to those in the living room, circling back to Hafdis on a regular basis. Arvid slouched against the adjoining wall, drinking beer from the bottle. Elin was out, but Marika was perched on the armchair like a Persian cat, a glossy magazine draped across her lap.

Arabella slipped onto the settee, setting her bottle on the side table. She shared the seating with a fully loaded guitar case. "Is this a new addition to the residents?"

"Yes, I bought it over for Hafdis," Jordan said. "Take it out, take a look."

Arabella unzipped the case. Marika started talking again, jabbing her finger at a photograph in the magazine. "Can you believe this woman? It's kind of disgusting."

"Why, what is she doing?" Hafdis asked, half an ear on the conversation.

"Does she pick her nose in public?" Jordan chortled, sounding like a school boy.

"I bet she shits in the garden," Arvid said.

"You two!" Hafdis laughed.

"No," Marika continued straight faced. "She's talking about having a baby."

Arvid laughed out loud. Arabella, now with the glossy new electric guitar out of its case and in her lap, the new babe to play with, glanced up and caught his eye, shared a secret smile.

"Marika," Hafdis stepped away from the curry to look into the living room. "It's a perfectly natural thing."

116

"She's thirty-five."

"It happens a lot to people in their thirties," Hafdis said gently.

"For her first?" Marika looked as though she'd just spotted a turd on the corner of the rug. "That's just selfish, if you want my opinion. Wrong."

Arabella glanced over her shoulder, half expecting to see Elin in the shadows of the corridor, sobbing her heart out. But of course, she was out at a gig. Why were the barbs in order in that case? She smiled to herself, shaking her head and strumming her fingernails across the metal guitar strings. It was in tune. A good solid sound. Of course it would never trump the banjo, but it wasn't too bad.

"This is the liberty of youth," Arvid raised his beer bottle as if to propose a toast. "Innocent to the reality of life."

Marika scowled. "Don't patronise me."

Hafdis rolled her eyes and turned back to the curry. There was a general unspoken silence in the room that said it wasn't worth getting into a discussion with the Swedish girl. She was at that age when she always knew best.

Arabella shifted in the settee, folding her body a little more neatly around the guitar.

"You going to give us a tune?" Arvid asked.

"Yes," Marika clapped her hands. "I'll get my violin. We can practice that set I was teaching you."

"No," Arvid groaned. "Let's do some proper music. Some rock..."

"Old daddy music?" Marika scoffed.

"We going to play guess that tune?" Arabella wavered on a note, flicking through a mental catalogue of popular tracks.

"I'm too young to know daddy rocking songs."

It was a strange comment, Arabella thought, for someone who played folk tunes as old as the rocks. Her fingers fell into familiar routes as she made her decision, plucking out a well-known guitar riff.

A cheer went up from Arvid and Jordan. Hafdis smiled to herself.

"*Money for Nothing.*"

Marika stalked out of her seat. "It's free?"

"It's the song." Arvid stared quizzically at her. "Have you not heard of Dire Straits, girl?"

"Sounds like you're in them," she muttered, not even sure what that was supposed to mean only that it was the solitary come back that had popped up in her mind. "I'm going to my room."

Arabella paused playing and leaned forward over the body of the guitar. "It's a good guitar, Hafdis."

"It had better be," the Icelander grinned and grabbed Jordan by the chin, pulling him towards her. "Or else there's going to be some trouble."

Was this happiness? Certainly if she was a giddy school girl there could be no doubt. Arabella caught sight of herself in a passing window and rolled her eyes. Calm down, she said, but she couldn't quite remove the smile from her face. She sauntered onwards, back towards the flat, swinging her banjo case by her side.

Things were getting better. Anyone facing redundancy could reasonably feel as though it was the end of the world. And anyone who had been through it knew that life went on. Crawl back out of that low patch. What had happened to her other than that she had been set free from a restrictive mundane nine to five job? She was back on her music, and it made her feel alive. It was the very blood that filled her veins. She was at a festival in Iceland for Christ's sake. She was performing at gigs, selling downloads of her music and at some point the CDs would be ready again.

A mental block had been pulled out of her head. Perhaps that old ill-fated engagement had screwed up her life more than she would have cared to admit. She hadn't been in a proper relationship since, choosing instead to hop from a string of one night stands and casual rendezvous. Usually there had been little about the men to recommend spending any longer in their presence than necessary. There were a lot of dull people out there. And when there was chemistry, something in her stopped. Oh, the distance would be too much. Oh, she was happy the way she was. Oh, she didn't want to risk it and for everything to fall apart.

That block had gone. She had enjoyed the past week immensely. Arvid had been to some of her gigs, and it had given her an inner thrill to see him there. They'd walked home to the flat together, talking about everything. The man was funny, intelligent and damn good in bed. She wasn't worrying about the fact that they didn't live in the same town, let alone the same country. She had let go of her worries. She was thirty and she was finally arriving.

She was feeling randy as she arrived back at the flat, and hoped Arvid was in. Man, she could tear the clothes from his body with her teeth, the way she was feeling. Standing her banjo case up in the corner of the living room, she strolled through to the room Arvid occasionally slept in. He wasn't there; in fact it was looking distinctly tidy. He must be out.

"Fucker," she muttered good-naturedly, fetching her banjo and heading to her own room. Flopping back on the bed she stared up at the ceiling and wondered what she was going to do with herself now. Maybe she could take a nap, because she didn't want to be sleeping much tonight.

Rolling to her side, she was met with a picture of an ugly looking cat licking its own nose in a contorted grimace. The brightly coloured postcard was propped up against her makeup case on the desk by the window. It certainly wasn't one of Arabella's possessions. Getting up, she walked over and picked up the postcard. Flicking it over, she noted Arvid's name at the bottom, and smiled, turning it back to the amusing picture. Certainly an ironic card. So, what had the guy to say for himself? Would they be meeting later on?

Hey you, the card started. "Jesus," Arabella muttered. "The art of the love letter's really died a death." She sat down on the bed and continued to read.

It's been a great week. You keep on playing, banjo girl. Setting sail again. Arvid.

She remained. The silence coiled around her. Her fingers pressed like vices to the edge of the card. She returned to Arvid's room and checked the drawers and the wardrobe. His hold all, his clothes, his toiletries. Everything had gone.

A key turned in the front door lock.

Arabella marched through to the living room. When he walked through that door, he was going to have things to explain. Angrily she rushed up as the door opened. It was Hafdis with her arms full of shopping bags, and Marika, checking her phone. The women stumbled up against one another, surprised and a little disorientated. Arabella backed off, muttering apologies.

"No worries," Hafdis spoke. "Were you heading out?"

"No, I just thought you were Arvid."

"Arvid?" Hafdis sounded confused. "But his shore leave ended. He sailed this morning. He said he was leaving you a note."

"When's he back?"

"When's he back?" Hafdis laughed, a little bemused by the question. "One never knows. Months, years. He was just visiting."

"Yes, but I..." she looked back down at the message scrawled on the back of a shitty cat postcard. This was the brush off. Thanks for the interlude, but I've got to get back to my life. Nice knowing you. And she thought of those whimpering faces, men she'd slept with who embarrassingly turned back up at the house, thinking that they were now going steady. But those had never been anything more than casual fucks. She'd spent the entire fucking week with Arvid.

Marika looked up from her phone. "He's a sailor. He has a woman in every port."

Arabella stared at nothing, feeling as though the plasterboard was beginning to peel and crumble off the walls.

"Anyway, you need to worry about your music," Marika advised, a glint in her eyes. "Maybe you should take down some of your MP3 tracks."

"What?" Arabella snapped.

"You're getting bad reviews." Marika passed her the phone so that she could see the website on screen. *What is this shit? It sounds like a cat in a washing machine on a distant hill.*

"I think I'd be just too embarrassed if I got bad reviews," Marika continued idly as Arabella passed her back the phone. "I'd have to take things off sale. I know they say there's no such thing as bad publicity, but... oh, you were just going out?"

Arabella ignored the question and continued down the staircase.

Did they never turn the fucking wind off in this fucking country? As wonderful as her purple flapper girl hat was, it simply wasn't up to the job. Arabella tugged the hood from her coat over her head, and shrugged her body back into itself. Her hands were stuffed into her coat pockets, her legs propped out in front, daring someone to come and tell her she was hanging over the edge too much. Just try it, she thought, just come and try it and see what happens.

She'd marched through town with no destination in mind. In truth she had nothing in mind. It was as if something had burst, and she was unable to grasp anything. A motive. A plan. A sound. Even the passing of time felt beyond abstraction. So she marched, until she found herself on the road that ran along Faxaflói bay. She continued walking, following the waters' edge until she arrived at the sun voyager sculpture. It was a skeletal metal frame forming a Viking longship, set on a disc platform with nothing but a heap of rocks separating it from the chilly arctic waters. The indigo water was choppy and bounding, crested with white foam. A person with a weaker stomach than Arabella's would have felt ever so slightly nauseous at the sight. She just hoped it was a lot worse out to sea and that tonight sailors would be heaving into buckets and toilet bowls, hanging over the edge of the ship and praying for an end. What had they done to deserve this misery?

She sat in front of the sculpture, away from the road and the very occasional passing pedestrian. Her legs were like sticks, straight out and over the edge of the platform. The wind pummelled the side of her body, pushing and pushing, go on, you want to go into the sea. Arabella growled back.

She'd checked the website on her phone once she'd sat down. Sadly Marika's announcement hadn't been misled. There were bad reviews. Really bad reviews. *If someone had actually even produced this mess, they really need to think about a career change*, one shopper wrote. *Total waste of money. She's got this the wrong way around. People are usually shit live, but all right when recorded.*

Arabella wasn't so stupid as to think she would never get a bad review. Since the first book, the first song, the first piece of art, in fact the first anything that was deserving of an opinion, there had always been someone who loved it, someone who hated it and a million other vague opinions filling in the space in between. Everyone gets bad reviews. Fair enough. But that was all she had. She'd given up scrolling after the second page and turned off her phone. Nothing but shit. You are wasting your time, girl. You need to think of a career change.

She squeezed her eyes shut and lowered her head. This was it. This was supposed to be the career change. Doing something she was good at. Not just playing the game and picking up her salary. Music was the thing that kept the blood flowing in her body. She had never felt she was a musical genius, but she knew for a fact that she wasn't too bad either. She could certainly hold a tune. She had been so convinced. Jesus, this is why she'd never turned pro. This was exactly why. Because they were lined up with their pins, popping the bubbles one by one, bringing her back down to earth. Actually you have no talent. Actually you have no point. What was left now? People had all but said she was getting too old for the dancing. She was redundant. She knew she'd just roll back into another administrative role she didn't really give a shit about, because hey, there were always bills to be paid. Then she'd go home to her rented room, day dream about the days she used to dance, strum on her banjo and hope no one heard her. She didn't have the life goals that other people took to bring meaning to their lives. Living through others: getting married, having kids. Get a dog, get a cat. Get a tank full of fish, a hamster, a rabbit, whatever the latest damned addiction was. She'd get older, Adam would either kick her out, die, or she'd have to marry him so she didn't end up homeless. Then at least she could say she'd managed to get a husband, even if she didn't love him in the way one ought to love spouses. A loveless relationship wasn't a good idea. She just had to look back at her parents to understand that.

But just as her music wasn't worth the fifty pence; Arabella wasn't worth more than a week. That fucking emotionally wanting Norwegian arsehole. Was she that boring, that mediocre that he didn't want to continue? Jesus, she'd forced herself to be brave and go for it, and she'd been left standing. It was impossible. The idea that you could genuinely like someone, and at the same moment the feeling would be mutual, was nonsense. Ludicrous. Everyone died alone.

She could carry on like this for a few more decades. Getting haggard, wrinkled, grey, flabby, miserable, sick. Same old shit. Or she could spare herself the inevitable and throw herself in the icy water. She wasn't a swimmer. She didn't give herself longer than a minute against that big bastard of a sea out there. She could do it. She'd always scoffed at the suicidal, but just now she couldn't think of a damned thing that was working in her life, that was worth continuing for. She had no curiosity as to how it might work out. She had a gaping hole in the middle of her chest.

Arabella watched as her white, blue-tinged corpse was pulled out of the sea, salt water pouring from her saturated clothes. They'd have to fly her body home, which would cost a bundle. She wasn't sure if her insurance had included it. Then there'd be the funeral. What a joke. Tinny music in a crematorium. Arabella Mangella, only made it to thirty. All the musical greats died young. Although wasn't that doomed age twenty seven? Too old for that.

What a load of bollocks. At least if Arvid had made some pretence of wanting to have a relationship with her, she could have had something to look forward to. Okay, so it wasn't love, not yet, but the lust and chemistry had been enough for a start, hadn't it? But he'd just fucked off and the world hated her music. Why did he have to do that? What was wrong with her?

Arabella tasted salt and panicked for a moment, shuffling on the platform to reassure herself that she wasn't drowning in the bay. She wiped at her eyes with the back of her sleeve, grateful that no one was present to see this little performance. No one ever got to see Arabella Mangella cry. Never let the bastards know they got to you.

She'd just have to start over again.

With nothing.

Why was she always alone?

She didn't need a man.

She was an independent woman.

"I will rescue myself," she declared, unintentionally shouting the statement out loud, as if the volume would make it into a legally binding agreement. A contract between the parties Arabella Mangella and her fucked up life.

"Anyone else shouting that would worry me."

Shit. She quickly dried her eyes, thanking the gods of fate that she hadn't been heavy handed with the makeup today. The panda look was always a giveaway. Twisting around, she looked up at Jordan Oates. In his long black coat, he looked like a mismatched gangster. The stripy blue woollen hat really didn't cut it as threatening.

"I got back to the flat a few minutes after you'd left."

"Oh." Her mind flashed through those last few moments. How would Hafdis and Marika have recounted the episode?

"I should apologise about those reviews."

"It wasn't you singing," she snapped. "Or what was it they said? Something about a cat on a far off mountain."

"No, but I had a hand in uploading the wrong file," Oates confessed, walking around the sculpture to sit next to her. "It was a corrupted file. It really did sound like shit. We'd got it fixed and then..." he held out his hands. There was no excuse. "Rushing late at night. Uploaded the wrong fucking file. One of the event organisers contacted me this morning as there'd been complaints. As soon as I had a listen I realised what had happened. But, you'll be glad to know the dodgy file's been taken off, and the correct one uploaded. We've emailed everyone who downloaded it, so they've got what they thought they were buying..."

"Did you see the reviews?"

"They weren't good."

"That shit is still live on the net."

"People will rewrite their reviews now."

Arabella shook her head and looked back out to sea. "I don't know what I'm doing. I really don't."

"There's an explanation for the bad reviews, it will get sorted. But..." he paused. "Everyone will get bad reviews at some point anyway. You can't go to pieces."

"I am not going to pieces."

"I know, I know," he spoke soothingly. "I heard. You'll sort yourself out." He watched Arabella. She was a good singer and performer but a dismal self publicist. She'd vanished for years, terrified of making a go of things. Fearful of those bad reviews. As if she was really just wasting her time. "Hafdis was worried about you."

"There's nothing to worry about. It was a corrupt file."

"You did realise about Arvid? Things are fleeting, never serious. I've known him for years, Hafdis for decades, but she can count on one hand the number of times she's actually met up with him. And they're friends."

"I'm not broken-hearted if that's what you think," she snapped defensively.

"Of course not. You've always struck me as a very independent woman. You'd have gone through with that misguided wedding otherwise."

"Exactly."

"Maybe better to stick to someone closer to home."

She shook her head slowly. "I burnt all those bridges."

"Oh."

"I told you I was made redundant, didn't I?"

"You did."

"And this isn't going to support me full time."

"Certainly not straight off. Put a positive spin on this. New beginnings."

"From nothing burst forth..."

"Something?"

"Fuck knows."

"Well, for starters, I've got a gig for you back in York when you return. If nothing else, this festival has shown you can do other things. I'm not knocking the banjo, but I hear your stint on the bass guitar with those Canadians went well. And you can sing. How about a fifties club night?"

"Singing?"

Oates nodded. "They're short one female singer. Put on one of those vintage frocks and go knock 'em dead. It's a dance and dinner event, a couple of hundred covers."

"I don't know..."

"We were just talking about fresh starts."

"Fine," Arabella grumbled, getting up from her perch. Her arse was growing numb, and the last thing she needed was piles. "I will do it." That illusive, undefined it that floated unfocused ahead. That was her future. Whatever the hell it was going to be.

Arabella's face wrinkled in disgust as an unpleasantness hit her taste buds. She spat the chocolate back into its wrapper and regarded the offending article. There were small black chunks in the spittle-chewed confectionary. Fucking liquorice. She lobbed the sweet into the bin and kicked the bag to the floor. What was wrong with this country? They had to put that revolting root into everything.

Like Lady Muck, she was curled in her bed, the duvet creased and massed like the mountain ranges of her kingdom. She was dressed in her pyjamas and had a vivid lilac eye mask pushed back on her forehead, tussling her hair. It never really got dark here at this time of year. The seasonal sun, plus the fact that a musician's life gigging didn't involve regular hours meant that Arabella was catching odd hours of sleep at random times in the day, generally with the sun pulsating through the window.

She was looking through the festival newspaper. She'd picked it up at the start of the event and not really had much chance to look at it. She'd probably not get the whole thing read – which she fully intended to do – until she was back home in the UK. There was the usual fare: gig listings, adverts, venue reviews, as well as interviews with every single artist and performer signed up as the paper had gone to print. Arabella had been a last minute signing, but even she had her page of fame, complete with a publicity shot taken five years ago. She looked oh so painfully young.

Just now she was reading through the article on Elin, the accordion-playing Swede and former flatmate. Quiet, unassuming and impressively deft with her fingers. Arabella had liked her, although found her a touch too full of angst to want to spend long periods of time with her. A few days shy of the festival end, Elin had decided to call it a day and fly back to the homeland as she was missing her husband. It had felt as though there was more to it, but she wasn't the type of person one could force a confidence.

She'd departed from the flat yesterday evening, many hours earlier than she really needed to. She said she was nervous about getting to the airport. Arabella suspected it also had something to do with the fact that there was only another hour or so left until Marika would be back. At least Elin bothered to say goodbye to some of her short term flatmates, unlike other worthless Scandinavians who had been staying with them.

"I hope she calms down and finds happiness," Arabella had said after Elin had gone.

"Mmm?"

"Did she mention the baby thing to you?"

Hafdis had winced. "Marika has been pushing her buttons about it."

"I know she's been a little fucker, but really, does Elin need to get that hysterical? So she's not stuck with a hoard of shitting, crying runts. I've never got the baby thing. There were people at my last job younger than me, and that was all their life was about."

"I guess we're all wired differently. Although Elin's not always been this bad." Hafdis had paused. "I don't suppose Marika's old enough at all, and I'm guessing you've not experienced it either yet."

Arabella had raised an eyebrow. "What?"

"Maybe you won't either."

"Maybe I won't what?"

"The biological clock," Hafdis had explained simply. "A whole cartload of terror hormones. It's not fun. Oh, I know, there are some women who have always wanted children and that's all they think about. But there are other women who aren't necessarily baby obsessed, and then they get the biological clock,"

"And have a personality change?" Arabella had suggested, sounding unconvinced.

"No..." Hafdis had said slowly. "But it's terrifying. Like a long panic attack. I can understand the angst."

Arabella remained unconvinced, even the following day when she'd had time to mull it over. Perhaps hormones really did fuck up people's brains, but she didn't like the idea of women selling themselves short. As if life was just about arranging your replacement. That it wasn't possible to experience, to live, without having to involve other people. Oh, what did she know? She was just an unemployed fuck up: redundant, no home of her own, no relationship, no startling music career and a dance repertoire that was never going to hit the big time. Arabella Mangella: short and angry about something, but who in the world gave a damn? No one.

"Arabella!" Marika shrieked, charging gleefully into Arabella's small room without even knocking on the door. "We're on YouTube."

"We're on the internet?"

"Yes!" The Swede leapt into her bed like a child at Christmas, curling up to Arabella and thrusting her tablet at her. "Look."

"Jesus, Marika," Arabella swore, taking the tablet. She'd not used one of these things before. It was disconcerting, like holding a little laptop screen and wondering who had run off with the keyboard.

"Look, watch the video." Marika jabbed at a curled arrow, replay, and the five minute video started again.

It wasn't too badly shot; probably from a proper stand rather than the wobbly, heavy breathing amateur film she had feared. It had been taken two days ago in the National Museum where the girls had done a duo performance one lunch time. The gig had been a medley of Norwegian and British folk tunes, with a bit of Americana, when Arabella got to sing. The video featured a cover of a song by an up and coming American folk singer. Arabella was perched on a bar stool (why did a museum have a bar stool?) her banjo set in the most natural position against her body, and she was singing into the microphone. There was joy, pleasure and a glow of simple living in her face. Marika did her body wave fiddle playing at the side. The pair of them skipped the light fantastic over the instruments' strings and grinned like loons as if this was the simplest thing in the world.

Marika leant up against her to get a better view of the screen. "I'm so glad I was wearing that green dress," she commented, keeping her voice low so as to not intrude on the music too much. "I've worn a couple of frumpy crappy things this festival. I gave away that skirt to a thrift store, you know." She shook her head in shame. "I can't believe I ever thought it was a good idea."

"The sound quality's pretty good."

"I know!" Marika nudged her shoulder. "It only got uploaded yesterday afternoon and look at the number of views."

Arabella's mouth widened as she double checked the figures. "Three thousand, two hundred and fifty eight?"

"I know!" she squealed. "We're going global, baby. And look, there's links to my website here. And yours underneath."

"My website," Arabella mused, idly stroking her finger over the screen and tapping the link. She was aware that Oates had been working on the site, but had left all of the technology and marketing to him. That was what agents were there to worry about. She was surprised when the website came up, wondering if it was the wrong link for a moment. This looked like the website of a professional recording artist. For the main page image he'd used a close up of her outdoors in the sunshine that they'd taken in his back garden shortly after she'd returned to the fold. The latest news was the YouTube video they'd just been watching. Below that were some photos from the Reykjavik festival; a few solo shots: one of her, Marika and Elin posing together; another of her and Johnnie O, unaware of the camera, laughing and sharing mischief together at the little cafe. There were page links to a sparse biography Oates wanted to flesh out later on after the festival; music downloads, and a corner box promising that a new album would be out soon. And a little apology regarding the upload of a corrupted file. All customers should have received a link with the correct MP3 file now. For nothing was perfect. Even so, she was rather touched that Oates had made such a good job of her website.

"I've got fifty more likes on my Facebook page," Marika was still babbling in the background. "Do you have a Facebook page?"

"What? Facebook?"

"You know, a performer page, so people can like you. Keep up to date with your news."

"I don't know. Jordan sorts all of that out for me."

"Make sure he gets it sorted," Marika told her, lurching back off the bed with her tablet as abruptly as she had arrived. "And when you do, make sure you add me."

Manchester felt like another planet. She had only been away a few weeks, although her nerves and sensibilities felt the time ought to be counted in years. It was bizarre being back in the UK, and also slightly depressing. She peered through her sunglasses across the airport train station. She felt like an alien, but things really hadn't changed. Iceland had been great, the break had taken its desired effect, but she really wasn't sure that she wanted to be back. The euphoria of making a new life plan had waned, and now the overwhelming project of enacting said plan loomed at her.

She'd taken a very early morning flight out of the Arctic land and returned to the UK mid morning. She had a couple of hours on the train to look forward to, then she'd be alighting at York station, walking through its Victorian ambience with a very heavy suitcase in tow. The figure on the airport scales had been a lot higher on the return journey. A sleep-deprived member of the check in staff had made her pay a fee for the unauthorised kilos. Like a foodie on a membership diet, she was sent away with a slip of paper to pay for her misdeeds.

The train journey was uneventful. Suddenly she was back home. The taxi driver grumbled at her about the council's ridiculous plan to shut Lendle Bridge. There was no point other than for the council to grab a bit of easy cash. They ought to stop this flea-brained scheme, he told her. Arabella closed her eyes; thankful she still had her sunglasses on. The perfect screening for rudeness.

The house was still standing. She had been deposited on the pavement, suitcase by her feet, banjo case in her hand. Her car was still parked on the road where she'd left it; a dinted red corsa keeping it company. And for a moment she couldn't move, didn't dare walk up to that building and put her key in the lock. Walk back into the mess that was her life. There was so much to try and resolve, and the unknown quantity of when and how it would be fixed was a little intimating. For Christ's sake, she scowled at herself. Stop being so pathetic. Arabella Mangella simply doesn't put up with this kind of shit.

She had marched up to the door and was just about to put her key in the lock when the door opened. Expecting to see either Adam or her mother, Arabella involuntarily leant back in terror when she was met with by complete stranger.

The woman, who was a similar age to Arabella, stood a good few inches above her. Judging from the expression on her face, she enjoyed the advantage. She was average looking, with particularly sharpened eyebrows, 50s secretary glasses and pastel pink glossed lips so well made up they look positively plastic. She regarded Arabella.

Arabella in turn took off her sunglasses and checked the house number in case she'd stupidly wandered up the wrong garden path. This was definitely home.

"Well?" the woman questioned, setting one hand on hip. "What do you want?"

Like a cat with its fur brushed the wrong way, Arabella icily snapped the arms of her sunglasses together. "I just happen to live here."

"Oh," the woman nodded, assessing her from head to toe. "You must be Arabella, the belly dancing whore?"

"Who the hell...?"

"I hear you've got a thing about gentlemen callers. A different one every day."

Arabella picked up her suitcase and barged her way into the house. She wasn't going to stand out on the doorstep of her own home and be insulted. She went to skirt around the clutter of boots, umbrellas and Adam's spare feet that resided in the hall, but was disconcerted to discover that the hall was empty. Disinfectedly so. She set her suitcase down where her jumbled collection of western boots were supposed to be resting. "What the...?"

"I've had a bit of a tidy," the woman said, shutting the front door. "The boots and umbrellas and other paraphernalia are in a bin bag. I put them in your room. I thought you'd want to sort through them."

"Just who the fuck do you think you are?"

"I'm Liz."

"I don't give a damn what you're calling yourself. I want to know what the hell you're doing here. I don't want you to clean up my boots like I'm some fucking child..."

"Don't act like one then."

"Shut the fuck up! We never have and we never will be requiring the services of a cleaner. Just pack up your mop and bugger off."

"I don't clean here. I live here."

"The fuck you do. I live up there. Adam lives down here."

"And so do I now." Liz folded her arms smugly. "Adam not tell you?"

Adam hadn't told her anything. In fact Adam had been rather uncommunicative. She'd sent two postcards to York and pinged off three or four emails whilst she'd been in Iceland, but hadn't paid attention to any incoming traffic. In fact, on reflection, she hadn't had a reply from Adam once. Arabella leered up at the ice maiden. "What did you do, murder Adam and bury him under the patio?"

"Adam's quite well. He's better than he's been in a long time."

"The fuck he is. I want to speak to him."

"He's out."

"How convenient. I am getting this sorted, and you're out." Arabella picked up her suitcase and started up the staircase. With a bit of privacy and she'd phone Adam at work to get to the bottom of this. The beast, Liz started to follow her upstairs until Arabella swung around, almost accidentally hitting her head with the banjo case. "Oh no. I pay rent to live upstairs. You keep that sour pickled face of yours down there."

"Speaking of which, we do need to talk about you renting those rooms."

Arabella ignored her and hurried up the staircase. She was glad that her back was to the woman, glad that she was almost in her bedroom and could slam the door shut and be alone. Her heart was suddenly pumping violently against her ribs and she felt an overwhelming need to be sick. This was not good at all.

Adam didn't answer the phone the first time she called. It went to answerphone. It went onto the answerphone the second, third and fourth times she called, all in neat succession. By the fifth call he'd obviously taken the hint that she wasn't going to disappear, and had answered. Most people in most situations would have turned the phone off. From experience, Adam had enough sense to override the fear and understand that the sooner he faced Arabella, the better.

"Arabella. How was your holiday?"

Normally she would have corrected him straight off. Working at a festival was hardly a holiday. There were more pressing issues today. "Just great. And I get home to find Mrs Psycho Bitch in the house. Do we have an intruder or have you hired a cleaner? I'm not paying..."

"Do you mean Liz, Arabella?"

"Which other psycho bitches might be turning up at the house?"

Adam laughed weakly. "She's a nice person, Arabella. She just has a strong mind."

"Who is she? Where the hell has she come from?"

"I met her online."

"You were advertising for a cleaner?"

"She's my girlfriend."

Arabella felt her head drop to her hand. She had been persisting with the cleaner line the moment she'd locked herself in her room, praying to God that this wasn't what it looked like. Adam was, as a general rule, terrified of women, and she had only been gone a few weeks. To go from nothing to something this serious was a lot for anyone to achieve, but for Adam it seemed impossible.

"Was she just staying the night?" She already knew the answer.

"She's moved in."

She dropped to the floor, feeling the base of her world start to crack. "But you must barely know her."

"It never stopped you, Arabella."

"I've never moved anyone into the house!"

"You've had a lot of people over."

Arabella the belly dancing whore. Doubt crept into her confusion. Where had Liz gotten that from? Had Adam said that to her? She supposed she'd had the occasional guy over for the night now and then. Had Adam noticed, had he been counting? Overnighters were hardly the same thing.

"Do you really think this is wise?"

Adam was silent for those first few crucial seconds. The seconds he would have usually filled trying to appease her. "Arabella, I'll have to talk to you this evening."

"This is really freaking me out."

"I have to work. Goodbye, Arabella."

She sat on the floor and stared at her silent phone in horror. Adam had actually hung up on her. What was wrong with the world? Was everybody actually going insane? Could anything else go wrong? Tossing the phone onto the bed, she tugged at the black bin bag that had been abandoned in her room, purposefully letting it spew her shoes and boots out across the carpet. Her domain had very definitely been swept upstairs.

"Not good, not good," she muttered to herself. Turning on the hifi at the wall, she was horrified to hear it automatically start up and begin playing the Nick Drake CD she'd left in before she flew to Iceland. She might as well just go find a rope and hang herself now. Rustling through the airport shopping bag, scrabbling through the packets of dried fish, Finnish chocolates and other assorted Nordic purchases, she clasped her fingers around the neck and drew out the bottle of Icelandic schnapps. There was a nervous tug in the deep centre of her chest and she needed something to calm her nerves. She checked her watch. Two o'clock. It was going to be a long wait for Adam to come home.

When she heard him step in through the front door, she was feeling considerably calmer, and slightly intoxicated. And very impatient. Leaving the music playing – it was Imelda May, to get her in the mood for the next gig in two days' time – she unlocked the door and headed downstairs.

Arriving in the kitchen she was disconcerted, for a moment wondering if the drink had affected her vision. This was not the kitchen. It was certainly a kitchen, but not the one she'd been using these past four years. Many items that had stood out on the work tops like faithful old friends had vanished, as had the rather ugly picture that used to hang on the wall. She couldn't say she missed it, only that Adam had stubbornly refused to take it down as it reminded him of his mother. A mug tree with matching mugs had appeared, as had the neatly arranged line of colour co-ordinated tea towels. There was a collection of colour charts and DIY catalogues on the kitchen table, signs that someone was planning an all encompassing renovation. Little things, here and there, that were sirens of doom to Arabella's eyes.

There was, however, a delicious smell of something roasting in the oven, which undoubtedly would not be for her. Liz stood at the oven and stirred something in a pan. Adam, smartly dressed, loitered close by, and turned as Arabella appeared.

"Arabella, nice to see you're back."

She couldn't help herself, immediately on the attack, snide and irritable. "Really? I feel like my homecoming has been an interruption. Don't you think, as flatmates, we should discuss things before others start moving in?"

"I'm sorry..." Adam started. He didn't look her in the eye; in fact it was unsettling just how uncomfortable he was with her very presence in the building. It had seemed as though he was about to start an apology or explanation but the words flickered out as Liz squeezed his forearm.

"He is your landlord," Liz reminded her.

"I am your landlord, Arabella."

"That doesn't give you the right to treat me like this. Jesus, you'd think I'd been away for years. You weren't even seeing anyone when I left, and now you've moved her in? Aside from the fact she's clearly a headcase, don't you think this is going a bit quick?"

"My, my, Arabella," Liz sneered. "Anyone would think you're jealous."

"Shut up, no one's talking to you. Adam, could I speak to you in private?"

Arabella backed out into the hallway, and Adam had started to follow her before Liz started to coo. "Dinner will be ready in five minutes."

She could feel the little red monster rising in her gut. It was at times like these she could lose control of her temper, ball up her fists, stamp her feet and roar like a beast. Her brain would shake in her skull and refuse to partake. "Let's step outside for a moment," she said tersely, marching out of the front door.

They headed down the street from the house and towards the river. It was just a little stream that ran down the edge of this district in York. Arabella stuffed her hands in her jeans' pockets as they walked, not sure if she wanted to cry or punch Adam squarely in the nose. It felt as though there were great black voids opening up on either side of her, and if she strayed from the line now, she would be lost forever.

"I've been writing to Liz on online for quite a few weeks, Arabella," Adam explained. "She moved in a week or so ago. She's very good for me. We're going to make a home together. She is helping me renovate so that I can move on from my mother."

That at least was something. Although his mother had been dead many a year, Adam had never really seemed to escape the woman's shadow. "She strikes me as a devious bitch."

"Don't speak about Liz that way, Arabella."

She groaned, exasperated, and stopped walking. "Look, Adam, I am worried about you. Do you not think this is all a bit quick? You've hardly known her two seconds and she's already living with you and planning on renovating the entire house. Your house, I should add, not her house."

"I don't want to be alone. Are you saying I shouldn't be with someone, Arabella?"

"No, I'm not saying that. But you should be with someone because they want to be with you, not because they get your house and you to manipulate. I think you're being used."

"I'm not stupid."

"You are naive."

"No I'm not, Arabella." Adam still refused to look her straight in the eye. "Things change and people move on. This is life."

"I don't want to see a friend get fucked over."

"I can look after myself."

"I beg to differ."

Adam's face had turned distinctly pink. He was angry, but despite everything that had changed in his life the past few weeks since Arabella had been in Iceland, he didn't quite have the courage to go out into a full out shouting match with Arabella Mangella. "I want to forewarn you that we're not all going to be able to live together."

"You're telling me. I'm not living under the same roof as that psycho bitch." The moment the flippant comment had tripped off her lips, she felt a lead ball sink in her stomach. She looked at Adam in horror. "You're asking me to move out?"

"I'll give you time to find somewhere."

"You want me to leave?"

"I have to get back, Arabella. My dinner is ready." Like a well-trained dog, Adam turned around and trotted steadily home. Arabella hung like a shadow on the gravelled path that ran along the riverbank. She felt as though she was going to throw up. Jesus Chris, what the hell was happening? She numbly walked along the path a few meters, and sat down on a low wooden bench. She curled her fingers up into fists by her sides and stared vacantly across the river. She pursed her lips tightly as her vision blurred. Motherfucking bastards. The tear escaped from the rim of her eyelid and twisted a salty path down her cheek. Life was a bitch.

Graham Nicholson, guitarist for hire, was worrying about entirely the wrong things. Either way she didn't care, because there were far greater matters pressing, but it did seem ridiculous how he peered in the mirror as if he wasn't quite sure it really was him.

"Do you think I look fifties enough?"

Who gave a damn, Arabella thought angrily. He ought to be checking that his guitar was in tune, and if he couldn't be arsed with that, he ought to be listening to her and coming up with some advice or at the very least making sympathetic noises. "Have you been listening to a word I just said?"

"Yes. You're living in the *Stepford Wives*."

"Stepford Husbands, I'll have you know. It's like the sequel. I've never seen anyone actually change their opinion on something so basic and important mid sentence. Wrapped around her little finger does not even begin to describe how bad it is."

"Hmmm." Graham lent back from the mirror. This was going to have to do. Both he and Arabella were rather last minute additions to this rockabilly group. Musically they were both proficient. Their performances wouldn't be a problem. He just didn't look the part. Arabella looked as though she'd been living the dream for years, in her very authentic sleeveless red dress, masses of skirts, vivid red lipstick, curled hair, killer eyelashes and a fake iris pinned behind her ear.

"Are you sure this isn't just a touch of the green eyed monster?"

"What?" Arabella peered at him, for a moment thinking he was referring to eye makeup. "You're talking about me? Do you think I'm jealous? Honey, Adam is a friend. If anything was going to happen there, it would have happened a long time ago."

"I didn't mean it like that. I've met Adam, remember," Graham said. Adam probably wouldn't even survive the night with someone like Arabella. "But he's not had a girlfriend since you've known him, and you've pretty much had him at your beck and call ever since you moved in there."

"I am not Liz."

"No, I'll give you that. She does sound like a nasty piece of work. The type that's only going to get with men like Adam. No one else would stand for it."

"Exactly. And Adam's not capable of standing up for himself."

Graham sighed, and walked across the room to pick up his guitar. "It's not your job to save him."

"How can you be so heartless? She's going to ruin his life."

"Or she'll be the making of him." He caught her expression and took a step back out of harm's way. "What I mean is that Adam needs to decide he doesn't need her. And when he's grown a backbone and thrown her out, he will be a better person for it."

"That's never going to happen."

"Arabella, everyone involved is an adult. You've told him what you think. He won't listen. Sometimes you have to let people make their own mistakes."

She felt another tirade brewing ready to spew forth, but was interrupted as the event planner poked his head into the room. "You two ready? The rest of the band is out here. You're on in a minute."

Graham smiled and patted her arm. "You're a good friend, but you've got to let Adam fuck up his own life."

Arabella rolled her eyes. He was useless.

They were performing as part of a band for a big dance and dinner 50s event in York. Tickets had been sold out months ago. Three fifties themed live bands had been booked so that the rolling line up of live music could play the whole night through without any musician passing out from exhaustion. Three weeks ago one of the bands had blown up. It had been an argument over nothing that was the final straw. The lead singer and guitarist, also a couple, had walked out. That left the drummer, bass guitarist and pianist with fancy clothes and convincing hairstyles, but completely unable to fulfil their contract. Graham Nicholson had been easily persuaded to cover the guitar, although getting dressed for the occasion had taken a little more work. They'd found a female singer who looked pretty enough, had a good memory and voice, but tended to stand behind the mic like a limp vegetable. It wasn't quite the fiery persona they'd wanted to lead the group. Jordan Oates had then appeared like an alternative fairy godmother and suggested they give Arabella Mangella a go. Two of them knew her – in the music circuit most people knew everyone else in Yorkshire – but they also knew that when Arabella was performing music, it was always her with a banjo or a guitar in her hand. She never just sang.

Necessity was proving to be the mother of a lot of things. From what they'd been told, her life had gone to shit of late, and she was clearly using this evening as a confidence booster. It had worked well at practice ever since the drummer had suggested she smile a little whilst singing and Arabella had told him what he could do with his drumsticks. Now they were getting on just fine. Arabella was a red siren centre stage, smiling like a showgirl, stage-flirting with her fellow musicians and shaking her skirts and shimmying her shoulders as they rolled straight in the first number: a fast, guitar led modern 50s styled cover.

The hall was buzzing. From the stage they surveyed the joy they directed. In the centre was a dance floor, filled with the beginners and daddy-dancers right through to the near professionals, women being spun three hundred and sixty degrees, hands grasped to spin one another around on the spot, sweat shimmering and gleaming. Many had dressed for the occasion, getting into the retro spirit, men in suits and duck tail quiffs, women in the tight-waisted, big-skirted frocks, bold makeup and curled hair. Around the edges of the room were the dinner tables, where people ate, drank, or simply sat and absorbed the atmosphere. At the back ran a long gleaming bar arranged as a fifties diner. Black and white photographs of film stars and music legends of the era adorned the walls. Considering it was just a one night transformation, a lot of work had been put in.

They played for three quarters of an hour. Arabella's lungs were throbbing by the end. She'd never performed music without an instrument. Up on stage with neither banjo nor guitar, she'd gone back into dance mode. Lost in the lyrics, she sang and danced, and by the time their stint was up, she could just about do a dignified stagger off the stage to the sound of thunderous applause. There'd be a ten minute break then the third group would be on. They'd be returning in an hour's time.

Backstage Arabella flopped into a chair and downed a bottle of water in one. The drummer and the bass guitarist headed outside for a smoke, patting Arabella's shoulder on the way. Graham's girlfriend had somehow managed to sneak in backstage, and was immediately on her man, flinging her arms around him and telling him how great he was.

Arabella pressed her back into the cooling wall as she watched the crazy shows of affection. She looked down at the empty plastic bottle in her hands. Maybe she was jealous. But of what exactly?

"Is there any more water here?"

The pianist, now stretched out on the sofa, shook his head. "No, we'll have to go to the bar. Can you bring some back for me?"

Arabella raised an eyebrow. Who made her the fucking waitress? Her eyes flitted from the pianist to Graham and his giggling girl. She could probably do with a leg stretch, watch a bit of the other band from the floor. "I'll go for supplies."

Weaving her way down the edge of the dance floor, taking the occasional back pat and 'you were great!' as she went, she made a bee line for the bar. Quite a crowd clustered at the middle point. Either end of the bar was quieter, like the old man's corner, spotlighted where Humphrey Bogart might have slouched with a scotch on the rocks, considering the world from a distance. Arabella wandered up to the end, deciding if the bar staff didn't notice her soon, she was just going to hop over the bar and take what she needed. They had been assured that refreshments would be provided free of charge for the performers throughout the night.

"I liked you in Iceland."

The tone of voice made her smile instinctively, before she even knew why. A reassuring welcome back. She turned to the sound. He was leaning against the bar at the far end, smartly dressed, an empty glass on the bar by his hand. James Bond. Ben Simon. She hadn't realised how much she'd missed him.

"I only saw you on YouTube. I don't suppose it captured the atmosphere of the live performance."

"No, but not everyone can make it to Iceland."

"Very true. So how is Iceland?"

"Pretty cool."

"Get chased by any Vikings?"

She smiled wryly. If only you knew. "I'm a fast runner."

"You're a folk star now. If you type banjo and Arabella into Google, it's you who turns up."

"Sounds like my agent has been doing something right."

A round of applause went through the hall like a Mexican wave as the next group took to the stage.

He smiled at her. "I feel as though I should ask you to dance."

"It sounds like there's a but coming."

"Oh no." He stepped away from the bar as if to take her hand and sweep her onto the dance floor. The message from brain to feet was intercepted and he staggered, looking as though he was going to tumble. Arabella darted forward to catch him, feeling his arms flop around her shoulders as she pushed him back onto his feet. He laughed by her ear, his breath reeking of alcohol. He was really tanked up.

"Jesus, Ben," she muttered, taking advantage of the momentum to get him out of the hall and into the reception area. "Having a good night?" He needed some cold sharp air to sober him up.

"I will have to admit I've probably had a bit too much to drink."

"No kidding." He was like a lead weight. She glanced around the reception, empty of people, searching for a chair she could drop him onto whilst she looked for something to sober him up with. She couldn't keep up this supportive waltz too long.

"I can't keep you away from the party," Ben muttered, hazily aware that the music was growing softer as the doors closed. "We need to get back." In a spurt of determination, he put his balance back onto his own feet, and slinging a leading arm around her shoulders, headed straight for the first door his eyes could focus on.

"Ben, that's not..."

They tumbled in through the doors into the cloakroom. Silent outdoor wear waited in neat lines. The door banged shut behind them, the music turning into an indistinct throb.

"We're lost!" Ben actually sounded worried, turning to hug her as if it were time to abandon all hope. "Arabella, I'm so sorry."

She hugged the poor wretched drunk back. This was just about the perfect ending to everything else that had been going wrong the last couple of months. The man was a mess. She'd been quietly, secretly hoping she would see him again. She'd never dreamt it would be like this. It was bloody typical. She rested her head against his and caught a waft of his aftershave.

Ben buried his face in her hair. "Oh Arabella, Arabella," he moaned. "Why won't you leave me alone? There's so many beautiful women in the world, but you..." His thought was cut off midpoint as he lost his balance again. Wavering on the edge of dignity for a second that felt like minute, he toppled backwards, ungraciously dropping into a pile of coats, dragging Arabella down with him.

She felt winded as she landed on top of him. Drunks were no fun when one was sober.

He ran his fingers through her hair. "Why can I not stop thinking about you? I drove up to York when I saw you were performing

142

tonight. I thought... I don't know what I thought. I might get to speak to you."

She propped herself up so she could look him in the eye. "This was sold out weeks ago."

"I snuck in."

"You've not even paid?"

"I'm a rogue." He smiled again, met her eye line and held it there before stretching forward to kiss her full on the mouth.

There were a million and one good reasons why she ought to get up and leave, but they all melted off the radar. Things went rather quickly, thoughtlessly but efficient. Arabella's knickers were in orbit somewhere down the far end of the cloakroom; Ben's belt was unbuckled, trousers and pants down and she was on top of him and they were grinding away in a mound of strangers' coats like a pair of randy back alley cats. For an inebriated man, he actually managed to perform, although it was functional and over far too quickly, leaving plenty of time for regrets.

Ben flopped back into his makeshift bedding, utterly spent from the final exertion. Arabella sat still; clutching the bottom of his shirt and feeling him go limp inside of her. What had she just done? Not like this, not with him. Aside from the fact that she had really, truly, hope-to-die sworn off one night stands for good this time, she'd just destroyed the one bit of far-fetched hope she'd had left. Idle day dreams on an evening, music in the background, reassuring herself that good things might come up in the future. Ben Simon had been on her mind and he had supposed to have been a dramatic romance worthy of the silver screen. Certainly not a quick drunken shag in a cloakroom. On the floor. Her eyes filled up with tears. She was a complete and utter fuck up.

"I think I'm going to throw up." He lurched up out of his slumber. Arabella slid off him and away, her skirts missing the vomit by millimetres. She staggered to her feet, backing up and hitting the wall. Ben rolled away from the warm splatter, shuffling to pull his trousers up. He looked up at her and felt nauseous in a completely different way. She was crying, not even trying to hold it in this time, her eyeliner beginning to dissolve. She could feel a sticky drip of semen that had rolled out onto the inside of her thigh. Sordid. Dirty. Meaningless. This really wasn't how she'd wanted things to be.

"Arabella, I'm so sorry..." he started.

"I have to go," she interrupted hoarsely, embarrassed by how tearful her voice was. She could barely speak. She never let anyone see her cry. It was a personal rule. Never let the bastards know what they've done. "I'm back on soon."

She fled from the room, out the back doors and around the building in darkness to sneak into the backstage area. She'd have to wash herself down, reapply makeup and then get up there with a fake smile slapped on her face and sing her heart out. And the moment her last number was finished, she was gone.

The following morning, sober Sunday, holy day of regrets, she still did not want to be alive. What was worse was that she was unable to sleep. She woke up at ten and her brain would not switch off. Why haven't you got a new job, it asked. Shut up. Ok, let's talk about where you live. Just bugger off. Of course, there's always the massive question mark over why you cannot deal with men like a normal adult. Arabella was silently screaming at herself, buried deep underneath her duvet, and writhing in fury at her unquantifiable enemy.

She eventually, begrudgingly accepted that she wasn't going to get back to sleep. A hand crept out from under the covers, locating her CD remote on the clutter of her bedside table to turn on the music. The Puppini Sisters serenaded her as her fingers tripped over the letter on their way back to bed. She remembered all over again.

If last night hadn't been bad enough, she'd returned to find an envelope with her name on propped up by her room door. It was hand delivered; as it turned out it had only been written downstairs. Probably dictated by Liz, possibly also typed by the witch, but most definitely signed by Adam. He was giving her notice. He wanted her to move out. It wasn't just the fact that she was shortly to lose her home, but that her friend, he whom she'd thought was her friend, was giving her a final slap in the face on her way out.

Digging out her copy of Wuthering Heights, feeling it was time to read about other people having a bad time and being generally evil to one another, Arabella settled in bed, intending to distract herself

144

from all of her troubles. There was a box of chocolates and a bottle of champagne she'd been given for her thirtieth, neither of which she'd touched since the big day. She consumed both, piggishly and alone, read her book, cried on and off and then reassured herself there really wasn't anything to worry about.

Now that Adam had given her notice, pride dictated she wanted to move out tomorrow. She was beholden to no one. She switched on her laptop to start looking for somewhere new to live. She thought she was doing well, finding so many four bedroom houses in York for rent that were within her budget, until she realised that they were all house shares. The rental was just for the room. Just a damned room: no private sitting room, no personal bathroom. No landlord who didn't raise the rent once in the whole damned four years she'd been living there. It was regressing to complete student mode. It didn't matter really, because no one would take her on without a job. Maybe she could just go and buy a damned house, but her redundancy payment wouldn't make much of a deposit, and even if she could have afforded to buy somewhere, the process would take months and she needed to move in next week.

She was thirty and thinking she was going to have to move back in with her mother.

Book fanatics would have gasped in horror as she put the book down on the pillow, face down and open. The spine felt a crease coming on. Groaning, she swung her feet onto the carpet and put her head in her hands. Melancholy, chocolate and champagne did not go well together. She was feeling dreadful. Her throat went rigid, and in a sudden spurt of energy she was up and running for the bathroom, arriving just in time to throw up in the toilet bowl.

"Oh Jesus," Arabella moaned into the lavatory. The second splatter of vomit she'd had to look at in the past twenty four hours. At least she wasn't tormenting anyone else with this. At least she wasn't doing this immediately after sex with someone. Her lips drooped and she pulled away from the toilet, knocking her head on the towel rail and bursting into tears. The whack reverberated through her skull. What was it they called this day? *Gloomy Sunday*. The most popular song to commit suicide to. Somebody please just take her away from all of this.

I used to be a credit controller, Arabella thought as she glowered at the computer screen. Now I'm doing a computer simulation test to prove that I know how to save a fucking Word document.

Finishing the simulation, all random requests for Word and Excel ticked off to the computer's satisfaction, she picked up the print out for the typing test. The next screen came up. The timer would start the next time she hit the keyboard. Five minutes of typing from a printed sheet to gauge words per minute and accuracy. The final test to complete all the facts and figures on basic computer skills for the database. Another step towards a monthly target of names added to lists. Probably not a damned job to offer anyone, but then Arabella had never rated recruitment agencies particularly highly. Needs must and she was doing the rounds today and hoping things were better than the last time she'd been forced to visit these bullshit merchants.

The staff at the central York recruitment agency hadn't changed. They weren't the same individuals she'd seen last time, but they all looked like they'd come from the same mould. A few years of steady employment and Arabella had hit thirty. This time it felt as though she was coming cap in hand to children to ask for a job. Some of the people working here didn't look as though they were old enough to have left school. When had she gotten so bloody old?

"Arabella Mangella?" A perky, short, skinny Northern Irish girl in a power suit appeared at the waiting area where the unemployable, the desperate and the temporarily between jobs loitered. Computer tests were complete. The nervous loiterers just needed to speak to an adviser.

"That's me." Arabella picked up her handbag from the floor and walked over to the girl. Summer had hit the UK with a sudden intensity. The only nod this building seemed to give to air conditioning was an open window. It wasn't a good day to be dressed in a suit, hoping the sweat stains wouldn't be noticeable.

She followed the girl through the open plan office to her desk at the back. Colleagues were dealing with other members of the public, or on the phone, hi tech headsets negating the need for a normal telephone. Everything looked intense and uber professional. They probably had shit wages and awful quotas to meet every month. Not a job Arabella would want. But at least they had a job, she grumbled to herself as she sat down in the uncomfortable chair at the girl's desk.

"I'm Meav," the girl told her. "Let's take a look at your test results." She was silent for a moment, gazing at her screen with an unreadable expression as she clicked through the information. For an awful moment Arabella wondered if she had misread all of the instructions and completely ballsed up the test. Well, Arabella, we were really aiming for words per minute – please note the plural.

"Really good. Those speeds look like a touch typist." She looked away from the screen. "Do you have any secretarial qualifications?"

"No."

"No bother, most people don't these days. We're the computer generation, right? So what have you been doing most recently?"

"I was in my last job for seven years. I worked in credit control."

"Great stuff. So you'll be used to dealing with difficult conversations. Good skill. Let's see, your highest level of education is a BA..."

"Spanish."

"You speak Spanish?"

"Yes."

"Great stuff. We may have some exciting opportunities coming up for Spanish speakers."

If this had been the first time Arabella had ever set foot in a recruitment agency, she might have gotten her hopes up. But she remembered from previous bouts of job hunting that there was a certain language all of these advisors had been trained in, regardless of which agency they actually worked for. They all had very exciting opportunities just on the horizon. Any skill you could bring to the table was exciting. To them everything was exciting. She wondered if it jaded their private life, made everything else feel like a big anti climax. Or perhaps it took the opposite effect and they settled permanently up on cloud nine.

"So what exactly are you looking for?"

"A job. Office work, administration. It doesn't necessarily have to be credit control."

"And temping or permanent?"

"Either. In the long run I want to get a permanent position, but I'll take temping work if it means I can get working now."

"Good motivation."

She half expected the girl to pass her a little name badge with her personality trait on. This place was begging to be labelled up in gimmicky headlines. You had to play the game, smile and enthuse and hope the cynicism was squashed far enough down, because you needed a damned job, and these people had you at their mercy.

"That's been great, Arabella," Meav told her, smiling in the polite but unfeeling way that a bank employee would just before declining the application for a loan. Thanks for dropping by, but we can't lend you any money. "I have your contact details here and I'll be in touch when we've got something for you."

She should have had a nameplate on her desk that read 'complete waste of time'. Arabella smiled out of conformity, shaking the woman's hand and spouting the usual pleasantries. She walked out of the office, feeling slightly unclean. Stepping out onto the street and the fresh summer air was like sweet release back to normality. The only good thing about that appointment was that she felt like she was doing something to get a regular job.

She idled her way through the centre of town and up to the Minster, a massive gothic cathedral and the centre point of York. There were clusters of tourists dotted around the site. A gaggle of school children were having a group photograph taken outside the main doors. Arabella sat down on a bench and switched her phone back on. Perhaps there'd be an exciting opportunity.

The phone buzzed as it picked up a waiting text message. She opened it. Sadly there were no job offers, just a message from Jordan Oates, her agent, to let her know that he had a delivery for her that she needed to pick up. Probably CDs, she guessed. It was still a little strange being in touch with him after those years of near silence. Odder still to back in England. Iceland had been a surreal interlude, a dream, an event that perhaps had never happened. She didn't think she could be bothered to see him today. She'd go round tomorrow. For now, all she wanted to do was go home.

What she wanted and what she got were two very different things. It was disturbing how quickly things could change. Home wasn't what it once had been, in fact home felt like an overly generous title. Adam hadn't spoken to her since that eviction letter had been left for her to pick up in the wee small hours of Sunday morning. Pointedly Arabella had been avoiding him. She kept herself very much upstairs, but she was increasingly feeling as though the only person suffering was her. Three days of nothing.

When she stepped into her sitting room, she paused, and looked around the quietness. Something wasn't quite right. It was nothing obvious, nothing she could point to. Merely a feeling. Someone had been here earlier, looking, riffling through, searching. She had nowhere to go yet, but she felt a building urgency that she needed to get out of here. She would start with her possessions. She ought to be able to store some of her more precious items at her mother's until she'd got the rest of the details sorted out.

Arabella spent a good part of the afternoon packing her music collection into available suitcases and boxes. Her belly dancing outfits and wigs were neatly folded away. She didn't have any more dance gigs booked in, and after what had last been said at the club, she didn't feel inclined. Suddenly she did not want to dance. I'm getting old, she thought to herself, and yet I'm still stuck in first gear in life.

She carried the boxes and cases down to her car. There was still space on the passenger seat, begging to rescue something. Stealing a few bin bags from the kitchen, she cleared her bookshelves. She'd go over to her mother's later, evacuation mission one.

The rest of the afternoon was spent on the internet. She wrote a couple of job applications for non-exciting (they weren't being advertised by recruitment agencies) adverts. Now that she was relatively calm and utterly sober, she decided to have another attempt at flat hunting. The prices were just as scary as they had been before. If she was going to live in York, she'd have to house share once she'd got the job issue sorted out. York had a bad reputation for high rents. Between the students, the locals and the people with jobs in the south with ample wages who were prepared to commute, demand was high and supply low. She could always move elsewhere, somewhere cheaper, but that would add a commute to her day. Either that or she could look elsewhere for a job. There wasn't necessarily any point in staying put. She pushed the laptop screen onto the keyboard. The computer went into hibernation mode and Arabella flopped back on the bed. So many possibilities but no idea.

She must have drifted off, for the next thing Arabella was aware of was a drop in temperature. It was still light outside, still warm, but that intensity of the heat of the day was waning. She was no longer alone in the house. There were voices downstairs, the mumbled, faded noise of distance. She couldn't make out the words, but from the tones, she could tell that both Adam and Liz were back.

Getting up from the bed, she wandered over to the window seat, taking in the fresh air. God only knew what view she'd be looking at in a month's time. She could be anywhere. The potential was endless, and it ought to have been exciting. A new adventure. She felt melancholic instead, sadly longing for a past that had moved on without her. Things lost. She picked up her banjo, nestled into the corner of the window seat and gently picked out a couple of tunes. Slow, sad melodies. That didn't work. She was familiar with the acoustics of this house well enough to know that they'd be able to hear that she was playing.

This was just making her depressed. In a change of tact, she switched to the lively song that she and Marika played in the YouTube video. She didn't bother singing, but the melody bounced along with enough complex parts to hold its own with neither vocals nor violin to back it up. She did feel a little buoyed by the mere act of playing, the sensation of vibrating strings going off by her finger tips, the sound reverberating off the body of the banjo. The movement and the increased blood flow through her hands lifted her mood. Things couldn't possibly be as bad as they seemed.

She had one ear at the window, waiting for the call of the guitar, but she heard nothing more than distant bird song. The shriek of swifts. Perhaps he wasn't that familiar with this track. It was a fast one, and if you were new to it, you might not dare to jump in. Ok, she thought, let's get back to good old faithful.

She started off with a couple of notes from the start of *Duelling Banjos*, an offering to initiate conversation. There was no longer any sound of talking downstairs. Neither was there any music. Of course, he would have to go and fetch his guitar and get settled in a chair before he started playing. Rather pathetically, she continued through the duet intro to the track, playing only her side of things and waiting for a response.

There was the sound of a chair being scraped on the floor.

Arabella smiled.

She was nearing the point where chords came in and things really sped up. He'd start playing now. Just the next bar and he'd join her. She continued, the guitar reply in her mind, her foot taps keeping the beat. There was silence from the ground floor. Her hand faltered and she missed a note. They'd always, without fail, made up over this song. She held her breath for two seconds. Nothing. Something broke inside her. She pushed herself into the main body of the song, fingers flying over the banjo strings. It was only a couple of minutes worth of music but it felt like hours. She had her pride to keep, and she would play the whole damn song through on her own. She'd started so she'd finish.

The house was painfully silent when she came to the end. Neighbours were sure there was something a bit different with the rendition that time, although they couldn't quite say why. Arabella stood up and put her banjo on the bed. Picking up her car keys, she left the house and drove over to her mother's.

"Arabella, darling, what a lovely surprise." Her mother appeared from behind the rosebushes that lined the drive. Briefly she looked bewildered, before striking a pose as if she were about to offer her a cocktail from the bar.

Arabella shut the driver's door, having just parked behind her mother's car. "I've been better. Listen, could I store some things with you?"

"Well, of course." The request was a little unexpected. She glanced from her daughter to the car and noted how it was stuffed with boxes and bags. "Goodness, are you moving out?"

"Starting to."

Her expression fell. "I was joking. Don't tell me you and that sweet man have had a falling out."

"Not exactly." Arabella rubbed her eyes as she walked around the car. She could feel a thumping headache coming on. "Although me and that sweet man aren't really able to communicate anymore. He's got himself a girlfriend."

"Oh," she responded as if this was rather perplexing news. "Is she the jealous type?"

"She is the psychopathic type. I've been given notice. I just don't... just don't feel comfortable there anymore. I'd feel better when I'm away from the place if I knew most of my belongings weren't there. I don't trust her."

"You must think of yourself." Her mother wandered back around the rose bushes to pick up the trug of cut flowers. "Renting is only ever temporary, rather like affairs, and when it ends, it ends abruptly. There's no point hanging on; one must move on. Don't look back." She set her basket of flowers and secateurs at the front door step. "I've just got the car out of the garage for the season, so you can use the garage to store whatever you want."

Only her mother would refer to the summer as 'the season' as if it were the beginning of a great fashion parade. Arabella took a couple of bin bags of books from her car and followed her mother to the garage. It was big enough to hold her belongings and the few items of furniture she actually owned. Then she could try and work out what she was going to do next.

"Let's get those cases out of your poor little car, it must be dreadfully overweight."

Between the two of them, they soon had the car emptied. Arabella's worldly goods were stacked neatly to one side of the garage. This was the beginning of the move. And the beginning again, just as when she'd finished university and had temporarily come back home. Another period of limbo until she decided what she would do. Even after the break down of her engagement, she hadn't needed to come home. Years later and it didn't feel like she'd progressed at all since the start of adulthood.

Pulling the garage door down, her mother locked it and passed her the key. "There's a spare in the kitchen, but you hang on to this. Then you can drop off things whenever you like. Are you coming in for refreshments?"

"Sure."

Her mother lived in a little village about a twenty minute drive north of York. Something of an eccentric hermit, she was probably still a local feature, despite the number of years she'd been living here. This house had never really been home for Arabella. She'd stopped here a few months after university, but no more than that. After the divorce, her mother had bought this bungalow and had gradually renovated it to her own bizarre tastes. Over the years it had transformed into a glamorous 1920s palace, trapped within the skin of a 1950s bungalow on a small village estate. It was thousands of miles from the traditional family home they'd started off together in.

"Would you like tea, or something cool? I shan't offer a cocktail because you're driving..."

Ever sensible. "I don't know."

"I'll make tea." She turned the kettle on and started to get the silver gilt tea set down from the cupboard. Entertaining guests and family, even if just with a cup of tea, was an event worthy making the effort for. "You've not yet told me about Iceland."

"Didn't you get the postcards?"

"Of course, darling, but it's not the same as hearing it from you."

"It was fantastic. Very busy. I even got to meet Johnnie O again."

"That delightful little blues singer? How lovely."

"Did you see the video on YouTube?"

Her mother gave her a pointed look. "You know how I feel about the internet. It is the beginning of the end of society."

"It's not quite as apocalyptical as you seem to think. Besides, it gives you access to all kinds of things you never would see otherwise."

"I'd rather see you play live. Have you done anything back on home turf since Iceland?"

"I was singing in a 50s themed evening last weekend. It was really great..." Arabella felt her voice break as she unconvincingly uttered the word *great*. Panic rose up and she was uncertain over whether it was due to the upset, or the very fact that she was showing this pain to someone else. Her brain felt tight over the tops of her eyes. She pressed her fingers to the centre of her forehead.

Her mother gently set the sugar bowl down on the tray. "Did something happen?"

"Nothing happened." The words struggled to get out past the wobble in the back of her throat.

"That doesn't sound very convincing."

"It's fine," Arabella sobbed, leaning back against the wall for support. She felt as though she was going to be sick. Tears were flowing freely down her face. She didn't cry in front of people. Arabella was always practical, always dealt with her problems like a grown up. "It's all a complete mess. I have nowhere to live. No job. And I... I've completely fucked up my life."

"Oh, now, darling." Her mother hovered in the kitchen for a moment. She had never been a traditional mother, and hadn't always been the greatest at comforting. The compassion was certainly there inside; it just sometimes struggled to come out in a form other people could make use of. She moved around the breakfast bar and went to hug her daughter. What on earth had been going on? She'd seen her the day she'd lost her job, so that was hardly news, and Arabella had been angry more than anything else when it had happened. Anger was Arabella's usual way of dealing with things. "I know it seems very dark now. I've been there. But these things work themselves out."

"I don't see any end to this."

She patted Arabella's back and felt ineffectual. Problems of the adult variety were rarely easily fixed. "What you need is indulgence," she decided. "You're to have a bubble bath and clear your head. I guarantee you'll feel so much better afterwards."

It didn't feel possible, but even just walking through the bathroom door brought her tears to a halt. It was irrelevant as to whether the promise of indulgence would cure what ailed her. The bizarre sight that met her was such a distraction. The bathroom had been a project her mother had saved during several years and it had only recently been completed. It was a bathroom fit for Cleopatra. The third bedroom, a box room, had been knocked into the original bathroom. The new space had been tiled floor to ceiling, the windows refitted with stained glass of pastel shades of frosted glass. Standard and essential bathroom features were carefully blended in; a toilet, towel rails and sink on a long plinth that also held a bowl of water with an orchid floating. From that the ambience flowed into the sublime. At the back end there was an open shower unit that looked as though it would pour like a small waterfall. And the bath, oh, mama, what a bath, Arabella thought. The floor had been raised in tiled steps so that the bath could sink back into the fresh ground. The tub was big enough for two, and with golden taps and hand shower, it looked like the centre of all decadence. Fluffy towels that could have been clouds from a summer's sky waited on the towel rack.

"You have a nice long soak," she patted her stunned daughter's arm. "And I'll get a little supper ready."

Steam twisted through the still air, beaten by the heat from the bath water. Bubbles, oiled surface, rolled over one another, creating a great mass of contained air. Arabella laid back in the warm water, closed her eyes and tried to calm down. She was ever aware of the gaping precipices that would open up around her. She was just that close from tripping and being lost forever. If only someone could assure her that it would all work out. She didn't even need to have the details: how she would make a living, where she would live. Just to know that the worry wasn't required. She would find solutions, solve the problems. There were just so many things to fix; it was difficult to know where to start.

Suitably wrinkled to a prune, she rinsed off in the shower. Borrowing her mother's dressing gown, Arabella wrapped herself up in the fluffy towelling and approached the mirror. Wiping a hand across the condensation, she peered at her own hazy reflection. Her hair was limp and heavy, the volume of styling lost. Her face was clean of makeup. She looked a little startled, eyes almost terrified. Pull yourself together.

"It's decided," her mother announced as Arabella padded barefoot into the living room. "Oh, this is for you," she added, pushing a large mug of hot chocolate in her direction.

Arabella flopped into the other settee with a sigh. "Would I be able to stay here a while until I get myself fixed."

"Of course, you don't even need to ask. But what I have decided, is that you must leave."

"Leave?"

"When something is over, it's over, and it simply isn't stylish to hang around. One must make the cut immediately and move on. You're not to stay in that flat another night. It simply won't do. Get your belongings packed up and move up here."

Arabella closed her eyes. Thank God. "Thank you."

"What are your plans for tomorrow?"

"I have to see my agent. He has some CDs for me to pick up. Otherwise just packing, I guess."

"Take a trip into York with me before that. I may have had an idea."

"Of course, I've never been inside, so this might be a simply dreadful idea."

Arabella and her mother had driven into York. They were in a housing estate in the next suburb on the clock face after New Earswick – where she had, up until very recently, lived. In comparison this district was much larger and had less of the old-fashioned village community feel. That wasn't to say it was a soulless hell hole either. It didn't go so far as to have the inbuilt, overwhelming cityscape to it. Instead it was a fifties estate of red bricked semi detached houses and bungalows. Residential rows that seemed to go on until eternity.

They had parked up outside a rather unkempt bungalow. Overgrown fir trees overshadowed the front garden and a shabby, ratty wooden conservatory ran along the front. There was a metallic handrail with concrete slope up to the front door giving the house a distinct and sad community centre feel.

Arabella, in a black and white polka dot dress, got out of the car and stared at the bungalow. "Why are we here, again?"

"I've not been here before," her mother confessed. "It's Great Aunt Agetha's house."

"This is a woman I've never met." Arabella paused, pondering on where she had heard the name before. "Didn't you say she'd died?"

"Yes, she's passed on." Her mother walked up to the house, taking a bunch of keys from her clutch bag. "She was a vile old woman when she was alive. I do wonder with horrified anticipation what she has in store for me here. She stopped speaking to me when I married, as did a great deal of the family. They didn't approve." She tried the first key in the lock. It didn't work. On to the second. "Rather bizarre, because when I eventually got divorced, they approved even less."

"Why didn't they like Dad?"

"Not for any reason normal people dislike him." She rattled the door in the frame. There was a click and the door swung open, releasing a waft of heated, stagnant air. The summer was coming in full force, and this greenhouse-like conservatory on the side would be a sweatbox. "They felt he was beneath them. The tradesman coming around to the front door and forgetting his place."

"Do you ever hear from Dad?"

"Not for years and years, thank goodness." She braved the heat and walked across to the actual front door in the house proper.

Arabella followed her inside, glancing around the surroundings. Rickety didn't quite capture the state of this odd side building. It was a flimsy wooden greenhouse attached to the side of the brick house. It looked as though there were gaps in the woodwork, which had been filled in with balled up sheets of newspaper. Jesus. A dead palm plant wilted at one end, in a face off with a dirty, stained cane chair.

Her mother paused, hand on key in lock and looked at her daughter. "Do you see him?"

"Not for several years. The last few times he was being a dick." She shrugged. "Just because you're related doesn't mean you have to like each other."

"No, but one only gets the one father." Her mother looked back to the front door. "Are we ready for this?"

Arabella shrugged again, not sure why they were here. "Sure."

The first thing that hit them, other than the feel of trapped heat, was the overwhelming stink of stale urine. Both women immediately wrinkled their noses and turned away from the door, gasping for air. Arabella's mother's face turned a delightful pink, as if she was embarrassed by the fact that someone might have pissed on the floor.

"I suppose this will teach me for having avoided coming here," she sighed. "Shall we go in?"

As intrepid explorers, they entered the reeking house. Once it had been a home to an elderly lady, now it was a piss-riddled shell. They passed an empty bedroom and followed the short hallway to an open door leading to the main room of the house. Sunlight beat in through the living room window, reflecting off the grimy glass of a large photo frame on the fireplace, bearing the photograph of a yappy looking little dog. The carpet carried a number of large brown stains, like nasty sweat marks; tide marks from a multitude of little accidents. Aside from the photograph, the room was empty.

Her mother pulled out a lavender scented handkerchief from her clutch and held it to her nose. "I had the clearance people in here as soon as probate was cleared," she said. "I never got along with Agetha and I certainly didn't want any keepsakes."

Arabella walked across the room, half expecting to sink into the spongy carpet as if it were a urine-soaked mossy bog. She stood in front of the photograph. I wonder if you're to blame for the stink, she thought, looking down at the little dog. She looked back at her mother. "Probate?"

"Yes, it's part of the legal process when someone dies." She left to look through the rest of the house. A second bedroom, empty. A

158

bathroom, very dated, brown tiles, and a stand in bath with a dead spider crumpled in the bottom. The kitchen looked as though it had fittings from the fifties, including the oven. From the kitchen window she could see a small triangle of back garden. There was a lawn with a washing line, and hip high back fences.

"Jesus, this entire place reeks like a rancid toilet." Arabella joined her in the kitchen.

"I know." Her mother opened the back door, savouring the feel of fresh air. "You'll have to rip out all of the carpets, perhaps even some of the floorboards."

"I'll have to rip out the carpets?"

"Well, yes, of course. You wouldn't want to live in this smell would you? I still don't quite understand why, but Agetha left me this house in her will. There was some mention of guilt about the way the family had treated me. Why they couldn't have said something whilst they were still alive, I'll never understand. But there you go. I am the owner of this festering toilet bowl. I thought you might like to live here."

Arabella watched her mother in horror as she stepped into the back garden. What exactly was she trying to say, suggesting she'd want to live in this piss hole of a house. She turned and looked back into the building. Of course, if she ripped out everything, got rid of the stink, and renovated every inch of it, the house could be habitable. It would be somewhere to live and with no flatmates. It was a lot of work. The house was repulsive just now, but she could turn it into something of her own. Her heart fluttered a little. This could be the start. She hurried outside after her mother. "You'd rent this to me? You'd let me do it up how I want?"

"Of course not. Well, of course you can do it up to your tastes. But I won't rent it. Honestly life is too short for all of that when you don't need to. You may as well just have the house. It would solve two problems. I don't want this, and you don't have anywhere to live. You can stay with me until you've got it habitable, but you don't want to be living with your mother long term. You have to get on with your life."

"But this is your inheritance."

She waved it aside. "I don't need the money, and I certainly didn't ask of anything from Agetha. Let's just make the best of this situation, and get you set up with property. Goodness knows you're never going to be able to afford to buy the way things are these days."

"You're giving me this house?" She still couldn't quite believe this was happening.

"Don't get too excited, there's a dreadful amount of work to be done here."

"But this would be my house?"

"Your home."

Arabella held her hands to her mouth, feeling tears well up in her eyes. She was so bloody emotional these days. But her own home. Her *own* home. She'd never even considered getting on this well.

"Morning ladies. Are one of you beauties moving in?"

Her mother turned. There was a disdainful expression on her face as she searched for the source of the slightly unpleasant, nasal noise. An old man with eager eyes, eyebrows on strings, and a dirty little moustache, was leering over the now suddenly far too low adjoining fence.

"Hello neighbours," he continued. "You're a right glamour puss. Lot better than old Agetha. Face like an old wash rag she had."

"I won't be living here." She wondered if this neighbour was Agetha's spiteful legacy. Here's a free house for you. And here's the pervert neighbour to go with it.

"Oh, I say." His eyeballs flitted to Arabella. "Now you are a right looker. You going to be living here, are you? You can wave to me from the kitchen as you're making a morning cuppa."

Not that Arabella was the best at formalities, jovially rubbing along with her neighbours, as the residents of New Earswick would testify, but even the basic courtesy of introductions felt inappropriate here. Never had she seen someone who personified vile quite so well. She merely nodded to him, it was as polite as she could stomach just now. "I need to get over to Oates'."

Her mother nodded, eager to get away. "Yes, we'd better dash."

Jordan Oates, agent to the generally unknown musical stars, worked from home. As this had been the situation for so long, he had renovated and shuffled around aspects of his abode to suit his life. Once you stepped through that door, you felt as though you were in the upstairs office of an agent to the superstars. Perhaps not the superstars, but actual artists at least, Arabella thought, glancing out of the window into his back garden and watching her mother rather dramatically take up residence on the garden bench in the sunshine.

The dining room had never been used for what it had been intended. He had even added an external door so that access was available without the need to go through the house. It was like a back alley as you had to scuttle down the side of the house, between brickwork and vertical six foot fencing. One half expected a neon sign to be dangling precariously over the doorway, blaring out the name 'Jordan's Notes'.

"Arabella," he greeted her as she came in. "Good, you're here to pick them up. How are you doing? Reacclimatised from Iceland?"

"Pretty much." She glanced over his desk, wondering if he'd recently been to an awards ceremony. There was a bucket in front of the desk holding a massive bouquet of flowers. He had a picture frame and a vinyl record on his desk. It looked as though he was trying to set up a display, but the record wasn't staying in position.

"It does get into the blood," he sighed, temporarily giving up with the record and laying it flat on his desk.

"Is Hafdis all right?"

"Yes, she's well. Hoping to come over in a month's time for a visit."

"So you had some CDs for me?"

"CDs? No, they're not ready yet."

"But the text..."

He pointed over his desk. "Those are what you need to pick up. They were delivered here."

Arabella took a step back to assess the bouquet of flowers. She wasn't the kind of woman who was in the habit of receiving flowers on a regular basis, but even she could see this was no mere bundle of carnations. She looked back at Jordan. "I've not got a nutty fan?"

"Probably a bit early for that. I think they're apology flowers."

Apology flowers? Who would send such a thing to her via Oates? Arvid. Her Norwegian holiday fling. She felt her heart sink. The reaction was a surprise because she had been rather into the man at the time. This was a damn sight better than the pathetic kitten card, and the man had been good in bed, but... She crouched down and extracted the card from the flowers. "What is Arvid doing bringing you flowers?"

"It was a local florist. Interflora."

"Hmmm." She flicked open the envelope and pulled out the card. No name. Still half-arsed. At least there wasn't another kitten this time. The card read: 'Arabella, I'm so sorry. I didn't mean for things to start this way.' What was that supposed to mean, she wondered sourly. His ship was pulling into Hull and he was getting some shore leave in Yorkshire? Needed a place to stay?

"How was the 50s gig?"

She nodded vaguely. "Good."

"I've heard good things from it. Graham said the band'll keep hold of your name. They may book you again. Of course, we're really looking to develop the solo side of things."

"Yes, but it'll be good for extra cash."

"You've not gotten another job yet?"

"Not a day job, no."

"Are you still doing the dancing?"

"No." She was surprised by how disinterested she felt about the subject. That talk with the club owner, Seth, just before she had gone to Iceland, had really thrown ice water on her belly dancing fire. "They took me off the regular rotation as I was going to Iceland and I've not called to say I want to be put back on the circuit. I don't know whether I want to continue."

"It does seem like belly dancing is falling out of favour. Not that dance is my speciality, but it all seems to be about the burlesque these days. There's a new performer, Cherry Malone..."

Arabella's face darkened. "Yes, I know," she muttered. "Only nineteen and a fucking genius."

"Jealous?"

She glared at him.

"No point spreading yourself too thin. Music is where you really belong; any idiot could see that at the festival. The website's getting good traffic. Good within Scandinavia, and the US, actually. A lot of yanks fly over to Iceland. The downloads are still ticking over, although traffic has dropped since the festival ended. We need to get your name about over here. I've booked you as the supporting act for a couple of acoustic gigs in September. They're at little arts centres in Yorkshire, but these can be good sellers. People are usually up for buying a CD in the interval, so we'll get enough copies ordered for that. I've got you in Helmsley, Pocklington, Saltaire, Richmond and Whitby. I'll email you the details."

"These are actual concerts?"

"Oh yes. You'll be supporting an Irish folk group. Bodhran, I think they're called. The agent's an old friend."

She'd never really done concerts in the touring sense, other than in Iceland. Most of her music had tended to be one off events and dances, playing in bars and clubs, backing musician, and a little bit of session work in the studios. "That makes me sound like a proper recording artist."

Oates rolled his eyes. "You are a proper recording artist. If this goes well, we'll look at booking you on your own tour. We'll keep it to Yorkshire to start off, keep the travel costs down and the need for accommodation out of the equation. It'll be the little venues, but we'll look at the folk festivals; Pocklington, Beverley..."

"That's great." She stared at him, a little in awe that things were actually happening. "You've gotten a lot better at this."

Oates raised his eyebrows.

"Nothing much seemed to happen last time."

"You got a lot of material recorded last time," he reminded her. "Besides, you didn't want things to happen."

"Yes, well." She stood up, severing the conversation. She didn't want to get into a discussion as to why things hadn't worked out last time. She supposed her early twenties had been a bit of a fuck up. She hadn't taken advantage of chances musically, gotten engaged to an idiot, and distracted herself with the dancing. Now she was unemployed and starting over, basically back at the point she'd been at fresh out of university. As if her twenties had been a waste of time. If she could just go back and relive those years, get things right...

"No one is the finished article in their twenties," Oates said. "Certainly no one with any depth of character."

She didn't have a smart retort, so let the statement hang in the room. Maybe he was right. "You'll email all the details? I'll get them in my diary."

"Of course."

"Oh, I forgot to tell you, I'm moving."

"You're leaving the one legged man?" He sounded surprised.

Arabella nodded grimly. "The girlfriend doesn't like lodgers."

"Oh dear."

She leaned over the desk, picking up a pen and writing on the top of an open realm of printer paper. "I'm going to be living here," she told him, writing out the address of Aunt Agetha's old place in Huntington. "The land line's not sorted yet, but you can get me on my mobile."

"Joining us mortgage slaves on the property ladder?"

She didn't dare tell him the house was owned outright. It seemed too much that she'd been so ridiculously lucky she had just been given a house. It was a shit hole, but it was her shit hole. Her mother didn't want to move in, and was prepared to forego any money from a sale. It felt more than one person deserved. "Something like that," she said vaguely.

"You'd better get yourself a job sorted out pronto."

"Working on it." She headed for the door. "See you later."

"Oj, Arabella!" he yelled after her.

She paused in the open doorway. "What?"

"Don't forget your flowers."

The next few days went by so quickly she barely had a moment to sit and feel sorry for herself. She bought a stack of packing boxes and went to Adam's house during the weekdays and packed up all of her remaining possessions. It took a few journeys to transport everything to the new place. By the end of the week she was finally out of Adam's house. The direct debit for rent and bills was cancelled. The cord was cut.

She'd returned to the piss house, determined that she would make it habitable. Under the usual delusion of someone who had very little experience of DIY she believed the task would be completed within a day. Without knowing how long it would be before she would have regular employment, she needed to be careful with her redundancy money, and would have to do the work herself. They were brave words for someone who didn't own any tools.

She took a slower walk around the property on her own, shocked by just how bad the smell was. Memory could weaken the worst of experiences with time. She unlocked all of the doors and windows, letting in the fresh warm air from outside to try and neutralise the wretched stink. It was ingrained in the house. The carpets were going to have to go, as were the couple of curtains still hanging inside. Then she'd need to strip the wall paper and possibly remove some of the floorboards if things had soaked through really badly. That was just on the interior. She didn't even want to try and consider what needed to be done with the rickety porch on the front of the house.

In the kitchen there was a drawer with random keys. Most found a home in the windows and doors. There were three that had no obvious use, and certainly none of them worked on the padlock on the front of the garage. She unlocked the door at the back of the garage and was surprised to find a small sailing boat in storage. What an odd possession for a solitary elderly lady to have had.

She made a trip to the local out of town shopping complex. Having wandered up and down the DIY aisles in a daze, she gathered what tools she imagined a practical kind of person would possess.

Arabella returned to the house, determined to achieve something today. She now had a cloth facemask, traditionally for those dealing with sawdust, plaster dust, asbestos and other breathing hazards. It would do for the smell in the house. Protecting against geriatric urine wasn't the listed as a benefit on the advertising packaging, but the mask did what she needed it to do. She spent the afternoon sweating through her clothes, mask and work gloves, ripping up carpets on her own with angry determination. Rolling up the mouldering fabric weaves, she dragged them out of the house, grunting with exhaustion as she dumped them on the drive. The fat bodied spiders that littered the overgrown trees in the front garden watched proceedings with curiosity.

Once the carpets and kitchen lino were out, there was only the bathroom flooring which she decided to leave for the time being. The entire bathroom needed to be ripped out, but even Arabella had enough sense to realise that a bathroom refit was beyond her. She walked through the house, surveying the bare floors. Everything looked all right, as much as she could assess, apart from the living room, where some of the brown stains had seeped through into the floorboards. This was the room with the worst smell. Shit. She was going to have to pull up half the floor.

She went to the kitchen to wash her hands. There was a bottle of hand wash from her previous bathroom, along with Arvid's flowers, currently displayed in a bucket she'd come across in the garage. Just to try and make things look homely. She turned on the tap and waited for the hot water to come. Pure icy water gushed out, which was actually quite refreshing in the summer heat, but she would need hot water. She checked the boiler on the wall in the kitchen, which didn't appear to be on. She tried the switch on the wall, but an electricity supply seemed to make no difference and when she prodded various buttons on the boiler, the front panel came loose and fell into her hands.

"Shit."

The garage seemed to be the only place her mother's clearance men hadn't been. Aside from the bucket and the boat, she'd found two metal chairs and round table, which she'd dragged out into the back garden. With her feet on the table, face mask pushed on to the top of her head like a bizarre hat, she'd flicked through directory enquiries on her phone, finding a local gas man who would come out on Monday evening to take a look at the boiler. She ordered a skip which would arrive the next day. Setting her phone on the ground and leaning back into the chair, she gazed up at the sky. It felt as though nothing had been achieved, or rather worse, more problems had been found. She'd spent several hours ripping out carpeting and still the house stank. What the fuck was she doing?

There was a small mew and a black cat hopped onto the low fence separating her garden with that of her semi-detached neighbour. She'd not seen or heard anything from next door. The cat stood on the fence, neatly balanced and observed her with feline distain. It mewed once, then jumped from the fence to the grass to Arabella's lap and gave her another dismissive stare before curling up to go to sleep.

"Don't mind me, will you?" She sniffed, ignored by the cat. It was still a better neighbourly introduction than the pervert she and her mother had met the first time they'd come to the house. As if he were a kind of subservient devil, the mere thought of him brought him forth. The old man crept out of his kitchen and into his own small back yard to leech over the fence line.

"Why, afternoon my dear," he cooed to her. "Is that your pussy?"

Arabella opened one eye to a slit-like glare. He was almost panting. He was like a *Carry On* film, but not even charming in outdated and politically incorrect innuendo. Just nasty. Another problem to add to the list. She ignored the man and picked up her phone, selecting a number from the phone book.

"Hello, Graham, it's Arabella. I think I have a job for you." She smiled. "No, not musical this time. I have a use for your day job." Her eyes flicked to the neighbour who was unashamedly staring at her chest. "It's not a big deal at all. Should only take an hour or so. Really? Great, I'll see you tomorrow."

Pushing the cat out of her lap, she returned to the kitchen, and took a quick tour around the house, locking windows as she went. That would be enough work for today. She needed to head back to her mother's and get this smell out of her hair. Leaving the rolls of carpets discarded on the driveway in preparation for the skip delivery – if someone wanted to steal them in the meantime, they were welcome to do so – she headed back to her mother's.

The next day, Saturday, was marked out for the continuation of stench removal and the blotting out of unwanted neighbours. Arabella was in the master bedroom, cross-legged on the floor hacking at the wallpaper with a scraper and swiftly losing the will to live. She heard a knock on the door, and she felt a jump of adrenaline, despite the fact that she knew who was calling. This was her first visitor.

Graham, in scuffed jeans and a checked shirt rolled up at the sleeves, was outside, along with the girlfriend. "Hey, Arabella," he greeted her. "You had a job?" he looked worriedly at the overgrown trees in the front garden. "Not here I hope?"

"No, it's out back. This mess..." she waved a hand at the front. "That's way down on the list so I'm not even thinking of it." She paused, looking to the girlfriend, who was in a print skirt, possibly silk, and a tank top. Not really work wear. She wasn't entirely sure why she was here, unless she was planning on sitting adoringly to one side, worshipping the work Graham performed. As far as Arabella knew, they were quite a new thing. She'd only briefly met the woman once, at the 50s gig, and hadn't been in the mood for staying back for the after party.

"You've met Miriam, right?"

"Yes, fleetingly the other weekend."

"Yes, hello again."

"Well, come on in," Arabella propped open the conservatory front door with a potted dead cactus. "I will warn you, it's a bit smelly inside."

Graham wrinkled his nose as he and Miriam followed Arabella . "I didn't realise you'd left Adam's." He glanced back at Miriam, whose face had turned a little red by the heat and smell. "You hitting the property ladder now?"

"Yeah. It's a bit of a shithole at the moment. Still, the smell isn't actually as bad as when I first came here."

"I saw you'd ripped out the carpets."

"All on my own, good job, eh?"

Graham glanced uncertainly across the bare floorboards. "You could probably do with getting rid of the gripper rods," he suggested, noting the lines of nails along the edges of the room that had been there to hold the carpet down. "Bit dangerous."

"It's on the list."

"Looks like you've bought yourself a big job here," he added, stepping into the living room. "These floorboards are a bit stained."

"I'm going to have to take them all up, aren't I?"

"Most of them probably. I'd get all the wallpaper off as well."

"I've started that," Arabella said, holding up the metal scraper. "It's taking ages."

Graham laughed out loud. "Just hire a wallpaper stripper; you'll get the house done in a couple of days. You'll be here till the cows come home with that thing. Looks like you've got plenty of other jobs to do once you've got the place fumigated. You're not actually living here at the moment are you?"

"No. I'm staying with my mother. Which is fine, but... it's like living on an MGM film set. My mother's an eccentric," she added for Miriam's benefit.

"So the psycho girlfriend got too much?"

"That and I got my notice from Adam," Arabella said. "I've not really seen him since, he's been avoiding me. I've packed all my crap up and moved out of there. It's just a shitty end. And he must realise I'm right if he won't..."

"He's an adult," Graham reminded her. "You have to let him make his own mistakes. Come on; let's see this fence you want sorting out."

By trade, when he wasn't playing the guitar, Graham ran his own one-man-band fencing business. Arabella sometimes wondered if it was a bad choice and he should be more wary of his hands. There was always the risk that the practical job could damage fingers essential for the art of the guitar. Thus far he had either been very lucky or very apt.

Arabella led the way through to the back garden and stood in the centre of the small garden.

"That," she said, pointing at a house that would be on a road further up from her own, its backyard attached to her garden, "is a pervert. I want him blotting out."

Graham looked across the row of little back gardens and yards, separated by low fences. "You're sure you want to do this? It won't look a bit unneighbourly?"

"I don't give a toss what it looks like. I don't want that old git looking at me."

"Okay. So which fence is yours?"

"Which fence?" Arabella looked at him as if he were speaking Double Dutch.

"You usually don't own the fences on all of the boundaries. I can't tear up any of this if you're not sure it's yours."

"Oh." She looked uncertainly around the garden. So many little trip hazards for someone who knew nothing about owning property. She didn't have the deeds yet, so she didn't have any paperwork to check. Her mother was in the process of signing the house over to her, and there'd been a letter from the solicitor full of much legal blurb, but nothing about fences.

The patio doors across the way clicked open and her offensive neighbour strolled out.

"Brought your friends over to say hello?" He called across, ignoring Graham and looking Miriam up and down.

Arabella marched up to the fence. It was like a tennis net marking the new boundary to the next battle. She moved as if she was going to swing a punch at him, but instead slapped her hands down on the fence. "Is this fence mine?"

"Oh no, this one's mine. Yours is over there," he said, pointing at the boundary separating her land from that of her attached neighbours. "But you can lean on my fence any time you like. Lean over to say hello."

Miriam put a hand to her mouth, covering the horrified laugh that was threatening to spew up. She hurried back into the kitchen.

"She ill?"

"I would think so," Arabella turned back to Graham. "There's nothing stopping me putting my own up on my own land is there?"

"As long as it's under six foot."

"Ok, I need this doing. You see where I'm coming from?"

"I've just got posts and planks in the truck. Are you all right with something basic."

"Will it be solid?"

"If you want."

"Here, what's this all about?" the old man interrupted. "You fencing me out?"

"I don't want any gaps," Arabella continued talking to Graham. "I need my privacy." She added, more loudly for her neighbour's benefit.

"Why, what'cha going to be doing? Sunbathing nude?"

"Jesus, I'm going to have to go back in. Are you ok to do this?"

"Sure. I can get it done this morning. It's not very big out here at all."

Miriam was in the kitchen drinking water from one of the mugs Arabella had brought over from her meagre kitchen supplies. "I hope you don't mind."

"It's just water. I have something stronger if you need it." She opened one of the dated cupboard doors and revealed a bottle of vodka. It was the only item she'd put in a cupboard so far. "After that little introduction to the locals, it might be necessary."

"I think I'll survive," Miriam smiled, setting down the cup and daring to peek out of the kitchen window. "I didn't realise relics like that were still about. It's not so pleasant in real life is it?"

"What isn't?"

"Being in a *Carry On* film."

Arabella shook her head. "I suspect I'm still going to have to hear it, but if I don't have to look at it."

"It'll be a start." Miriam gazed around the kitchen. "This is kind of funky, very retro."

"I don't know if I'll have to rip it all out. Although the smell in here doesn't seem to be too bad."

"I think it's just what's coming in from the rest on the house. I think your living room's the worst culprit." Miriam crouched down, opening a cupboard and peering inside. "I guess you're looking to do this up on your own."

"I don't have a lot of spare cash."

"I wouldn't rush to get rid of this. They look like proper solid cupboards. You could always paint them up. I'm a great upcycler."

"A what?"

"I do old furniture. Old anything really. Find new uses for things. I don't like waste, and besides, I find renovated second hand has so much more personality than production line manufactured crap. Do you know what I mean?"

Arabella didn't. She had never had to worry about owning furniture other than her chaise longue, but nodded vaguely regardless.

"This will be great once you've got the wallpaper off and those floorboards out. Once the smell is dealt with, you'll be able to start on the design..."

Arty type, Arabella thought. If only it was possible to do a house up on banjo notes. A G cord to get things going; vibrate all the dust and crap out. An F sharp to add a fresh lick of paint.

"I know it must feel like an overwhelming project right now, but I'm quite jealous," Miriam continued. "You'll be able to put your mark on everything. It really will be your home. You should get on freecycle. You'll be able to pick up some free furniture there. And there's the community second hand furniture store. You can get bits there for ten, twenty quid. If you paint stuff up they can look quite funky. I got a chest of drawers there last month. I've repainted them and stencilled a quote from Alice in Wonderland on the front."

"And what does stuff cost on freecycle?" She'd ordered an oven and fridge freezer on the internet, but when she walked through the empty rooms, doing a mental inventory of all the things she didn't have, she realised this was going to cost a fortune. It was a bit of a shame her mother had let the house clearers in before she'd decided to offer Arabella the house.

"The clue's in the name. Although you really need to give something away before you start taking up other people's offers."

Arabella felt a little deflated. What did she have to give away? "I have a boat I don't want."

"A boat?"

"It's just sat in the garage. Funny, I can't unlock the padlock at the front. The key must be lost. Do you think Graham would have something for breaking it off?"

Graham did have a set of bolt cutters. He was taking them out of the truck and moving around the skip towards the garage when

Arabella's neighbours – the ones in the end terrace house who shared the plane of concrete driveway with her – pulled up onto his drive in his gleaming four wheel drive.

"Hey!" The man tumbled out of the driver's seat when he saw Graham lift up bolt cutters to the padlock on the white wooden garage doors. "What do you think you're doing?"

The three of them turned as the man hurried across. Arabella stepped forward. "I've just moved in here and I'm getting into my garage."

"That's my lock."

Were all her neighbours arseholes? "Why would your lock by on my garage?"

He huffed his way up to her, irritated that the house had already been taken over. It didn't look as though they'd have a quiet little old dear this time. "Because that's my boat in there. You'd better not have damaged it."

"I haven't touched your bloody boat."

"The old lady was very good and let me store it here."

Arabella pursed her lips. The inference: you are neither old nor good. And you've been here barely five minutes. You're trampling on my rights. "I don't believe you," she finally said.

"What?"

"Prove it to me."

"That it's my boat?"

"Unlock the padlock."

"If it will stop you people destroying my property," he grumbled, shuffling through his bunch of keys to select the correct one. The padlock clicked open easily, and he pulled it off the garage lock as if to demonstrate for even the simplest of minds that he had most definitely unlocked the door. "See? I really don't see what the problem is. It's not like anyone's using it."

"Maybe so, but if you want to carry on keeping your boat here, I'm going to have to charge you rent."

Graham laughed, a little awkwardly. Arabella had always had a bolshy streak and he suspected the heat wasn't helping. "Come on, Arabella, you don't want to alienate all your neighbours. It's not like he can move it yet, with the skip in the way."

Arabella looked over at him, stony faced. "When the skip goes, the boat goes."

"So which of you people are moving in next door?" the man asked, directing his question to Graham in the hope that he was the husband in charge.

"Just me," Arabella answered on Graham's behalf. Why did all conversations like this eventually end up between the men? Just leave the hot headed silly women to dance around in the background. They were not worth worrying about. "I think I'm going to go inside and start pulling up gripper rods."

The atmosphere was growing uncomfortable. They hadn't reached the point of fighting. Everyone was ready to step back and get on with whatever it was they had been occupied with. But no one wanted to break the tension. Miriam hopped awkwardly from foot to foot. "I'll give you a hand, Arabella," she offered. "Let's get them ripped out. You don't accidentally want to put your foot on one of those."

Indeed, Arabella thought, indeed.

"Don't listen to anything she says."

Arabella heard the suggestion that was toned as a request, but said nothing as she watched the twenty-two year old assistant facilities manager disappear through the door. The girl, Hayley, was friendly and perky enough, but she hadn't yet learned to hide that niggling lack of confidence. Her uncertainty was the little chink people like Georgina would relish.

"She really doesn't understand what's required of this job," Georgina continued primly, rearranging the papers Hayley had left on the reception desk. "I don't know why they gave her such an important job. She doesn't know what she's doing."

Arabella looked over at her and smiled weakly. For someone who had looked as though words were glued to the inside of her mouth with an unpleasant tasting adhesive whilst Hayley had been in reception, she was being distinctly vocal now. Jesus, it was only her first day and already she had one colleague she wanted to slap. She'd not even been working with Georgina for an hour yet.

There was some truth in what Georgina was prattling about. Hayley did appear out of her depth. Arabella had clocked the lack of experience the moment Hayley had met her in the foyer this morning. But Georgina spoke with such bitterness; one would think Hayley had gotten in the habit of shitting in her kitchen. It was classic old woman sourness, but as Arabella watched Georgina turn around – and damn, that was a massive arse – she had to worry whether she too had experienced such moments herself. Getting riled and irritated by the Marikas and the Cherry Malones of the world. Was she just a younger Georgina, bitching at the next generation? Or did she have genuine grievances? Perhaps the question was more how one went about expressing these feelings.

"Now, let me show you how we really should be dealing with the visitors' book." Georgina set down the book in front of Arabella and carefully smoothed the pages open. "We want to get this right."

Arabella had become so focused on renovations and planning what she needed to do next in her little house that the realities of the day had been forgotten. It had come as something of a shock when Meav, the recruitment agent, had called on Sunday evening, trying to sound calm whilst advising Arabella of an 'exciting' opportunity. She had immediately thought Arabella would be perfect for it. She needed to start the following morning at seven thirty. That wouldn't be a problem, would it?

Either someone had let her down at the last moment, or she'd fucked up. Arabella wasn't green enough to believe that this 'opportunity' had miraculously appeared at five o'clock on a Sunday evening. Still, a job, any job was welcome news. It was only two weeks' temping to cover the main fulltime receptionist was on a month's sick leave (it sounded like someone had let Meav down part way through). A two mere weeks hadn't seemed like much to get excited about, but having met Georgina, it was already the light at the end of the tunnel that this wouldn't be forever. The fifty-something part timer worked ten till two so that Arabella could take her one hour lunch break. She had arrived on Monday in a bit of a temper.

Having just got the first temp trained up and out of most of Hayley's bad habits, she was going to have to start all over again.

At least Arabella was getting paid for this. Maybe Meav would be so grateful, she'd dig her a proper job up after this. At least she could stick a finger up at her former employers. Other people wanted to give her a job. She was able to move on. At least, at least, at least. At least Georgina was finishing at two.

The week rolled on switching from paid work as a receptionist to unpaid work as a beginner DIY queen. She went back to sleep at her mother's house. The stink was pretty much gone from the house now, although Arabella had been forced to take extreme measures. Carpets and gripper rods were all out. The wallpaper filled wet sacks that festered in the skip. She'd spent a productive and therapeutic evening ripping out the floorboards in the living room, after a day when Georgina had been at her most condescending. Pissy bitch. Pissy floor. The skip was full. Arabella called the skip hire company and told them they could collect the container.

The gas man had been by and checked out the boiler. It was fucked. The lack of heating didn't seem the greatest issue just now as the air was baking through the height of summer. She also knew that she didn't like the cold and damp, and she knew that winter was coming. With a quote that would take its hungry chunk of her redundancy money, she had booked him to come in a couple of week's time to install a new boiler. The kettle would provide hot water for now, and it wasn't too much of a problem as she wasn't yet living there. The new fridge freezer and oven had run off with their own fists fulls of dollars, but the new appliances looked smart in her otherwise shabby kitchen. There was just the new bed to arrive on Saturday, then she'd be down to hunting for second hand furniture, not wanting to break into the last portion of her redundancy.

On Thursday evening she'd had some fun with a bag of plaster, an old washing up bowl and a trowel, fixing up the walls in the master bedroom in preparation for a paint job. On Friday she came back with two cans of aquamarine bedroom wall paint, but that would have to wait until Saturday, for tonight she was entertaining. Nicki, from her old cursed job, came over to view the new property.

"Jesus Christ, Arabella," Nicki exclaimed, actually taking off her sunglasses to underline the shock. "I know you said it was a bit of a wreck but I would have thought you'd at least have a floor."

"I did that the other evening."

"You did that?"

"The floor was piss-soaked. She had a little dog. Judging by the stains he didn't get out much."

"As long as it was just the dog."

"I wouldn't like to assume. But the floor had to go."

"I brought this as a house warming gift," Nicki offered her the purple moth orchid. "But looking around I feel like I should have brought you a plank of wood."

Arabella grinned. "I can put this in the kitchen." She almost skipped down the hallway, with the thought on repeat in her head: *my* kitchen. She placed the orchid in the centre of the kitchen windowsill.

"I see you've already been getting flowers."

The bucket on the kitchen work top held what was still reasonably fresh from the bouquet. A number of the flowers had found their way to the green bin. Considering it was over a week old, and the summer was hot, it was impressive that any of the blooms had survived. "Yeah. Perhaps not the most stylish vase, but a girl has to start somewhere, and there were more important things to sort out, like this." She ran a hand down the side of the fridge freezer.

"I never had you down for a domestic goddess. You had a life-direction change with the redundancy?"

"Maybe, but not like that." Arabella opened the fridge door. "I'm only interested in this appliance this evening because of this." She took out a jug of margarita cocktail mix. "Let's go outside."

The back garden, small as it was, had swiftly become a personal space, all thanks to the six foot fences Graham had put up for her last weekend. Arabella had strung fairy lights across the top. They had been her purchase a couple of years ago for communal Christmas decorating and she'd be damned if Liz was going to use them.

When dusk started to fall, Arabella liked to sit out in the summer evening, sweat-stained from an evening hard at work in the house, and switch on the lights.

"So you're coping all right since the redundancy?"

"Surprisingly, yes. I always thought redundancy would be a disastrous thing. But life just keeps going. I've not got another job yet. I'm just temping at the moment."

"Yeah, but you always had several jobs on the go." Nicki watched as she poured out the drinks.

"True, although I've quit the dancing."

"Ian was blethering something about that. I didn't think it was true."

"Ian? What would he know?"

"Apparently he'd been asking at the club. They told him you'd decided to retire from dance to focus on your music."

Arabella nodded sagely, sitting down. "That's pretty much it. And if it means I don't have Ian leering at me anymore, what can I say? Christ, I don't miss him."

"Things haven't changed. Well, most things anyway," Nicki sighed and wistfully gazed into the void for a moment. "I don't know whether you'll have heard, but Laura had her baby. A few weeks premature, but all's well."

Arabella nodded sagely. It was good to hear she supposed, but she wasn't particularly interested. She had never been able to feel that hysteria over other people's babies that many women did. The moment the word baby was uttered, or a miniature cardigan was shook forth from a bag, the squealing did commence. Heaven help people's eardrums should a photograph be passed around, or the actual creature wheeled into the room. If Arabella had been more of an insecure woman she might have worried there was something missing in her genetic makeup. She was a woman; why didn't she react like this? Babies just didn't make her excited. "That's nice."

Nicki laughed dryly. "You're lucky it's just me telling you. Cooing was obligatory when we were told in the office."

"Hey, you know me. I just don't get excited about babies."

"I can't say other people's babies do it for me either." Nicki took a drink from her cocktail. "Not that I know of any other types of babies." She paused, considering Arabella. "Would you ever want to go down that road?"

"Children?" Arabella looked horrified. "No," she responded without even thinking. "Well, I don't know," she relented a little. "I'm not a natural baby-crazy-lady, so I'm not supposed to say yes, am I?"

"Just because you're not crazy about other people's kids doesn't mean you wouldn't be crazy about your own."

It was too surreal a concept to really contemplate. Responsibility, little people. Some poor small bugger looking up to her as if she had all the answers. That would be some start in life, having Arabella as a mother. "All I hear is that children is what you're supposed to do. I don't want to run with the crowd so I can't say I've really given myself any time to think if it's actually something I'd want to do," she said, surprising herself by the sudden openness. "Not that it's relevant; I can hardly have kids on my own. Maybe in the future, I suppose," she waved it off like it was a mildly irritating fly. "Not now."

"I hate to say it, but the future isn't away there over past the hills. It's right here. You're not in your twenties anymore."

"Jesus, I am only just thirty!" Arabella gasped.

Nicki nodded, setting down her glass on the table. "I know, you have a good ten years or so. But you are getting to the point where you have to decide."

"Do I need to remind you that I'm single just now?"

"What I'm saying is, it doesn't hurt to take some time out and think about what you do want. So if the opportunity does come up, you don't miss it. I know the world's overpopulated, and the last thing humanity needs it another unwanted child..." her speech fizzled out. She wasn't sure where she wanted to take it. This was a subject that sometimes came up on her own list of questions, although at forty-two she felt that she'd pretty much missed the boat. She had gone through a couple of angst-filled periods in her life when the biological clock had started, but she'd never been in a stable relationship at the time. It hadn't worked out. As with many things, sometimes it didn't matter what you wanted. You just had to take whatever opportunities life decided you were going to get to play with.

"Screaming poo sacks."

Arabella's cynical comment broke through Nicki's thoughts.

"It's a terrifying thought, just arranging your own replacement like that. That's all it is, isn't it? Your own youth is now over. Onwards with the next generation."

"That will happen whether you have kids or not," Nicki sighed.

"It's just tiring, all these arseholes you don't even know just assuming you want children, and feeling they have the right to tell you that. Hey, I have a womb, that must be the sole purpose of my existence. Why aren't I preparing my body for child bearing? And really, I should have done this years ago, because it's kind of disgusting that a woman in her thirties would have her first child."

Nicki laughed out loud. "Where have you been hearing this shit?"

"All over the place."

"In fairness, I heard all of this ten years ago. Maybe this is the benefit of getting older. People stop hassling you about children. I get the pity stares now, like I've failed in life. Missed my joyful moment."

"Have you?"

Nicki lowered her eyes. "I don't know. I'm just saying from my own experience, give yourself some time to decide for yourself if you do or don't. Don't base it on not doing what everyone else says just because you're stubborn."

Arabella set her drink down on the table. "I don't know why we're getting so serious this evening. It's not like I'm pregnant or in a serious relationship where the question's come up. I feel like I've always got to defend myself against arseholes. I am not an incubator. I don't think I'm the mothering type. Or maybe everyone has it within them given the right circumstances. The hormones'll look after it. You just parcel yourself up and put your essence in the attic. Become a mindless slave to the children. Because we must think of the children." She finished on a fake gasp, putting her hands together and striking a saintly pose. "Mothers are annoying."

"I think that's a slight generalisation. Besides, look at your own mother. It's not as if she ever gave up her personality. Was she a Stepford when you were growing up?"

"My mother has always been nuts."

"Thing is, I think there are all types of parents. Some women are desperate for babies the moment they can put a thought together. And I suppose that's fine if that's what they want out of life. But I do think we need more of the women who don't want to have kids, to have children."

"Put us in our place?"

Nicki shook her head. "Not at all. The women who don't immediately want to start having children are the ones who get out there and do things. They have interests, experiences.... girls need more role models like that."

"I suppose," Arabella said off hand. This discussion was growing rather heavy. She suspected there was something more behind it, but it felt as though Nicki wanted to keep it firmly in the hypothetical. She wouldn't push a confidence. Perhaps it was time for a change of subject. "How are things at work otherwise then? Are they done with the redundancies?"

"For now, so it looks like I'm safe," Nicki said

"And no one else had to go after I'd gone? Everything ticking over? How's Robin doing?"

Nicki waggled her head as if she didn't really want to answer the question. "You don't want to know about that old place now. Move on."

"Christ, you're not saying he's coping?" Arabella looked horrified, a momentary lurch of that professional competition back up.

"I don't know," Nicki averted her gaze. "I think it's too much for anyone person to take on. But you don't want to stress out over that anymore. You've got new things going on."

"I guess." Arabella stretched her right leg out, her sandal flopping loosely off her toes. "Work wise it's not amazing. Two weeks temping, one week already done. It's not exactly impressive. But I have to earn my keep. The music isn't ever going to be my bread and butter."

"I don't know. It sounded like you had a good time in Iceland. And your website, very impressive, my dear," she clinked glasses. "And you've just inherited a house. That's some going, even if it doesn't have a floor. To not have to pay rent or a mortgage. I wish I was there. You are only thirty."

"I know, count my blessings. So what about you? Anything new?"

"Not with work or where I live..."

"But..."

Nicki grinned. "I have started seeing someone."

"Oh my god," Arabella shrieked, taking a moment to drain her glass before continuing. "I always thought you were a sworn celibate."

Nicki laughed. "What gave you such a stupid idea?"

"You've been single a few years, never been into flings."

"Arabella," she scolded gently. "That doesn't mean anything. Not everyone wants one night stands."

"Neither do I," she responded primly. "Anymore."

"Yeah, well." Nicki arched an eyebrow, as that was all that could be said on Arabella's messy trail of what might vaguely be called a romantic life. "I met him online, which you're not allowed to laugh about. He's called Marcel, which you're not allowed to laugh about either."

"There's nothing wrong with the name Marcel. The flowers in there," she pointed at the kitchen, "are from Arvid."

"Arvid?"

"It's Norwegian."

"You're seeing a Norwegian."

Arabella shook her head. "It was a brief week thing in Iceland."

"A bit dull, was he?"

"No," she sighed. "Actually it was me that was a bit dull. Or a bit dim. He wasn't interested. Let me know with a fucking kitten postcard. I mean, what kind of arsehole dumps a holiday fling with a kitten card?"

"The flowers were to apologise for his dreadful ways?"

"Something like that," Arabella stared thoughtfully at the kitchen. She'd not heard from Arvid since the flowers, despite the slightly cryptic message on the card. Not that she particularly wanted to see him again. "Anyway, when everything's sorted, I'm going to have a house warming, then you'll have to bring Marcel."

"And when that's going to happen?"

"Soon. I guess. I've got a few things to sort out. You know, paint the walls, maybe buy some curtains or something," she nodded to herself. "Get the damn floor put back in."

Nicki snorted into her drink. "Floors are kind of important."

"Yeah," Arabella mused. "If you've not got something to walk on, you're kind of screwed."

The way the sunlight danced upon the wet lacquer of her metallic blue toenails was rather pleasing. Arabella mused on the little pleasures in life as she stretched her bare feet out of the kitchen doorway. Saturday afternoon in the new house and the nausea had just about worn off. Too much heat, too much work, and too many damned paint fumes.

She'd thrown up in the dingy bathroom, surprised that the evacuation of her stomach hadn't made her feel better. Perhaps it had been the margaritas last night. The first layer of turquoise paint complete in the master bedroom, she'd wobbled to the kitchen, deciding it was probably a good time to give the DIY a rest. With a sugary-sticky lollypop out of the freezer, she'd sat down in the open kitchen doorway, savouring the fresh air and warmth on her face. The cooling ice was drawn up and down inside her mouth. Sucked on to within an inch of its life. If her pervert neighbour had still been able to see her, he would have had something to say. The sweetness disposed of the lingering taste of vomit.

Lollipop consumed, she'd decided to paint her toes. If the house was getting a spruce, why shouldn't she? When the minor paint job was complete, she had waddled inside, toes stretched spread-eagle. She fetched her banjo and returned to the kitchen doorway. She sat down and retuned one of the strings. It had been a week since she'd last played. Such a period of silence was unheard of for Arabella. Temping and doing up the house had taken up every waking moment recently. It was good to get back to the solid, reassuring feel of the banjo in her hand, the round body propped against her thigh. Old friend.

She worked her way up through the notes, then strummed through all of the strings, humming to herself. She naturally fell into the intro of the *duelling banjos* tune, even though there was no one to reconcile with, and no reply to call back to her. Her friendship with Adam was over in the time it took to make a cup of tea. Even now, after a few weeks and a new house, there was still something sad about how it had ended. It reminded her of the impermanence of all things. People one assumed to be friends could be anything but when the lynch pin was extracted. Here she was on her own in the kitchen playing *duelling banjos*. It was a monologue of a duet. Arabella was thinking over all the good people she'd managed to piss off, the people who'd pissed her off, and the permanent separation that followed.

A smile crept onto her lips as the tune went up tempo. She'd just have to be some kind of mad banjo lady. When she had the money and had fixed everything else, perhaps she could rip out that crappy conservatory porch construction at the front, and replace it with a proper American style open air veranda. The widow's walk for the woman who had never married. She could mourn the men who might have been. She could get herself a swing seat, sit there and play the banjo, directing evil grins at passersby and terrifying her neighbours.

She finished the tune with a dramatic flourish for no one's benefit, just as the sound of a heavy knock at the front door echoed up the hallway. Arabella twisted, staring suspiciously into the house. She wasn't expecting any visitors. This had better not be any damned neighbours coming to tell her to keep the noise down.

Laying the banjo on the empty kitchen work top, she padded bare foot across floor boards to the original front door, a solid panel that kept house from porch. Pushing it open, she entered the hot house of a porch, the humidity taking her back like a punch. From here she had a full vista of her short drive, her parked car and the street beyond. In her subconscious she could see what was ahead, but it took her conscious side a few seconds to catch up.

An unfamiliar car was parked outside. It had pulled up onto the footpath and blocked her own vehicle in. Presumably its driver was the figure outside the door. A man, dressed in dark jeans and a light T-shirt, stood with his back to her house. The thumb of one hand was hooked in a belt loop. The other hand held a pair of sunglasses, dangling loosely in his fingers. He turned around as the sound of the current front door creaking open took him out of his day dream.

"Well," Arabella leant against the door frame with her arms folded. She was a little bemused by the way today was going. Perhaps this was a mirage, for she had never expected to see him again. It was so unexpected that she didn't have chance to acknowledge the surge of emotions that came with recognition. She just had to put her confident face on and go out there. "Mr Ben Simon."

He grinned sheepishly at her. "Arabella."

She couldn't help herself, smiling like a love struck fool. Idiot. "I hope you don't think this sounds rude, but I wasn't expecting to find you on my door step."

"Yeah," he winced slightly. "I hope this isn't a problem. Your agent gave me your address."

"Jordan?"

"Yes. I don't think he normally would have," he added quickly, realising handing out private information could get an agent into trouble with the client. "I just think after the flowers, and..."

"The flowers." Arabella said slowly.

"Yes. He did pass them on?"

The flowers, of course they hadn't been from Arvid. She'd just assumed. She had simply presumed they had been from the Norwegian, because of the connection back to Iceland, Oates and Hafdis. But a man that broke up with a kitten postcard wouldn't then bother with such a bouquet weeks later. She would be old history now as far as Arvid was concerned.

"Yes, I got them."

"Maybe they were ill judged, I don't know. I couldn't decide if it was better to do that or try and apologise in person. But I had no way of contacting you. I sent those to your agent but I got to thinking it was a bit weak, so I came up to York."

"You came up to York to apologise?"

"Well, yes." He paused. Arabella seemed a little dazed. "About the other week, at the dance event..."

That dreadful shag in a cloakroom.

"I was very drunk..."

"I noticed."

"I really never meant for that to happen."

"You didn't want to?"

Ben put up his hands. The tone of the question was innocently put, and perhaps she didn't mean anything by it. But he'd fallen into these word traps set by women before now. "Not like that is what I didn't want. I'm not actually that kind of person."

I am, Arabella thought miserably. Or rather I certainly have been in the past.

"It was the final utter fuck up to finish off the crappy year I've been having. I am making positive moves to rectify everything. I am here to say sorry."

She mused over what he had said, feeling a little woolly-minded. It must be the heat. She watched one of the locals wander past with the dog, unashamedly staring in at her and Ben. "It takes two to tango," she finally said. "You don't need to apologise."

"I didn't want to treat you like that."

"Let's just draw a line under it," she quickly interrupted him, feeling uncomfortable. People being too nice often made her skittish, searching for the catch or the punch line. Kindness and sincere attention wasn't justified a lot of the time when she had been involved.

"I'd like that."

She stepped up from the doorway. "Do you want to come in?"

His eyes widened slightly as the heat in the front porch hit him. It was oppressive. No wonder the cactus was dead. Footsteps echoed down the hallway, void of carpeting, wall paper or any other nicety. "Have you just moved in?"

"Yeah, I'm in the process of doing everything up. Everything takes longer than you think."

"Oh shit."

Arabella turned around to find him at the living room, a look of amazement on his face.

"What happened to your floor?"

She'd gotten used to the gaping hole in the front room, but she supposed it would look drastic to newcomers. "The old woman who lived here before, her and her dog must have used that room as a toilet. It reeked. I had to rip out the floor."

"It doesn't smell now."

Arabella opened her mouth to issue some warning as he went into the living room and disappeared from view. She hurried forward to discover him in the middle of the hole, examining the remaining floor boards and the lats underneath. "The timber here still looks all right," he told her, running a hand along a lat. "It's some job, but it could be done in a day."

He turned to look up at her. She was a little bewildered by how thrilled he appeared to be over the mess her house was in. "It's on the list," she said vaguely. "I have to admit you're the first visitor who's felt the need to jump in. Most people just stand and laugh."

"It's a challenge, but it's satisfying getting things like this fixed," he said as he clambered back out of the hole. "I've been getting odd bits fixed in the flat to get it ready for the estate agents. It's supposed to go live next week."

"You're selling your London flat? Are you upgrading?" Arabella wandered in to the kitchen. What she really wanted to ask was if he was moving in with someone. He was getting engaged and no longer needed the bachelor pad? Are you seeing someone? She couldn't quite force the question from her mouth. Just what are you doing here? Come to apologise and tie up loose ends before you move in with your sophisticated London lady?

"I don't know," Ben replied, unaware of the increasingly horrific scenarios boiling in Arabella's mind. "I've not got that far. But property prices in London are crazy, so it will probably be an upgrade with the money elsewhere.

"Well, I'd offer you a drink," Arabella started, opening the freezer and thinking what she really wanted was another fruit lollypop. "But I had one too many margaritas last night. That and the painting today have left me a bit woozy."

He'd noticed the smell of drying paint. Seen the bright blue room by the kitchen. "I don't want anything to drink, anything alcoholic, I mean. I'm staying away from the booze for a while. I'm sorting things out after a crappy year."

"Drink problem?"

He snorted as if the suggestion he couldn't control himself was a great offense. "Lifestyle problem. Work style problem. Long hours, boozing up demanding clients. I was burning out."

"Lollypop?"

"Oh." He took it without thinking, the last thing he'd expected her to thrust in his face. "Thanks."

Arabella soon had the wrapper off and the stick of ice in her mouth. It felt so good, she had to close her eyes for a moment. It was thirty degrees today. A temperature that meant little in many countries, but for the Brits it was hot. A day for doing nothing, certainly not painting in a hot house.

"Why don't you just get another job?"

"I've already quit," he said, following her out into the small back garden. "I was sick of my life, sick of moaning but never doing anything about it. So I quit. I'm going freelance. A couple of the decent clients have followed me."

"So you're an independent marketing guru?"

He smiled at her description. "Something like that." Just now they were like a couple of kids, sat side by side on the weed-pocked lawn, legs stretched out. They each had a garishly coloured popsicle, melting in the summer sun. "It's not quite as exciting as playing the banjo for a living."

Arabella waved it off. "Not a living. Music doesn't pay the bills. I'm just a receptionist temp at the moment. I got made redundant. I was a credit controller before that. It's all just office shit. I'm actually really rather dull."

"I don't believe that," he said quietly.

Arabella's lollypop crumbled in her mouth. She crunched on the liquefying ice crystals, relishing the cool water running down her throat.

"I heard the banjo when I pulled up at your house."

She nodded, finishing her iced treat. "I'd been painting, but the heat and the fumes had gone to my head. It's the summer, felt like I needed to just chill for a bit." She lay back on the grass, draping a forearm over her eyes. "This heat is just repressive. Usually I'm ok with the sun, but it's knocked me for six recently." She felt utterly exhausted, her eyes thankful she had finally pulled down the eyelids.

"Hot summer days aren't meant for doing much."

"I need to slow down," she muttered, feeling her brain switching off. "Got to stop obsessing about getting the house finished."

She wasn't sure what the time was when she next opened her eyes, or how much time had passed. Only that there had been a lapse when she'd been out cold, for the sun had moved across the sky. Her legs were now in full, late afternoon sun, gently warming. Her head was in an oval of shade. Disorientated, she propped herself up on her elbows, looking around the garden in confusion. How had she gotten here? The metal table and chair in the garden had been shifted. A black umbrella was opened out and propped up at an odd angle on the chair. How strange, she thought, until she followed it across and realised that the umbrella was casting the oval of shadow across her face. Her banjo stood in the open kitchen doorway, propped against the wall.

Yawning, whilst stretching out her arms and curving back her spine to wake up like a cat, Arabella got up and padded across to the kitchen. She gave the interior a cursory glance, noting the clutter. Someone had been cooking. Had she been cooking dinner and then fallen asleep in the garden like some old biddy? Jesus, hitting thirty really was getting old. She sat down in the kitchen doorway and took the banjo back in her arms. She was awake but she still felt as though she was caught in a dream.

She started to play, clawhammer style, mid way through a song of star crossed lovers by the sea, disapproving brothers and ultimate death. Melancholic but with a catchy rhythm. She quietly warbled one line to herself before involuntarily jumping as a footstep creaked into the kitchen.

Her brain rushed into the here and now. "Oh," Arabella gasped, the banjo falling silent. "You're still here. Sorry I fell asleep. Kind of embarrassing. I don't usually sleep in the middle of the day."

Ben smiled gently. "If you're tired, you're tired. Don't worry about it."

"Clearly I have a lot to learn about being a house owner. I don't think you're supposed to go to sleep when people come to visit."

He laughed. "That's probably in the rule book somewhere. I always preferred people who weren't bound by conventions." He re-entered the kitchen and continued with his work.

Shit, Arabella thought, it wasn't me who had been cooking either.

"I wouldn't worry, I've kept myself busy. I was out on a short adventure. I managed to find a supermarket." He glanced over at her as she got up and put herself down on the kitchen stool. "You didn't seem to have a lot more in other than ice pops."

189

"I'm not actually living here yet. I'm gradually making it habitable. I got a bed delivered today, but it's still unpacked in the spare room with all my other boxes of crap. I'm not as far on with my room as I'd thought I'd be. I only got the first coat of paint done today."

"Your agent seemed to think you were living here."

"Soon. I'm staying with my mother at the moment. Everything takes longer than you think."

"All good things come to those who wait."

She watched him finish off in the kitchen. "You don't have to do this."

"Yes I do, I'm bloody starving," he joked with an undercoat of truth. "I've driven all the way up from London."

Arabella put her hands on her face. "Oh Christ, don't make me feel any worse," she groaned.

"Come on,"

He'd put his hand on her shoulder, naked as the halter neck straps left her shoulders bare to the sun. It was a familiar action, just to encourage her off the stool and out into the garden. And yet a very new sensation, a small electric shock rippling over the surface of her skin and waking her up with a spark. Ben was already outside at the little garden table. "I hope you're hungry."

"Starving," Arabella admitted. "I've been eating nothing but lollipops all day."

Sunday morning felt like the right time for a little 90s diva pop, and Arabella had Annie Lennox belting another classic out from the CD player in the hallway. She sang as she worked, changing the broken glass to broken floors in the lyrics as she plunged the roller in the tray of turquoise paint, loading the sponge up with colour. Back to the wall for the second coat. It should be dry by the evening. Thank god, Arabella thought. It was high time to fly the nest and move into her own space.

Her mother had acted out last night. It was unfair of her to think like that, but she couldn't give it a better term. The bottom line was that they got along fine when they didn't live together. Arabella hadn't really lived at home since she was eighteen, and the proximity was trying both of their nerves. She needed to move out and give them both their space back before they fell out properly. She'd told her mother that she was going to start living in the house as of tonight, and had packed her car up with as much of her crap as she could manage. When the paint was dry, which shouldn't be too long considering the heat, she'd unwrap the bed and move it into the bedroom. There was an ugly built in wardrobe in the room she fully intended to upcycle with paint and new knobs, but in the meantime she'd just live out of a suitcase. It would be no bother.

Yesterday evening had been pleasant but odd for Arabella. It had been many years since a man of a similar age and no musical working connection had socialised with her and not expected sex at the end of the session. Granted the state of her house didn't invite one to get down to business, but she hadn't even been kissed. It had ended like a couple of friends finishing off a pleasant dinner. She'd stood in the porch, watching him drive off, burning up in her own frustration. She had literally no idea where she stood. Was he slowly trying to seduce her, or did he really just want to be friends and nothing more? Or maybe he had just needed to assure himself he wasn't an utter bastard by doing the date he should have completed before the shag. Now there were no more outstanding obligations. She didn't even know if she was ever going to see him again. In the past the possibility of a hunt might have appealed, and if he didn't show, there were always others to bring down. Today other fish weren't good enough. What an arsehole, she growled to herself, stretching up to reach the corner join with the ceiling. Was she not good enough for him?

The room was soon finished. The walls glowed in their rich Egyptian turquoise. Pure lapis lazuli. Arabella washed out the tray and roller in the kitchen and laid them in the back garden to catch some sun and dry out. What to do now? She wandered down the hall and paused on the cusp of the living room. Floors were pretty essential and she ought to move on to this basic feature. Surely it ought not to be any harder than buying some wood and nailing it down. She just needed to measure the hole so the sales assistant would be able to work out how much she needed.

There was a knock at the door and Arabella felt her heart leap. It might be him. It wouldn't be, he'd be off back to London today, guilty conscience thoroughly erased. She hovered in the hallway, dragging out the moment. Whilst that door remained shut, it could be him. After it was open, the anticipation would be gone. It was probably the neighbour about his boat. You're pathetic, she scolded, forcing herself to the door. He's just a man, and the only time you had sex with him it was dreadful. Truly dreadful.

Her tension leapt into the back of her throat, making her internally awkward and ungraceful as she opened the porch door. He was back. Second day in a row. Ben Simon had come to her. He was in jeans and a casual blue shirt, the top few buttons undone in honour of the temperature and to aid ventilation. And the side effect of giving her a tantalising sneaky look at the curve of his collar bones, the start of his chest. Arabella felt her pulse rise, and a want deep inside to rip those remaining buttons free.

Ben just grinned at her idiotically, utterly oblivious. "I've bought you a present."

It was infectious. She was grinning like a fool. A present for little me. Really? What could it be? "That's very..."

He held up a plank of wood.

"Wood?"

He nodded back over his shoulder. "There's more in the car. I've brought you a lot of wood. I thought I'd help you with the floor."

"The floor?"

He raised his eyebrows. She didn't seem quite with it. "I believe there's a big hole in your house."

He's come to put a lot of wood in my hole, she thought, closing her eyes and taking a deep breath. And I'm turning into the pervert innuendo neighbour next door. Fated to be equally frustrated.

"You didn't have other plans for today, did you?" he asked, the smile dropping. For the first time he sounded uncertain. "I should have asked yesterday, but I thought I'd surprise you."

Arabella smiled politely and opened her eyes. "I had no plans," she admitted. "I've just been finishing off some painting. But you really didn't need to do this. I should pay you for the planks."

"They weren't much; don't worry about it. Besides it's a present." He stepped up into the porch as she moved to the side to let him in. He paused, turning to her. They were in particularly close proximity. "I thought this was what all women wanted men to bring them."

She raised her eyebrows questioningly.

"Some wood."

Oh, you're just teasing me now.

"There's more in the car if you want to grab an arm load."

And with that she was dismissed. She was dressed in her flip flops and the same old halter neck dress from yesterday, which was clearly so old it had lost all of its seductive powers. She walked down the drive. His car was unlocked. Flipping up the boot, she drew out three planks of wood. Wrapping her arms around them, she returned to the house. Inside Ben was already in the living room hole. In the time it had taken her to go fetch a couple of planks of wood, he'd found the saw and tape measure she'd bought on an earlier tool gathering mission (an unplanned shopping trip gathering DIY paraphernalia, half of which she still had to use. She was very new to all of this). He was measuring up at the far side, already working out what length he needed to cut.

Arabella pursed her lips. He'd been itching to come and play here since he'd first seen it yesterday afternoon. "Did you miss your calling in life?"

Thigh deep in the flooring, Ben turned around and looked up at her.

"You work in marketing but you should have been a joiner?"

He laughed. "Maybe. I do like fixing up things. This isn't a problem is it? If you don't want me to help I can leave it be."

"No, help by all means." She might as well take what she could get. "It needs doing. Sooner rather than later. I've officially moved in, so if I go sleepwalking tonight, I don't want to end up under the floor. I've got some nails in the kitchen."

"Screws are better," he told her, pulling out a packet of screws from the back pocket of his jeans. "If you ever need to pull the floor up, you won't have to rip up the planks."

"You really have thought of everything."

"I'm in the mind set at the moment," he explained as he snapped the tape measure against a length of wood. "I've been fixing odd bits in my flat, getting it ready to sell. I've got to get back down to London tonight, get the last of my belongings into storage. Then the viewers will start coming in."

"You've got to head back today?" Arabella crouched down, setting the planks of wood on the floor in the hallway. She felt disappointed. That familiar Sunday feeling but intensified.

"Yes." He marked the length on the plank before popping the pencil behind his ear and looking at her. "Don't worry; we'll get this done today before I head off. I don't want to come back and find you've broken your legs walking into the abyss in your sleep."

"You're going to come back?"

"Of course." He had his back to her as he shifted the plank to cut off the last twenty centimetres.

Arabella lowered her eyes, running a finger along the edge of the wood she'd brought in. Considering they'd actually already had sex, the awkwardness ought to have gone. At least according to tradition. Instead it felt as though neither dared be blunt about why he was really here. As if creeping too far onto the matter would bring them back to the subject of that embarrassing moment in the cloakroom. The disgust would return and one would reject the other. Actually on retrospect, you're really not what I'm looking for.

"I'll bring in the rest of the timber," she told him.

It took several hours to get the floor in. There was some mild bickering over who would do what, Arabella giving up the saw when she held up her attempt, with a disappointingly uneven plank end that Ben had to re cut. She obviously didn't have the patience to saw at right angles. Drilling holes for the screws was easier, and she went along the lats, preparing them for the new floorboards. They ate lunch – leftovers from the previous night and the last of Arabella's lollipops. Suddenly it was the late afternoon, the floor was in and he had to start the drive back to London. She'd rather forlornly followed him out to the car, with nothing more than a chaste kiss on the cheek before he'd gone. Arabella was left with frustration and the realisation that although he'd taken her mobile number (there was no point coming to visit if she was going to be away) she still had no way of contacting him. Was this revenge for her initial unwillingness to initiate anything with him? She remembered the time they'd met at the burlesque in Leeds, and she'd been stand offish, pointing out that London was just too far away. She'd turned him down point blank.

It was too far away now.

Locking the porch door, she wandered back into the house to discover the little black cat of uncertain abode had returned to pay her a visit. The cat had strolled casually in through the open kitchen door and was now in the hallway. It regarded her, mewed once then padded into the living room, complete with new floor. The cat did a circuit of the room to assess the layout, then returned to Arabella, purring and rubbing itself around her legs in figures of eight.

"At least you don't mind getting close to me," she sighed, crouching down to fuss the cat a little and feeling generally weepy. What the fuck was the matter with her? "Shall we get the bed sorted out?" She asked the cat. "I've got a brand new king size in there that needs unpacking. Might as well have somewhere comfortable to sleep." If nothing else, the cat could play with the cardboard packaging whilst Arabella dragged the two base units and mattress through to her empty bedroom. Then Sunday would be over and it would be back to another week of routine. Roll on Monday.

Was she really the woman with the mouth of Quentin Tarantino? It had been a well-meant jibe, although strictly speaking not that accurate. She wasn't anywhere near fast taking, smart arsed and foul mouthed enough to live up to that ideal. But the joke had been made, and as Arabella had strolled past, muttering 'you fuckers', she wondered if they had a point.

It had only been today, the last shift of her two week temping stint on reception duties, that she'd been rude to someone. Granted, it had been in self defence, and she liked to think that she had been making a point for womankind. But in reality her opinions weren't going to change society overnight. Nothing would change and the same old shit was going to be spun around society for the next fifty years. One angry little lady wasn't going to be taken seriously. Part of the problem, but that was the status quo.

Two women who worked in the back office had strolled in after their lunch break. Arabella still had no idea what their names were. They were chattering and laughing. One of the women carried the pronounced bump of the pregnant. Arabella hadn't paid them much attention, and was mid yawn when they entered the lobby, her eyes shut and her neck arched cat like. It was hardly the spritely welcoming face of the organisation, but she'd just been hit by a wave of exhaustion.

The first woman had given her a sympathetic smile. "Is he not letting you get any sleep?"

Arabella had opened her eyes, at first assuming they weren't talking to her. The two women had stopped by the reception desk and were expectantly watching her. "Sorry?"

"I remember what it was like having a six month year old," she had continued, with a knowing, we're-all-in-the-club look. The pregnant woman beside her had started to shake her head. "My second was just a nightmare."

Arabella had squinted. "Are you talking about babies?"

"Well, yes, I..."

"It's not Lucy," her pregnant friend had pointed out. "She's still off on sick leave." She had shifted her attention to Arabella. "You're covering Lucy's post at the moment. She got signed off for a month's sick leave, depression and stress. I think she's struggling with her baby to be honest with you."

"God, of course," the first woman had laughed. "And she's only got the one. It's crazy. Besides, she'd barely been back a month before she was getting signed off. Still, you'll know what I mean anyway, won't you? You have kids."

There had been silence in the entrance hall, the women waiting for confirmation that they were all of a similar life choice. Arabella had stared back. "I can't say that I do."

"But then how can you be tired? A woman without a screaming baby doesn't know what tired is. Don't worry," she had petted her forearm reassuringly. "You'll find out soon enough."

"Are you saying I'm fat?"

The woman had faltered a little at the direct question. "Well, no. In fact I am rather envious of your figure." She had sighed, as if she had just realised something. "Of course it's obvious that you don't have kids yet. But you will one day."

"Because I'm a woman?"

"Well, everyone wants a family, that's just..."

The pregnant woman had looked a little distressed as she listened to this faltering conversation, as if she was only just being let in on a secret, too late after she'd gotten herself in this predicament.

"I know it seems daunting," the first woman had told Arabella. "But we're women, this is our purpose... And yes it's hard work, and oh so tiring. Like I said, nurturing a little one is the real meaning of tiredness. You won't know about that yet but you can trust me on that point."

Arabella had smiled sweetly and without sincerity. Condescending dull bitch. Why did she get dragged into these prehistoric conversations? "I wouldn't know. I find nurturing my own brain takes up my time, but I sense you wouldn't know about that either."

The two women had stared at her as if they'd just been slapped with a wet fish.

"Now move along ladies, I'm afraid your brand of retro sexism is against company policy."

She'd never have been that rude two weeks into a job, not even Arabella Mangella, if it hadn't been the fact that it had also been her last day. She was sick of taking on people's preconceptions, batting off their well-meant insults and put-downs. Just patronise me a little more so you can feel better about the fact that your own life hasn't turned out quite as well as the fairy books promised.

Still, perhaps she a little too aggressive at times. She was aware of the battle lines that had been drawn up between womankind. If each side continued to press their case too vigorously, maybe women as a whole would never move on. The mothers were keen for everyone to experience their joy. Some were perhaps worried they'd missed out on something else in life. But all mothers were tired of being looked down upon by the career girls, the women who were child-free by choice, the militantly verbal, the women inexplicably without children. They were all an unquantified threat just like the single girl in a crowd of ladies with men. The difference wasn't to be trusted. Women without children were frigid and afraid to admit to their own feelings. Apparently.

Deep down, Arabella knew that not all mothers thought so unkindly about other women. Although they did get her back up when they'd laugh condescendingly about the fact that she couldn't know what tired meant.

Arabella knew people who had moved further in the decision making process that she had. They'd definitively decided that children weren't for them. Some of them were quite aggressive, tired of the patronising parent brigade, and had decided that all people with children were dull, mindless and not worth knowing. They sneered down at the women with kids, or the women who wondered over whether they would like a family. If you had a child, they didn't want to waste their breath talking to you. Was making such a generalised judgement like that any better than telling a woman she wanted children simply because she carried a womb in her female baggage? There were extremes on both sides of the argument. But there was great variety in the human race, and you couldn't just label a woman simply as a saintly mother or a child hater. There were infinite other types of women in between. Perhaps in this case women were still trying to be their own enemies.

It was a subject she could philosophise on for an eternity and still not come to a concrete solution. In the meantime people continued to piss her off and speak to her as if she was a moron.

The reception job was finished, she consoled herself. She was already on to the next gig, a Friday night one-off to pay back Graham for helping out with the fencing at her house. She'd paid him for the fencing, but felt a little indebted for him turning up the day after she'd called. When he'd rung in the middle of the week and asked her to step in for a last minute gig he'd agreed to take she hadn't really felt she could say no. It was just going to be a night of covers, with Graham in lead, but she'd still got Oates to post it on her website, already bored by the temping job and having a burst of promotional energy for her musical work.

It was a three piece band. They'd all played together a lot of times in the past, an infrequent occurrence speckled over the years. Graham was at the front with his guitar and sunglasses, looking like the dude: lead guitar, lead vocals. Arabella was demoted to the background, mostly covering bass guitar this evening, and set a little further back. She didn't mind. It meant she could mess around a little more with the drummer, and not have to worry about interacting with the pub audience between songs. Even though she was the background and back up: back up guitars, backup vocals; she was the best looking thing on stage, in her jeans, high heels and a strappy scarlet top that looked as though she was wrapped up in strips of bold red silk. Just to the left sat the drummer and the jazz man. He was the only one of the three of them who did manage to claw a living out of music. Christ knew how, but he never stressed about the next day. He had a sleepy eyed, relaxed daze of a face. His dark flat cap, like Yorkshire's answer to the beret sat at a jaunty angle on his thinning hair. He had dark hair curling on his bared forearms. He was the kind of man who threatened to turn into a walking shag pile carpet in middle age. He had Greek ancestors.

It was a loud, cheery pub night, jumping with a mixed audience, packed, drinking and sweating. They were playing a medley of upbeat, rocky music. Just now they formed an alternative Yorkshire answer to the Fun Lovin' Criminal's *Korean Bodega*; Arabella's backing vocals adding a more feminine touch to the song. Jeff, the drummer, was bouncing behind the drum set as if sat on a space hopper, sweat running down his face. He mostly played in jazz bands, but enjoyed picking up random jobs, letting it all loose for rock. Arabella's legs were bent at the knees, allowing for a dignified bounce. She loved the guitar riffs in this grungy NYC rock of the late nineties. Graham wasn't quite the American rapper-singer that the standard of music would have required, but no one in the building could have really cared less.

As they came to the end of the track, Jeff decided to pull his microphone over for something more than just joining in the roaring on the rock songs. "I've got to introduce the band to you good people," he shouted. "At the front we have Graham Nicholson, guitar maestro. What he don't know about flamenco, nobody does. And to my left I have Arabella Mangella, best known for her banjo and her Quentin Tarantino mouth..."

She swung around, neglectful of the microphone. "What the fuck?"

A cheer went up from the audience. She had fallen straight into the trap. "See what I mean. After all this aggression, me and Graham thought we needed to chill a little..."

Arabella saw him pick up his oboe from the back of the stage. Now what?

"Arabella's so used to gigging we don't need to work out a set list in advance. She'll be singing lead on this." With that final cryptic note, he started to play the intro.

Arabella recognised it immediately. The Carpenters' *Down at the Bayou* of all songs. Seriously, on a Friday night pub gig? This was definitely tongue-in-cheek. Still, the audience seemed to be going for it. Shrugging out of the electric guitar strap, she went to the back of the small stage to fetch her banjo. They would play a jazzed up version. It was true enough that they didn't work out set lists in advance, but they had played their own rendition of this one on numerous occasions. She put her lips to the mic.

From the Carpenters they got through some Foo Fighters, Dire Straits, Kula Shaker, Green Day, P J Harvey, White Stripes and other retrospective favourites. As they were nearing one in the morning, Graham decided they'd close on a Paulo Nutini number. Arabella switched to Graham's acoustic guitar. Graham was just down to vocals and a tambourine for this finale. The song had a slightly melancholic Simon and Garfunkel feel, but it was also a bouncing, jolly-along melody that finished off evenings rather well. Arabella played and sang backing vocals, eyes wandering over the crowds, thinking she was ready for bed. She'd have to get a taxi home. She spotted Miriam, Graham's girlfriend, in the crowds waiting for the gig to end. She'd help him get home with his three guitars and one amp. She'd be company. She'd be... Arabella sighed back into the backing vocals. It must be nice to have someone come for you. She was so independent she had never asked that of anyone. These days it was more than a matter of pride. She couldn't help herself.

She'd not heard from Ben all week. She couldn't call him because she'd neglected to ask for his number. She was simply holding her breath for him. She could be waiting for weeks. He was selling a flat in London, setting up as a freelance or a consultant or whatever the hell he saw his business as, and she was... she was Arabella. Beyond that she couldn't say.

She closed her eyes; close in to the mic for the finale drifting vocals. They finished to a tremendous round of applause in the pub. Jeff hopped up from behind the drums and they lined up for a bow. Arabella pushed the guitar around to hang down her back. They joined raised hands and bowed, feeling a rush of euphoria from the clapping. Then an evening's diversion was over and people were back to their drinks. Miriam was up at the stage talking to Graham. Arabella shrugged out of the guitar strap, passing the instrument to Graham.

"I'll transfer your cut over to you tomorrow."

"Sure, whatever." She headed to the back of the stage. Jeff was juggling with his drumsticks, his flat cap at a slightly drunken, jaunty angle as he flirted with a couple of female members of the audience. Pre recorded music poured out of the pub's tinny sound system.

Arabella crouched down and packed her banjo away in its case. She zipped the soft case up around her electric guitar, popping her guitar picks in the side pocket before hoisting it up on her back like an oversized rucksack. Collecting the banjo case, she turned to leave.

"Hey, Arabella, you not stopping for the after party drinks?" Jeff winked at her.

She smiled weakly. There had always been a sense of unfinished business with Jeff, and he'd probably sleep with her tonight if she put herself out. After a year of saying she was done with one night stands whilst doing the exact opposite, she felt as though she'd actually arrived at her intended destination. "Not this time. It's been a long week."

"No worries. We'll get together soon, do another gig. This has been fun."

"Sure."

She slinked her way through the crowds of drinkers, suddenly feeling a need to be alone. Her inner party animal was elsewhere tonight. She stumbled out of the front door onto the uneven street of central York. The night sky twinkled down upon her. The merry cries of party goers in town filled the air.

"Arabella, can I give you a hand with that?" Ben appeared from the pub doorway.

"Ben. Where the hell did you come from? Were you inside, at the gig?"

"Of course I was. I was trying to catch your eye, but I don't think you noticed me. I did try calling you earlier..."

"I forgot my phone." She'd actually left it at home on purpose, tired of checking for messages and missed calls and getting nothing. "How did you know I'd be here?"

"Your website. I thought of it when I couldn't get hold of you. Let me take that." He took the banjo case from her. "If it wasn't for your agent..."

"A lot of things wouldn't happen." She paused. "I was just planning on heading home, I don't..."

"Let me give you a lift. I'm just parked outside the walls." He caught a look in her eye. "Don't worry, I am unbelievably sober." He flashed her a smile. "Come on, it's just this way."

She joined him up the medieval street, footsteps tapping through the summer night. The sun-blasted stone slabs and cobbles were cooler now, most of the heat radiated back out into the atmosphere. They headed towards Monk Bar, one of the gate ports in the medieval stone walls surrounding the city centre. "Have you just driven up from London?"

"Not exactly. I've moved out of London."

"Already? I thought you'd only just put your flat on the market."

"Property sells quickly in London," he shrugged. "It's subject to contract. It'll still be a few weeks before I have to move the rest of my things out. But now it's done I thought I'd start looking forward."

"So what are you doing? Renting?" They walked through shadows under the bar gate, and up to the traffic lights to cross the road.

"No. I'm house sitting at the moment, over in Leeds. One of my friends has had a bit of a crisis," he scoffed at the word. "Listen at me, like I'm any better. He's buggered off for three months to go travelling and find himself. The timing's good for me. Gives me a base whilst I try to figure myself out."

"Then you'll buy your own wreck to do up."

"Yeah, something like that."

His car was one of the few still left in the car park at that time of night. The roads were quiet of traffic aside from the meandering drunks and the steady stream of taxis. They got smoothly out of the city centre and up to Arabella's house in particularly quick time. She wished they'd gotten stuck in traffic.

He pulled up outside her house. "You're living here properly now?"

"Yes." She clicked off her seatbelt. "I've even got all of the rooms painted. Nothing more done in the living room though."

"Floor still there?"

"Still looking good." She paused, awkwardly trying to think of something more to say and drawing blanks. "You could come in and check if you wanted to."

He drummed his fingers on the steering wheel. "I should probably just..."

"Another time," she interrupted, scrambling out of the passenger seat. Idiot. She wished he'd fuck off. She didn't want to be friends. This was just cruel. Opening the back door, she leaned in to retrieve her instruments. "You've still got that drive back to Leeds." Now she sounded bitter. She lowered her eyes. "Thanks for coming tonight."

He turned off the engine as she pushed the car door to. "I would be remiss if I didn't walk you to the door."

"That's very sweet, but I think the biggest threat here is this shitty porch falling in on my head. There's not much chance of being mugged." She passed him the guitar case to hold whilst she unlocked the door. The sky was clear and the moonlight cast the interior in a slight glow. She hadn't sorted out curtains yet, and only the bedroom window had any covering, being serviced by a bed sheet for the time being.

"As you can see, the floor is just as you left it." She wandered into the living room, setting the banjo case on the floor. Leaning over, she slipped off her shoes. Her feet were throbbing, the balls of her feet no longer able to take any more pressure. "Renovating in general just takes so much time. I can't decide if its time or money that's my biggest obstacle to getting anything done."

She trotted past him, painfully conscious that she was chattering nervously, covering over the fact that sober he didn't appear to have any interest in her. It had been awful when he had been drunk, truly dire, but at least he had been candidly adoring. She flicked on the hallway light. For a second there was clarity, followed by a flash, and the bulb went, tripping the entire lighting circuit in the house.

Arabella groaned, slumping back against the cupboard door in the hall. "Still got a few things to work out."

"Do you know where the fuse box is?"

She shook her head, rather pointlessly as he probably couldn't see her. She'd given up and closed her eyes. "I'll fix it tomorrow."

"It's usually found somewhere like the kitchen," he said, moving into the hall way. "Or in one of these in built cupboards." He'd stepped up beside her and gently tapped the door she was leaning against.

She didn't want to get involved in any more home improvements with him. "I'll sort it tomorrow."

"Do you want me to go?"

She took a deep breath. "You really don't need to feel obligated to help me fix everything because of your regrets over what we did. Seriously, I said we'd draw a line under it, and we have. So you don't need to sort out the fuse box. It's fine."

"Do you want me to go?"

He stood very close to her, not quite close enough for their bodies to meet, but enough so that she could sense the heat radiating from him. She looked up, her eyes growing accustomed to the poor light. "Not especially."

"Not especially? That's very vague." He slipped across the front of her body, a hand moving through her hair. "I only regret how I performed last time." He searched out the curve of her neck, his lips hovering over her pulse. He could feel Arabella's hands moving to his waist, fingers creeping up under the loose edge of his shirt, finding raw skin. Arabella's heart was hammering in her chest. She didn't dare push this too fast for fear that it would disintegrate like sand between her fingers. Yet she couldn't remain in this state of limbo much longer.

He kissed her neck. She raked his back with her finger nails. "If I was to open that door," he started, moving up to her mouth. "And throw you through," a pause for a kiss. "Is there any kind of bed in there?"

"Ample." She pressed the palms of her hands to his back. The skin was hot; the sensation of his heart beating was pumping frantically. Was he just as nervous about this as she was? "Come with me."

By autumn, into late October, the house was coming together. The front porch was still a dated wreck to be dealt with one day in the future. But when one passed through that mask and entered the bricks and mortar, things were looking a lot better. Arabella had bought second hand pieces of furniture, painted up several and finished off her living room and bedroom. Clean, sweet smelling carpets were down on the floor, the dog's mess a mere unpleasant memory, growing ever distant. This was turning into the home that Arabella had built.

In through the front door and Arabella paused, gazing straight down into the living room. The settee issue had been resolved, at least temporarily. After Ben had sold his flat, he'd put a certain amount of his furniture into storage. She was still using her second bedroom as storage, and had suggested he might as well use the space for any surplus. That had included his settee, which had rather quickly been promoted from the storage room to the living room. He was still flat sitting in Leeds, but his furniture had certainly moved in with her.

Turning the corner, she headed to the kitchen with her shopping bags. Ben was at the sink swilling out a couple of coffee mugs.

"Afternoon."

He glanced up at her. "That was very well timed."

"Eh?" She put the bags on the worktop. "I told you I was going to be out all morning at rehearsal. And I did stop off for food on the way home."

"I've just had the most surreal lunchtime of my life."

"Really? I thought you were just working."

"I went out to the post office to get that tender in the post. When I get back there's this crazy woman sitting at the table with a cup of coffee. I wondered if it was a ghost. She looked like some femme fatale out of an old Hitchcock film..."

Arabella winced. "I take it you met my mother." The turbans and kaftans were gone for the present in favour of two piece matching skirt suits and silk scarves."

"She acted like *I* was breaking in."

"I have told her about you."

"She said I must be the young man," he continued, pulling Arabella across the small kitchen space so they could stand hip to hip, his hands resting on her bottom. "I told her I'm too close to forty to be anyone's young man."

She rolled her eyes. "Give over; it's all in the mind."

"That's easy for someone who's still just thirty to say. So, you never told me that your mother has a key."

"She doesn't. She used to do this where I lived before. One of us would come home and she'd just be sitting there in the kitchen having a coffee."

"This happen a lot?"

"I have no idea. I don't know how she managed to get in. For all I know she did it every day we were out at work. She moves in mysterious ways."

"Just as long as she's not planning on strolling in when we're in the middle of anything."

206

Arabella's phone started ringing. "That's never happened. She doesn't turn up when people are at home." She quickly kissed him before taking her phone out of her back pocket. It was Pritesh's number, from the club. It had been a long time since she'd spoken to him.

"What do you want?"

"Arabella!" He sounded momentarily offended. More worrying was how he also tried to keep the irritation out of his voice. "That's hardly a friendly greeting. And it's been so many months since we last saw you."

"And that's because you know I've retired."

"Yes, I know, that's what I was ringing about. There was nothing wrong when you left us. I think it was prematurely done."

"I'm not coming back."

"Thing is, if you're going to retire, you should do it properly, don't you think? One last final tour. The goodbye performance."

Arabella gritted her teeth. Ben was looking at her quizzically. "Who's let you down now?"

"What makes you think I'm desperate?"

"The fact that you're calling me after months of silence."

"Arabella. Seriously, I've always admired your work...."

"Cut the bullshit and get to the point or I'm hanging up."

"Cherry's fucked off," he said bluntly. "She's got a contract down in London and she's gone running to them at the drop of a hat. How's that for loyalty? We had a schedule."

Arabella smiled to herself. So Cherry Malone and the burlesque act was working. The girl wasn't even twenty yet, and she had a calling to London. It sounded like she was going to make a success of it. Funny, this time last year such news would have made her furious, but she didn't care now. "I'm sorry to hear that, but it's hardly my problem."

"I'm thinking of you."

"I'm thinking I've retired. Ask Jennifer or someone else."

"I already have," he muttered. "She's up the duff. Definitely a non starter."

She laughed. "Sounds like I'm bottom of your list."

"Believe me, I am a long way off rock bottom."

"That's such a compliment," she joked. "But I'm not at the top of your list either. Still, if I'm not at the bottom, that means you still have options."

"Come on, I need some quality on the stage next weekend."

"And I told you, I've retired. The answer is no. Good bye." She hung up on him before he had chance to protest.

"You've retired?" Ben asked. "Is there something I don't know about your music?"

"No, it's not the music; it's the dancing I quit."

"Dancing? I didn't know..."

"Of course you do. I thought that's how we first..." she paused, thinking back to their first meeting. No it had been a music gig in York. "You never have seen me dance, have you?"

"No. So what was it, burlesque?"

"Not likely. I was a belly dancer."

"Really?" He grinned lecherously at her. "That's not like stripping or anything?"

"No it is not." She slapped his arm, slipping out of his grasp. "It is a respected art form and my costumes stayed on at all times. I was never some cheap little gratification thrill. But with the day job, the music and the dancing I was spreading myself too thin. So I decided to quit the dancing." He didn't need to know that she had been pushed out. Going out of fashion, getting too old.

Wandering down to the spare bedroom, she quickly located the packing box she wanted and carried it to her bed. She hadn't opened this since she'd moved in. The box contained all of her belly dancing gear. Tugging at the concertina flaps, she opened an Aladdin's cave of wigs, sheer scarves, coin belts, embroidered bras and tank tops, skirts and glamorous costume jewellery. She picked up the wig of long anime pigtails, the synthetic hair threaded through with ribbons. Christ, the crazy get ups she had. Laying the hair out on the bed, she worked her way through the contents, shaking out scarves, holding up strings of coins and beads to the light. She had no intention of taking to the stage again, but these clothes were gorgeous. It was a shame they were completely inappropriate and out of context for the real world.

Picking up a slit skirt that hooked up at the front, she shook it out to its full length against her legs. The dressing up was certainly one of the many wonderful aspects of belly dance. Unhooking the skirt, she put it around her back and went to button it up against her low waist, horrified to see there was a good three inches between the two sides as she tried to fasten it.

"You been letting yourself go since you quit?" Ben joked from the bedroom door.

"Sod off," she muttered, feeling an uncomfortable sweat break out on her forehead. "This was never meant to be worn on top of jeans."

"Don't worry, I still love you as you are," he said, wandering off to the living room.

This is actually very serious, man-pig, she thought angrily, not paying him much attention. Unbuttoning her jeans, she wriggled them down to mid thigh, then tried to fasten the skirt on. Still a good inch and half too narrow. It wasn't going to fasten. Her hands were clammy. She wasn't dancing, so of course her exercise levels had dropped dramatically, the toning of her body would suffer. This sweat was the product of more than a lack of exercise. She was having an awful moment of realisation. How could she have been so bloody stupid?

Dropping the skirt on the floor, she sat down on the bed. What did this mean? Other than the fact that she was a moron, for how could she not have thought of this for so long? Her period was late, not just a few days late, but potentially a few months. This was bad, especially for someone who was very vocal on the wonderful variety of contraception, on the fact that these days, a woman could easily avoid getting pregnant. What an idiot. She was on the pill, but she knew that she'd missed a couple of days here and there around the time of coming back from Iceland. Getting upset over Ben all over again. She'd just buried her head in the sand and told herself it was nothing to worry about.

So, how far gone could you be, she asked herself. It had been a while since she'd last suffered from a bout of nausea. On the occasions when she'd felt sick, babies hadn't been a potential explanation. She'd always blamed it on the heat, the stress, misery, stomach bug... shit, even volumes of alcohol. How long had it been?

When had she had her last period? If she went too far back, she wouldn't even be able to say who the father could be. There was Ben. But there had been Arvid, and if this was really far gone, it could have been that ugly guy from the nightclub. No, not him. She'd not missed any days on the pill back then. She closed her eyes. This was really important. She needed to know. When did she last bleed?

She'd bought tampons in Iceland. Yes, she felt her heart leap. She had used them. On her last day in Iceland, therefore after the last copulation with Arvid, she'd suffered with period pains as the blood had come on. There was one worry off the list; she wasn't going to have a little Scandinavian sailor baby. And perhaps with all the recent stresses, her body had just been messed up and taken a pause from regular periods for a few months. Maybe everything was all right.

Who the hell was she trying to fool?

She listened to Ben moving about in the house. What was she supposed to say to him? He might think she was trying to trap him. Did she even want a child? Did he? Maybe she could just deal with this and he'd never need to know. They could continue in this happy bliss they'd found themselves in. She really didn't want to fuck things up. If I tell him about this he'll think I'm trying to trap him. Maybe he'd be happy to be trapped. He was over in York a lot of the time. His settee had moved in with her months ago.

What to do? What to do? She had to know the facts before she did anything. She would have to make an appointment with the G.P and find out what was going on with her body before she terrified Ben with any potentially life changing news.

She buried her head in the sand for a few days, then by the middle of the week found the courage to make an appointment with her GP. The results were as expected, although making it official, printed out on the computer screen, terrified her. Arabella Mangella, Madame Angry, Mrs I'm-Fine-on-my-own, was most definitely pregnant.

The appointment itself hadn't been pleasant. Whilst waiting in the limbo of the waiting room she had found herself in an awkward standoff. Dr Mark Thaw, not her assigned G.P and certainly not the one she had been booked in to see that day, had appeared in reception for some other purpose. He had clocked her, taken a moment to realign his centre, before approaching with a shield of confidence.

"Miss Mangella."

Arabella's eyes had flicked upwards, the taste of bile and irritation lurching up her throat as she recognised him.

"It's been a while since we last spoke. Did I mention last time that I'm engaged?"

The last time I saw you, you were a pathetic whimpering obsessive puppy obviously going through some kind of mid-life crisis. Like I give a shit. She smiled without any hint of compassion. "Was this when you were standing up to your knees in river water and duck crap?"

A couple of elderly ladies at the other side of the waiting room tittered, making no effort to hide the fact that they were eavesdropping. The doctor's smile dropped. "I have work to do," he informed her, as if she was hindering the good work.

"Don't let me stop you."

What an arsehole, she thought as she left work the following day. Why did people feel the need to rub their success in her face like a defence mechanism. Yes, Arabella, I'm better than you! Aren't you jealous? Her own life wasn't perfect but it was finding a balance of some kind. In many respects she couldn't really complain. The paperwork was through, and she owned her own home. She was working, although it was only a temporary contract for six months. It was good money, and not too stressful, working in admin in the physics department at York University. She knew fuck all about physics, but the professor seemed quite taken with her, and she was given all kinds of interesting tasks to do. It made the time pass better, and as a general rule, her work no longer put her in a bad mood with the human race for the rest of the day.

There'd been a lot to think about in the last few days. She'd even bumped into Adam this morning in the corner shop. She'd stopped off for a couple of things before driving on towards work. It had been a strained moment, for since leaving the house they hadn't spoken once. It had been a silent parting, paying off final rent and joint bills. No forwarding address left. They'd been friends whilst they'd shared the house, or at least Arabella had considered them friends, and it had been sad that not only had she lost her old home, but a friend. Perhaps it had all proved to be an important lesson. In work and rental agreements keep your distance. People will only disappoint you.

Adam had looked thinner, a touch gaunt as if he was starting to grow old. They'd politely acknowledged one another, simultaneously asking if they were well without really wanting to know. Details were not exchanged.

"You got some post a couple of days ago," Adam had said, pulling a green envelope out of his satchel and passing it across. His voice had seemed neutral and confident. Different somehow. "I wasn't sure what to do with it."

"This is all that's come?" Arabella had looked down at the envelope. Handwritten, locally posted. It had looked like a greetings card envelope. It hadn't been her birthday for a long time and it was too early for Christmas.

"So far," he had said. "What do you want me to do if anything more comes for you?"

"Just forward it on to my mother," she had answered, distractedly ripping open the top of the envelope with her finger. "Although I don't think you'll get anything. I thought I'd told everyone." Inside there had been a greetings card. She had pulled it out, confused as she considered the message. 'Sorry you're leaving!' What the hell? It was a good long while before the job with the university was due to end. She hadn't been at any of the temporary positions long enough for anyone to care. Pushing the sides of the card apart with two fingers, she had peered inside. Her eyebrows had jumped up as she had seen the multitude of brief signatures and messages, recognising several of the names and realising where this had come from. Her old job, where she had worked as a credit controller, had sent her a leaving card. They had made her redundant, and really a message to say sorry you're leaving would have been inappropriate at any point in the miserable process. But several months after she had gone? Where was the point in them saying thanks for the work and good luck now? Bad enough that they hadn't bothered at the time, but it was even more insulting to resurrect the bad memory now. She had pushed the card back into the envelope and ripped the entirety in half. She had smiled tersely at Adam. "Junk mail."

Walking past an open eating area on the university campus, she watched a toddler waddle away from its mother; brave exploratory steps in the world. Was this scene supposed to make her heart melt, if she was meant to have children herself? She didn't feel any particular interest, the fact of which worried her. What was someone like her doing getting pregnant?

The toddler must have heard her thoughts, for he was heading in her direction. He tripped on an uneven paving slab and toppled over into whimpers. As his mother rose in a panic, scurrying across, the crying child looked up and met Arabella's eye; the gaze of which put him into hysterical retching screams. Even children hate me, she thought as she hurried away. She really wasn't a baby person.

By the time she had arrived back home and was walking through the door, she had almost convinced herself that there wasn't a problem. She saw Ben in the living room. She paused in the doorway and couldn't think of a thing to say. She had to tell him, but either he would walk out, shouting that he wouldn't be trapped by a devil woman like her; or he'd be sobbing, 'oh god, I always wanted a son. Let's have ten more'. Then Arabella would run screaming from the house. I can't live with such a soppy jelly-brain! It was enough to make a girl sick. Arabella could just imagine the third reality; the embarrassing tears and snotty nose, and her having to explain that she wasn't maternal. He'd make her have it, then he'd take it away, the courts granting full custody, because they couldn't leave a kid with a crazy bitch like that.

Ben looked up at her and smiled.

"Hey."

"Hey yourself. Come on in and tell me about your day."

She almost passed the threshold, but worry pulled her back. She couldn't do idle chit chat, knowing what she did, but she didn't quite think she had the energy to speak the truth. She made a vague noise, retreating in to the shadows and heading for the kitchen.

"Are you all right?"

"I'm fine."

I'm not, but I can't do this. She poured herself a glass of water.

"Arabella?"

She jumped, spilling a little water down her front. His voice was alarmingly close. He must have followed her down to the kitchen.

"You've been acting weird all week."

"No I haven't."

She heard him sigh. "Trust me, you have. Weird. Even for you." He waited a moment, giving her a cue to say something. "Okay, I'm just going to be blunt and put it out there if you won't. I am well aware my friend's back in a week's time and I've got to be out of the flat. I am not expecting to move in here."

Arabella turned around, horrified. She'd just assumed he would, hoping it would happen organically without her needing to say anything. She wasn't good with words when they involved emotions, serious issues, life, or even a hint towards the fact that she might have vulnerable points. Swearing and arguing she could deal with, but this kind of stuff could terrify her.

"I will find somewhere else."

"You don't have to."

He raised his eyebrows. He hadn't expected that. He'd just thought she didn't want to give up her independence. "That's nice to hear. And you're not worried that it would be too soon? We have only been going at this for a few months..."

She was going to be sick. Moving in with me is nothing compared to the shit I'm about to lay on you. Too soon? When exactly was it the right time? Ought one to wait a certain number of dates before sex? A year at least before moving in? A year after the wedding before the birth of the first baby? She had completely fucking jumped the gun on all of those. And for all the people who did things at the 'right' time, did that make it any better? Was the relationship stronger? The fuck it was: just consider all those divorces and break ups she'd witnessed over the years, starting with her parents. There was never a right time, just as there never was a drum roll and burst of fireworks for the big life events. Things happened and the world continued. If you waited with baited breath for the 'moment' all that would happen would be that you'd run out of oxygen.

"I don't want circumstance to push you into something you don't want."

Arabella closed her eyes, not sure if she was going to cry or vomit. She felt him step up to her, put his hands on the small of her back. She leant into him, her forehead resting on his shoulder.

"There's that weirdness again."

Oh you sweet man, she thought. Even if there was never a definitive right time, there were always wrong times. She'd never been a good judge of things when it came to working with other people. I really don't want to fuck this up. I am fated to screw up everything.

His hands moved up to cradle her, around her shoulders, fingers in her hair. "If it's not about living arrangements, you want to tell me what's up?"

Do it! a voice screamed in her head. There's no point holding back on the inevitable. She summoned up what little determination she had left, the remains from every false-start conversation she'd tried to have with him over the week. "Okay," she finally spoke, her voice sounding awkward. "Sit down and hold on to the table. I've got news."